Ruby Tuesday

Jennifer Anne Kogler
AR B.L.: 5.2
Points: 10.0   MG

I've never put much stock in the saying that all things have a beginning. After all, I can't tell you exactly when I realized that my friends at Laguna Heights didn't read as much as I did. I don't know when I began to like the way my legs looked in a skirt, the smell of gas stations, or the company of my mother. And while I'm unable to locate the inaugural date of my adolescence, I guess, when I think back on it, I started to become a player in my own life on Jack's wedding day.

Ruby Tuesday

Jennifer Anne Kogler

HarperTempest
An Imprint of HarperCollins*Publishers*

HarperTempest is an imprint of HarperCollins Publishers.

Library of Congress Cataloging-in-Publication Data
Kogler, Jennifer Anne.
Ruby Tuesday / Jennifer Anne Kogler.— 1st ed.
p.   cm.
Summary: The 1988 World Series win by the Los Angeles Dodgers sets off a chain of
life-changing events for thirteen-year-old Ruby Tuesday, as she travels to Las Vegas, where she
learns some surprising truths about her family members and their careers as gamblers and
musicians.
ISBN-10: 0-06-073958-4 (pbk.) — ISBN-13: 978-0-06-073958-4 (pbk.)
[1. Family—Fiction.   2. Self-perception—Fiction.   3. Gambling—Fiction.   4. Musicians—
Fiction.   5. Los Angeles Dodgers (Baseball team)—Fiction.   6. Las Vegas (Nev.)—History—
20th century—Fiction.   7. Laguna Beach (Calif.)—History—20th century—Fiction.]   I. Title.
PZ7.K8215Ru 2005   2004021507
[Fic]—dc22

Typography by Christopher Stengel

First HarperTempest edition, 2006

To my parents, for miraculously giving me the madcap source material for this novel without any of the potentially costly psychological problems associated with it. With your support, everything is possible.

Nine gamblers could not feed a single rooster.
—Yugoslavian proverb

The dogs bark and the hounds begin to howl
Watch out strange cat people
Little red rooster's on the prowl.
—from "Little Red Rooster"
performed by Mick Jagger

Ruby Tuesday

One

It began the day my father sliced off his index finger. I was thirteen, and that was the hottest fall of my life. Summer that year had refused to take its own scheduled vacation. As my older brother Jack's October wedding approached, our conversations were mired in talk of the perfect honeymoon locale and multilayered carrot cake options.

I've never put much stock in the saying that all things have a beginning. After all, I can't tell you exactly when I realized that my friends at Laguna Heights didn't read as much as I did. I don't know when I began to like the way my legs looked in a skirt, the smell of gas stations, or the company of my mother. And while I'm unable to locate the inaugural date of my adolescence, I guess, when I think back on it, I started to become a player in my own life on Jack's wedding day.

My brother's reception convinced me that weddings are a tricky business. If they go as planned, some people go home happy, some drunk; the luckiest teeter home both. But like anything that involves planning, there's always the element of surprise, and Jack's big day was no exception. There is no such thing as a pleasant surprise at a wedding.

Jack met Mae on a sunny day in June at Mission Beach. The waves were glassy barrels curling two feet overhead, and she liked the way he carved the surf with his board. A few Mai Tais at Woody's Wharf and a salty kiss later, they were in love—at least, that's how they told the story at the rehearsal dinner.

In keeping with my family's tendency to avoid normalcy, Jack and Mae had decided early on to get married at the beach, scorning floral arrangements, stained-glass windows, bow ties, and frocked ministers.

"This ceremony isn't progressive, it's preposterous," my Nana Sue began. "I should *not* have to wear SPF forty at my grandson's wedding." She huffed as she spoke, clutching the peeling paint railing, following my father and me down the earthen stairs toward Woods Cove, a well-hidden beach in Laguna. Nana Sue limped with both legs, but her odd march made her that much more intimidating. Around the weathered banister, a mat of phalecia, lupine, and bright golden poppies wallpapered the hill, swaying in the breeze—a dazzling backdrop to our steep descent.

"This is the only wedding I've seen where I have a better chance of catching melanoma than the bridal bouquet," she wheezed. My grandmother laughed at her own joke with a gentle sucking of air that exploded into a cackle.

I had been told by most everyone who knew her that Nana Sue was beautiful when she was young—so beautiful, in fact, that I wondered if her now-cragged face made her bitter when she stared at it in the morning mirror. Whenever I looked at her, I thought of the faded photo perched atop our TV. In it she stood holding my infant father, Hollis, enveloped by a parched Reno desert, her face shaded with the unmistakable softness of youth. Now she looked jagged and cynical in pictures.

Nana Sue always smoked half a pack of Virginia Slims in the morning and drank at least four tumblers of Knob Creek, straight up, by the time she went to bed. The day of Jack's wedding, she wore a collared ivory shirt with tiny anchors across it. Navy slacks hung loosely from a tan belt over the SAS deck shoes that women her age often wear. A visor shielded her face. Her hair was the smooth color of Xerox paper, and her face was a dehydrated version of Hollis's. Still, she was spry for a seventy-four-year-old, and she'd made the five-hour trek in her black '78 Mercedes from her home in Las Vegas without complaint.

When I had finally reached the roped-off section of the beach at the bottom of the cliff, it was half full with guests mingling in bikinis and swim trunks. Some of Jack's friends were bumping a volleyball in a circle, killing time. Old beach chairs were strewn in uneven rows around the seaweed-draped podium. Rainbow-colored paper lanterns swung from poles like airy tetherballs in the coastal breeze. I lagged behind as Hollis and Nana Sue plodded toward the matrimonial sandlot.

"Why, that woman's in a thong!" Nana Sue shouted, looking half amused and half appalled at the procession of scantily clad guests.

"I still can't believe Jack scheduled this thing during game one of the Series," my father grumbled. "The kid grew up bleeding Dodger blue." It was true—the two things the entire Sweet family watched together were Dodger games and sunsets. I'd been initiated at an early age.

In fact, the Los Angeles Dodgers were as close to a religion as we Sweets had. While other girls were learning to crimp, tease, and braid, I was learning to recognize the top-spin of a curveball from our field-level box seats at the stadium. A good portion of my life was spent staring out at nine players in Dodger uniforms. Sometimes my eyes would venture toward the faint lights of LA's urban sprawl outlining the hills of Chavez Ravine. It was understood that

Hollis, Jack, and I would be at each home night game. We'd sit side by side, content to spend three hours together fixated on Orel Hershiser's pitch count. During the season before Jack's wedding, Hershiser had wowed us, pitching fifty-nine consecutive scoreless innings to break Don Drysdale's major league record. In between Dodger Dogs and seventh-inning stretches, I had discovered that watching baseball with my father was a way of surreptitiously peering into his past. My father had grown up on legends like Sandy Koufax, Don Drysdale, and Maury Wills, and he prided himself on his knowledge of even the most obscure Dodger trivia. He talked warmly of hot afternoons watching games with Nana Sue when they'd made the trip from their home in Reno to Los Angeles.

"I just wish the wedding wasn't during the Series, that's all," my father said, tugging my ponytail.

Nana Sue stood fully upright as her arm shot toward the pocket of Hollis's pants. She clenched a handful of his yellow linen trousers, searching for something.

"You don't have a radio on you, do you, Hollis?" Nana scowled. "Because, I swear, honey, you'll break Jack's heart right open if he sees you listening to him say 'I do' in one ear and the broadcast of the bottom of the fifth in the other."

Hollis stood silent.

"You aren't in play? You don't even have a double saw-buck on the game, right?" Hollis and Nana Sue's conversations were often sprinkled with strange words like *sawbuck* that I rarely understood. Still, I could tell by Nana Sue's venomous tone that she meant business. "Hollis, look at me: Couldn't you spare a day? *This is your only son's wedding*." My father's face gave him away—he grimaced like he was suffering from a migraine, and his expression read like a confession.

"Oh my word, Hollis . . . you do have money on the game!"

"It's not what you think, Nana Sue," Hollis said. I wondered if he'd ever called her Mom.

"I'm worried about you, Hollis—and this is coming from *me*—a railbird who split time between Reno and Vegas her whole life. This isn't natural. Are you in the hole? Are you in trouble?" Nana Sue's anger straightened her spine.

"No, of course not, Nana. It was last winter when I placed . . . I had no way of . . . it was a future on the World Series. Look, it's a long shot that might pay off big." Hollis glared sternly at Nana Sue and then at me. It was the kind of glare parents have been directing at children for generations—a signal that this discussion was not suitable for young listeners. My ears immediately pricked up.

"Don't worry, Sue. I'll watch the highlights later on

Channel Seven like everyone else here. No radios. It's just me, you, and Ruby here, enjoying Jack's big day."

Hollis shot me a knowing look—a look that I can still visualize. I was the only one privy to my father's scheme for the evening, partly because it included me: Once the preacher introduced Mr. and Mrs. Jack Sweet and the party began, Hollis would switch on the transistor sleeping in his front pocket. Assuming I could avoid the pubescent table and jockey for a seat next to him, he'd slip me a side of his earphones and we could listen to the last innings of game one.

I hoped I was up to the task.

We continued down the beach in search of Jack—my father's tall shadow stood against the twilight, my grandmother's short silhouette lost in his, with my own trailing behind.

Hollis spotted Jack in the corner of the makeshift beach chapel. His green Hawaiian shirt and Dockers looked brand-new.

"Dad, Nana Sue . . . right on time." Jack grinned, his bleached teeth shining in the orange rays of the setting sun.

"Are you going to pull this thing off before it gets pitch black, Jack?" my father asked. "Or are we going to have to rely on the moonlight?"

"We have plenty of time. The sun won't set for another fifteen minutes."

"Should be charming," Nana Sue added, putting on a saccharine smile. Her perfect dentures looked odd against the backdrop of her sagging, liver-spotted face.

"Where is Uncle Larry?" I asked, directing my question at Jack.

Nana Sue bristled. "You have the child calling him 'uncle' now, Hollis? For shame!"

"Larry is *not* your uncle, Ruby," Jack said, his face lit with amusement.

"That *greenie* is your father's *bookie*," Nana Sue snapped.

"Dad's *what*?" It was more of the same—words that mystified, phrases that loitered unexplained. I made a mental note to write any new words down when I got home.

"Never mind, Rube. I'll explain later." I knew he would do no such thing. The subject change had an immediate permanence.

"Speaking of unlikely guests, Jack," Nana Sue began, "is Darlene expected?"

"I don't know. But she does know about the wedding. I invited her."

My father's jaw dropped, and Nana Sue clicked her tongue at the news of Darlene's invitation.

None of us, Nana Sue included, was on good terms with my mother. Whenever she popped in on Jack and me, she lugged in presents that defied the conventions of gift giving. Once it was a portrait of her made entirely of tree bark by an Amish artist, another time a gift-wrapped sack of jalapeño beef jerky from an Indian reservation near Tucson. Then there was a Jackson Browne album with the signature of Jackson himself on the cover. Like all things associated with my mother, the authenticity of these offerings was tainted with a maddening uncertainty.

The way we figured it, Darlene Sweet required three things: her independence, the Rolling Stones, and Johnnie Walker by the handle. Hollis had a standard response whenever her name was mentioned. He called her a social chameleon—she changed from hippie to hard rock in an instant, always the most stylish person in any room. She just didn't take to children. "Can't choose who you love," he would say, but he never seemed to give up on her entirely.

To me, Darlene was like the Santa Ana wind. She blew in about twice a year, made my face contort into strange expressions of discomfort, and then disappeared. In her wake she left the debris she had dressed up in wrapping paper. Worse than a completely absent mother, she came around just often enough that I couldn't forget her.

I turned my attention back to Jack's handsome face and asked him if he was nervous. I thought this was a question

I should ask—someone had done it in every movie I'd seen that involved a wedding.

"Nah. My part is simple. I just have to repeat what someone else says." Jack patted my head in a fatherly fashion. He had taken to doing this in the month since he'd moved out of our house, and it only made me miss him more.

"Jack, I'm proud of you. You're the luckiest guy here." My father rarely spoke in superlatives, but today he was all parental pride. He gripped Jack's shoulder with brawny affection in that way men do.

"I should get married more often," Jack said. "I'm liable to drown in all these compliments."

"I wouldn't worry, Jack," Nana Sue said, laughing. "You're far too shallow to drown."

This was the kind of nimble, harmless banter characteristic of every Sweet gathering. And I loved it.

Jack turned to leave. "Well, I should probably go take my place."

He stopped halfway between the podium and the spot where the chairs for the wedding party had been set up.

"I'll see you after it's official," he said with a wink.

Of course, it wasn't a matter of *if* my mother would arrive, but *when*. Darlene didn't appear until a few minutes after Jack had taken his position by the podium at the end of the seashell-bordered aisle. She sauntered toward us from the flowered cliff, waving, her eyes shaded by Jackie O sunglasses. Most everyone on the beach, even the youngest guests, focused their gaze upward as she approached.

The last time I'd seen my mother, she was in town to catch Rod Stewart at the Coach House, and she called to say she wanted to spend the afternoon with me. I remember sneaking upstairs as she approached the house wearing purple leg warmers and a baggy tee. I didn't want her to see that I'd been looking out the kitchen window for hours, waiting for her Thunderbird to motor up our hill. We spent the afternoon at the Salvation Army sifting through old clothes that smelled like wet pavement. She was convinced we were both minutes away from a "great find." I came away with a hat that said "Sun Records" to complement her "Elvis Lives" rhinestone belt. She dropped me off in front of the house and told me to "send Hollis her love," like always. It had been years since she'd stayed the night at our house, and I knew it would be months before I saw her again. Six months had passed between our shopping trip and the day of Jack's wedding. I often wondered why she bothered coming at all.

Today Darlene's hair was an unconvincing shade of blonde, and her tight red halter-top sundress clashed with her broiled skin. Huge iridescent sea horse earrings dangled to her shoulders like a pair of competing wind chimes.

Before any of us could manage an awkward greeting, the wedding march boomed out from enormous Bose speakers on the ocean side of the beach, and people began adjusting their beach chairs to view the windblown procession. The stately chorus struggled against an off-key orchestra of rusty hinges.

Five bars later, the sound of an approaching siren swallowed every other noise. Mae had arrived, chauffeured in a lifeguard jeep, red lights ablaze. As the jeep jitterbugged across the sand, she stood, gripping her lavender bouquet of El Moro Canyon wildflowers with one hand and the roll bar with the other.

I had met Mae a few times before at tense family dinners and decided she was pretty, but as I looked at her in her white appliquéd lace bikini, she became a gorgeous sea siren. Her short, shell-encrusted veil flapped in the wind behind her tall glistening frame as fountains of sand sprayed in her wake. The lifeguard killed the engine and rushed to the other side of the jeep, helping Mae down from the passenger side. She stared at Jack as she made her way to him from the parked jeep, and soon they stood hand in hand. They were a couple of glamorous beach bums, barefoot and squinting at each other through the orange dusk of a slouching sun.

"May you ride the perfect wave, catch the perfect tube, and forever be committed to the endless summer that is marriage," the preacher-surfer hybrid concluded, smoothing his rumpled Hawaiian shirt. He ended by pointing to the location of the buffet, set near the rising tide. Scattered folding tables sank slowly in the white sand, alongside a wedding banquet offering a choice of fish taco *especiales*, pinto beans, guacamole, cheese wheels, crackers, and fresh sliced California-grown oranges and strawberries.

As we walked toward the food with the other sunscreened guests, I could feel my palms turn clammy and my stomach rumble with nervous hunger. It was easy to forget that Jack was now a married man in the excitement of my father's and my World Series listening gambit.

"Alright, Ruby, as soon as we sit down with our plates, I'll hand you your end of the earphones." Hollis whispered to escape the attention of Nana Sue. "Slip the cord behind your earlobe and put the speaker in your ear." Hollis viewed this game's outcome as the best predictor of the Series. If the Dodgers won the first game, they'd win the whole thing. As always, the odds backed him up.

We both piled our paper plates with watermelon and corn tortillas stuffed with charbroiled ahi and green cabbage and sat down at the nearest sand-anchored table. We were soon flanked by brittle relatives: Nana Sue on one side and my mother Darlene on the other. The silence led me to believe that, at least for the moment, everyone had chosen his or her taco *especiale* over conversation. I was relieved.

As I grabbed for the earpiece under the table, I felt a naughty exhilaration. This was better than smoking a forbidden cigarette or shotgunning a warm beer with Jack behind the garage. Cupping the earpiece in my hand, I pretended to scratch my ear. Seamless. Contact had been established. I had performed as well as expected. The Dodgers, however, were losing to the Oakland Athletics, 4–2. As I looked at the mixed company around me, I remembered how quickly things could turn from silence to a searing argument at any Sweet gathering. Both Hollis and I tried to keep up with conversation between spoonfuls of pinto beans and earfuls of the Dodger game.

Darlene stared at my profile and leaned toward my father.

"Hollis, Ruby looks as pale as a ghost. You should send her outside more often. She reads too much." She waited for Hollis's answer. "Hollis? Hollis, are you listening to me? I'm trying to communicate with you here."

Nothing.

"Hollis? Are you deaf? Are we going to spend our son's wedding in silence?" There was a look of serene pleasure on Hollis's face. He had not heard a word of Darlene's umbrage—he was under the spell of longtime hall-of-fame Dodger broadcaster Vin Scully.

"Answer me! What in the world is wrong with you? Are you calculating over/unders on how long the party is going to last?

"Fine, ignore me. That's mature. It's worked for you in the past." Sitting up slightly, she reached into her frayed yellow purse and produced a silver hip flask. She poured three seconds' worth of brown liquid into her bottle of Dos Equis and then downed a significant portion. Nana Sue darted her hand across the table.

"Mind if I borrow a drop or two?" Nana Sue said, flashing her dentured smile.

"Sure, have four. We might as well try to drink Hollis's misbehavior off our minds, right?" Darlene snickered to herself. My father snapped to attention.

"Let's not turn this into one of our clashes. . . . And by the way, Darlene—Ruby is pale because the sun causes cancer. Maybe you haven't heard the news. The statistics are quite compelling." Nice save, Hollis.

Normally Darlene would have deferred to the line she used whenever Hollis's penchant for sarcasm found its way into one of their divisive talks. *Sarcasm destroys families, Hollis.* This time she snapped back on topic.

"I'm not encouraging you to marinate her in the sun—but she looks like she's dying. Her skin is translucent—I mean, I can practically see through her." Being the ball in one of my parents' games of verbal Ping-Pong had stopped bothering me long before that moment. I did what I used to do best: I kept silent and let the argument run its course.

"She is also going to live a long, cancer-free life. Darlene, you really should read. . . ." My father trailed off as a crack from the earpiece tickled my ear. It was the sound of a bat making contact, piped in through the earphone. The Dodgers had just scored another run, making the score A's four, Dodgers three.

I nudged Hollis's knee to remind him that Darlene expected him to finish his sentences. My heart was pounding, knowing full well the volatile table would erupt into all out verbal warfare if we were found out. The plan began to seem foolhardy, and I wondered if we'd even make it through an inning. Hollis was talking to me now, and not about the wedding but the World Series playing out in his ear.

"I know, Ruby. Four, three—it's a real barn burner!" I put my face in my hands, frustrated, near tears. Nana Sue spoke next.

"What in the world are you talking about, Hollis? Four three what? Maybe you better lay off the hooch." Nana

Sue's southern accent kicked in full force, as it always did when she was stern or angry. Hollis spoke again.

"Four three two one." He offered up a dumb smile to the table.

"Lately Hollis has been countin' when he's excited," I added, taking my father's lead. "That's what Dr. Toni Grant tells people to do."

"Since when has Ruby Tuesday been calling you Hollis, Hollis?" Darlene demanded. This made me angry. My mother was now on the offensive. I looked at my father. He wasn't with us—he was with Scioscia, at the plate with a three-two count in the bottom of the seventh. I tried to step up and save him.

"Well, that's his name, right, Darlene?" It was the first time I had said my mother's name out loud to her face, and it felt good. Everyone was staring at me. I continued. "Hollis says if I want to be treated like an adult, I need to start acting like one. You don't call Hollis 'husband,' do ya?" I was really on a roll. Heck, Nana Sue had laughed. But Darlene's glare was toxic.

"Now you see why I can't live with her full-time. The child's spoiled. She has no manners. Soon she'll be swaggering like some Vegas cocktail waitress." She marshaled her flask back from Nana Sue and took a swig. Then she closed her eyes and let out a burning alcoholic sigh.

"Oh, I don't know if that's so bad, Darlene," Hollis began. "It's what you were when I met you." I heard my mother's voice echo in my head. *Sarcasm destroys families.* Things were heating up. Darlene's eyes got smaller.

"I don't mean that, Hollis. I mean if she doesn't have any discipline she's going to end up like you or me or like the rest of this family!" Darlene raised her hands above her head. "Even Jack—I thought he'd turn out all right; he's got a good head—but look at this nonsense." She waved her arms at the tables full of bathing suit–clad revelers with sunburned cheeks now mingling in the dusk. Hollis raised his arms toward the blackening sky.

"This is our son's wedding. Why don't you show some class."

"Oh, yeah," Darlene countered with a boozy leer. "Nothing says class like a bride in a bikini."

"Why do you insist on being so critical of this family?" Hollis tried to muffle his anger.

"Ruby shouldn't talk like she does. She's only twelve."

"I'm thirteen." It was the first time I can remember interjecting my own opinion into one of their displays of marital unbliss.

It wasn't long before Nana Sue weighed in too. She was good at playing the peacekeeper, able to keep the passion of my parents at bay with one well-timed utterance.

"Let's keep things civil. Ruby, do not talk back to your mother," Nana Sue scolded me. Scioscia had grounded out to second base. The seventh inning had ended. And Darlene remounted her attack.

"You've got money on the game tonight, don't you, Hollis?" Darlene was relentless. "You're always betting on something, aren't you, you fool? In fact, I'm surprised you're missing the game. Your whole life revolves around whether some round object is hit by some idiot over a stupid fence, or put in a hole, or through a basket." The drunker Darlene got, the more insulting she became. "You are pa-thetic. Our only son's wedding." My mother's face was glowing with an arrogant expression. Her garbled speech had quieted the table. I tried to block out everything else, concentrating on Vin Scully and the Dodgers in my ear. The Sweet family silence lasted through the break in between innings—a pitch for Farmer John Bacon, Union Oil, and season ticket packages. Nana Sue spoke first.

"Darlene, we haven't yet asked what you have been up to. How rude of us all," she said. I knew it was taking all of Nana Sue's resolve to be courteous for Jack's sake. Reluctantly Darlene set her grievances aside and answered the question.

"Actually, I just left the Sawdust Festival. You know that macramé planter that hangs from the porch eave? I sell—"

"Well, guys, how does it look?" Jack approached, flashing his silver screen smile and wiggling his ring finger. He had been making the compulsory rounds and had saved our table for the end. Mae had split off to mingle with a table full of her own adoring relatives.

"Look, the band's about to start playing." Jack seemed to sense that conversation hadn't flowed in his absence. "Promise you won't sit here for the rest of the night—dance a little. For me. Please."

He turned away, and I envied him. Jack was married now. His escape had a permanence that I could only imagine. Now he would only have to sit at the Sweet table for weddings and funerals. Mae and Jack were a *we* now. I was jealous.

Men in white shirts and white pants moved about lighting the large Tiki torches that surrounded the tables and the dance floor. It had grown dark. Guests flocked toward the band as they began playing The Platters' "Twilight Time." The Dodger game had reached the ninth.

"This isn't music with any beat to it," Darlene slurred.

"Darlene, you're drunk," Hollis told her. She turned away from him and faced the cover band jamming in their matching OP shirts and shorts.

"I've heard better dance music in elevators—how about a little 'Summer Romance' or 'Everybody Needs Somebody to Love'! 'Honky Tonk Woman' would be better than this garbage." My mother's heckling disturbed a few nearby guests, and once again Hollis played the diplomat for a drunk Darlene.

"Ruby, how would you feel about going over to the buffet for some more guacamole, then having a dance or two?"

Hollis didn't wait for my answer. He grabbed my hand forcefully and walked us toward the food. We kept our backs to Darlene and Nana Sue, who were still discussing whether to dance, eat, or sulk. The small wire connecting Hollis's right ear to my left kept us close. We tried to match our steps in the cold sand, like contestants in some kind of three-legged race, and I no longer worried that someone might see the slender cord that held us together. My father waited until a significant distance separated us from our disgruntled family group before he spoke.

"Bottom of the ninth, four to three, Dodgers trailing with two outs. Eckersley walked Davis. Lasorda's bringing in Gibson to pinch-hit even though he can barely walk—the game's on the line." His face was flush with the thrill of a close contest. I squeezed his hand until he spoke again.

"Come on. Let's go pillage the cheese and fruit and hear the end of the game in peace."

The full moon shone like a flashlight in the sky directly

behind Hollis, leaving what looked like a snail trail on the water. His eyes were dilated with excitement. His cheeks no longer sagged from the forced smiles and congratulations of the day. The reception line in front of us cast dancing shadows against the Woods Cove cliffs. The linen-covered buffet table was the closest thing to the water.

In my ear, narrating events thirty miles away, Vin Scully described the gimpy Gibson dragging his injured leg to home plate. It wasn't long before Eckersley had Gibson down no balls, two strikes. Hollis stood to my left, mindlessly cutting thin slices of cheddar cheese. I shoved sesame crackers into my mouth, not chewing but soaking them with saliva instead. The crowd roared in my ear as Gibson fouled two away and took three pitches for balls. Eckersley was throwing nothing but fastballs. The count was now full: three balls, two strikes. I looked back at my family among the drunken revelers.

Nana Sue and Jack stood at arm's length, moving in firelight dim enough to hide any trace of awkwardness. Darlene stood on the side of the dance floor, glowing with pride as she tried to catch the eye of her son waltzing. They all looked happy, their faces bright with a beaming mix of moon and twilight. But then Vin Scully's excited voice piped in and brought my attention back to the roar of fifty-six thousand fans at Dodger Stadium.

Gibson had connected with a hanging slider.

"Way, way back, back to the track . . . it . . . is . . . gone." The broadcaster's voice was barely audible above the madness of the crowd. It was a noise so loud, for a moment I could hear nothing else. It was deafening and it was wonderful. "In a year of the *improbable*," Vin Scully shouted into my ear, trying not to be drowned out, "the *impossible* has happened!" My father jumped three feet in the air, painfully yanking the left side of the earphones out of my ear.

The screaming delight of thousands of delirious Dodger fans gave way to the solitary, unnatural howl of my father. I looked at him. He was staring wide-eyed at the buffet table. His face had drained as his eyes turned over in their sockets like rolling marbles.

And there it was.

At what point during Vin Scully's call of Gibson's home run my father missed the cheddar cheese and, instead, sliced off the top of his index finger, is anyone's guess. It was severed right above his knuckle. Resting there, the finger might have blended innocently with the edge of the cutting board if it hadn't been for the shimmering pool of bright red blood spreading across the white tablecloth like an accelerated shadow at dusk. Transfixed by the detached portion of Hollis's finger, I moved closer to it. It looked abandoned—a little white death adjacent to a half-eaten wheel of cheddar cheese.

Hollis stopped howling and covered one hand with the other, blood dripping from the wound through his clenched fist, spotting the white sand beneath us.

The band stopped abruptly and a crowd gathered around us, dozens of eyes bouncing in unison from my father's gory hand to the loose earphones that dangled from his ear, to the cheese, to the knife, and finally to the bloodless tip of his index finger, now completely surrounded by a scarlet island of stained tablecloth. The woman closest to me let out a murderous shriek. A lady with graying braids dropped her plate of cantaloupe and keeled over backward like a falling domino in the sand.

Darlene and Hollis had never been silent when together in a confined space, but as my mother drove her mint-green, mint-condition Thunderbird through a maze of red lights and red stop signs on Pacific Coast Highway, an absolute stillness filled the car. Hollis's finger rested between them, packed in a Ziploc full of ice from the caterer's beer cooler. When we arrived at St. Joseph Hospital, Darlene gingerly carried the finger inside.

Mae and Jack arrived a few minutes after we did, perhaps slowed by the clanging tin cans attached to their bumper and the "Just Married" sign reflected in the rearview mirror of Jack's jeep. The waiting room wasn't as exhilarating or as dire as I expected. Small clusters of people just like us waited for news. We finally got word. Hollis's finger could not be reattached. It would be a stump. And it would only be a matter of months before his loss was reduced to a punch line at family gatherings: *Your finger just called, Hollis, and it wants you to know it misses you. Do you have any finger to go with the crackers? How 'bout a high-four, Hollis?* Once word got out to the kids at Laguna Heights—which was a certainty considering much of Laguna had been at the wedding—the fingerless jokes would be flying at school too.

"You know Dad's going to be just fine. No one dies from a fatal finger wound, Ruby." Jack tried to comfort me, but all I could think about was the rubble of shaken guests and bloodied napkins that our family had left at his wedding. I wished the Sweets could do something—anything—in a normal fashion.

"Aren't you mad that all this broke up your wedding?"

"Nah. I mean, I think I was about to be roped into dancing with Mae's mother. And that, Ruby, wouldn't have done anyone any good." Jack's happiness, usually as infectious as a winter cold, had no effect on me that night. My father was released in a little over three hours. His right hand was now a mound of gauze. His eyes were pools of dejection.

"How much did you have on the Dodgers, Hollis?" Darlene's question came without a trace of humor once we were back in her car.

"What makes you say I bet money on the game?" He had never directly discussed his gambling in front of me before. I willed myself still.

"Oh, maybe because you snuck a radio into your son's wedding. Maybe the fact that you're an appendage short now because they won. You may bleed Dodger blue, but you don't bleed *for* Dodger blue." Hollis chuckled for the first time since he and his finger had parted ways.

"It was a future on the Series I placed at Caesars months ago. Forty to one odds."

"How much did you lay down?"

"A lot."

"Translate 'a lot' into dollars."

"Enough."

"It's been a long night, Hollis. I'm tired. You're tired. Our son got married. You chopped off your finger. Excuse me if I don't want to dance around this with you. How much?"

Hollis whispered into Darlene's ear, close enough to kiss it. They were telling secrets. They were married.

"Holy—I mean, Hollis! That's a fortune. That's an absolute fortune."

"I know." Hollis looked down at his bandaged hand. The white gauze was already bloodstained. They had all but forgotten me, silent in the backseat. So had I.

"Why, you could do anything with that. That's a college fund. That's a mortgage payoff. That's a future." Darlene was stunned, almost proud. Quiet flooded the car. She glanced at me in the rearview mirror. Hollis finally spoke.

"The Dodgers haven't won the Series yet. Just game one. There's no use even talking about it."

"I wish that you weren't so good at what you do." Darlene paused. "I mean, you don't have a job. I'm no example. I stopped trying long ago. But you could start with this. You could stop."

"We've had this conversation before. You said it—we're both tired."

"You know it's not real, right? Putting money down on a bunch of morons playing games—it isn't a career. It isn't even legal." Darlene was never shy about voicing her opinion—to her, Hollis was a waste. The blinker ticked away like a metronome keeping the rhythm of our silence. We turned onto Bent Twig Road, and we were home.

Like most houses perched on the hills overlooking the

beaches of Laguna, ours appeared as if one hiccup of the earth would loosen it from the hillside and send it tumbling into the sea. Darlene left the car running and opened my side door. She kneeled down and wrapped her arms around me. Then she pushed me an arm's length away and gave me a purposeful stare.

"Ruby Tuesday—this is good-bye for a while. I'm going to miss you while I'm gone." I couldn't bring myself to do more than stare back at her.

"Look. You don't have to listen to me, but I want you to do two things while I'm away. Do what Hollis says. You try to get as smart as you can, and you can get out of here. Hollis will send you to college wherever you want. Do you understand, Ruby?" Darlene said it with the kind of tone that begged for my full attention. She wanted her words remembered, cherished, reflected upon. Maybe she did care. Maybe I cared. Both options bothered me.

I nodded and she pulled me back to her, squeezing tightly. As fast as I could get away, I slammed the car door and left my mother and her familiar good-bye behind me. Hollis opened our front door with his good hand, and I followed him inside.

We went straight to the kitchen and Hollis plopped on the first of three bar stools at the counter. Jack, Hollis, and I had spent countless nights on these cold, metallic stools, leaving them warm with body heat when we left to go to bed. Jack's stool was empty now.

I grabbed two bowls, two spoons, and a box of Frosted Flakes from the cupboard and sat next to my father. When he finally spoke, his voice seemed distant and hollow.

"I bet we're both starving. Cereal. I've always thought cereal was a large step for civilization. It has a simple elegance to it. The bowl. The spoon. The milk. The flakes." Tired creases returned to his face. He began to look like himself again as he spooned flakes with his good hand.

"Hollis?"

"Yes?"

There were so many questions I wanted to ask. Like how the Dodgers winning the World Series was going to pay for a future. Like what my father did if he didn't go to work. Like what life at the end of Bent Twig Road was going to be like without Jack. Looking back, I'm glad I didn't ask any of them. I would find out soon enough.

Two

I guess I should explain who Uncle Larry was—and was not—before I explain why Darlene and I hopped on a Greyhound bus to Vegas when he turned up dead after the Dodgers won the 1988 World Series. I don't remember the first time I met Larry Brenn, but that doesn't strike me as odd—he was family. He stopped by our house on Bent Twig Road for the occasional visit the way I assume most uncles do.

Uncle Larry was a large man, about six three, with calves that resembled flesh-colored sandbags and a head so bald that it picked up light like an oversized bike reflector. When I picture him, he's always wearing a bright velour jumpsuit and thick, square, orange sunglasses. He really only wore that getup occasionally, but his seventies garb was so out of place in our sleepy beach town, it defined him. He was a town caricature, a rich guy who constantly donated money and made waves in our sheltered community.

But he was an ever-evolving caricature—everyone had a different and morphing explanation of who he was and what he did. Mrs. Lerner, who owned the EbbTide Art Gallery on Main Street, would tell anyone who would listen that Uncle Larry made a fortune breeding quarter horses at Los Alamitos—it was why he could afford a house in both Laguna and La Jolla. *It's why he never seems to be doing anything,* she would say in her espionage voice. PTA president Ms. Curtis thought Uncle Larry was just a business-savvy guy who'd benefited from a bull market–fueled economy. Sheriff Heppinger was convinced he was Larry Brenn of the Connecticut Brenns, a blue-blooded New England family that had "more money than God." How Sheriff Heppinger figured out how much cash God had, I don't know, but it explained Larry's philanthropy and his generous tipping habits. It also explained why Sheriff Heppinger never missed an opportunity to suck up to Larry. The president of our Neighborhood Watch group, Mrs. Mazuri, opted for the Larry Brenn as a no-good mobster theory. There was his penchant for fancy cars and the menacing men who followed him around, accentuated by the lack of a Mrs. Brenn and his fuzzy-at-best occupation. Some whispered "organized crime," others "venture capitalist," still others "trust fund." Larry was the talk of Laguna—a town that always seemed to be talking.

Hollis kept quiet on the issue of Uncle Larry. He never denied the things people said about him and never made excuses for him. Hollis just didn't respond when the topic came up.

Shortly after Jack got married and Hollis cut off his finger, things returned to normal around the Sweet household. I went to school. Hollis walked me there and picked me up. Some of my classmates made comments behind cupped hands, but there was little finger furor. We would order takeout for dinner. Hollis and I would sit and talk for two hours sometimes, leaving the Styrofoam dinner dishes and Lo Mein remains piled high until he returned to his converted-bedroom office, and I cleaned up. We'd talk of the missteps of Dodger general manager Fred Claire and rumors of how much money Steve Sax was holding out for next season. Hollis stayed cloistered in his office for hours after dinner, usually until he tucked me into bed.

Every so often Darlene would surface via curt scribbled postcards and abbreviated phone calls. Hollis always took care of any mail that arrived for her when she was MIA—said he would forward it on to her, though he rarely seemed to know where she was.

Two months after Jack's marriage, about two weeks before Christmas, Darlene called early in the morning from Right, Minnesota. She was there to witness the annual

Wrong Day celebration. Hollis and I tried to guess what the festivities might include as we sunbathed, sipping lemonade by the pool. I imagined a town-wide Jeopardy-esque contest with credit given for incorrect answers. He guessed a huge street carnival with prizes for missing the hole, the milk bottle, or the lily pad by a wide margin. Darlene was always traveling to far-off locales to experience strange commemorative bits of Americana—the weirder, the better. Maybe I'm lucky she ran off to do things that Hollis and I could joke about—it was easier than moping over the fact that she'd left us.

It was on that day that Uncle Larry came to deliver his customary holiday gourmet offering of thirty-two frozen Omaha Steaks and a little something special just for me. He wore a green velour jacket over a bright yellow T-shirt. I remember voices drifting to me softly where I lay on the deck when Hollis met Larry at our front door.

"Happy Christmas, Hollis!" Uncle Larry's tone wasn't any different than it usually was—he always acted like there was a holiday on the horizon. His gift's vacuum-sealed packaging dripped freezer frost condensation in the unusually hot Southern California winter. I was air drying on the back porch, having just doused myself in the cool, chlorinated water for some temporary relief.

"Where's my Ruby? I want her to open my gift now,"

Larry said to Hollis.

"Larry, it's not even Christmas Eve, and you're going to get her all frantic. The kid already has one doting grandmother. She certainly doesn't need another."

"I know you don't like intrusions on holidays, Hollis. And this way I can see her open it. Besides, you can't classify Nana Sue as a 'doting' grandmother. That piranha would eat you if it meant a victory at the felt table."

"Don't forget yourself, Larry. I don't disrespect your relatives."

"I wouldn't mind if you did. Can I see the munchkin or not?"

"You can give it to her soon enough," Hollis said firmly. "Do you have the ticket for me? And what have I told you about bringing your goons with you?" I peered harder through the back window toward the front of the house. Larry's Mercedes was parked in front with a long-haired bearded man reading the paper behind the wheel. From my vantage point, he looked greasy and intimidating.

"He's just a runner of mine." Larry swiped his arm across the air, in front of Hollis's face. "Calm down, Hollis—you're getting paranoid in your old age."

Hollis's voice was stern.

"It's been two months since the Dodgers won the Series. I would like the ticket. Now."

"But I thought we were going to sit on it awhile. Wait till things cool down."

"It's been long enough."

"You're not even allowed in Vegas—they'll throw you out the minute you set foot in the Sports Book—how, exactly, do you think you're going to cash it in, anyhow?" Uncle Larry sounded puzzled and angry.

"I'll have somebody I know do it."

"You don't trust me? What about my share?"

"You'll get your cut. Just let me handle this one, okay?"

"Fine." Uncle Larry reached in his pants, fishing out his wallet. I watched as he handed my father a thick envelope. "Here's your cash for the week. Should be three g's. A lot of pheasants laid the points in the Houston game and we won big."

"And the ticket?" I saw my father thrust his hand toward Uncle Larry, once more. Uncle Larry reached deeper into his wallet and slapped a small white slip of paper into Hollis's open palm.

"You be careful not to lose that thing. I know I don't have to tell you what it's worth. Double the vig, right?" Larry questioned.

"Of course. Like we agreed. You'll get double the vigorish."

I had heard this word, *vigorish*, from time to time. But

I didn't really take note of it until my eighth birthday. That year my present from Darlene was a yellowed *Webster's School Dictionary* complete with a Fort Worth Library card that had been stamped with dozens of dates. After Hollis bid me good night, I looked the word up using the Indiglo of my watch. The closest entry was *vigor*. It meant intensity, which, despite my efforts, I couldn't bend into the context. The next entry was *Viking*—equally useless. So I wrote the word down on the inside front cover of my Webster's Dictionary right next to the Fort Worth Library card. From then on, every time I heard an oft-used, never-understood word, I added it to my list. But it was hard to come by definitions that fit the whispered sentences my father and his friends formed with words like: *greenie*, *felt*, *exactas*, *hedging*, *railbird*, *sawbuck*, *teasers*, *slickers*, *squawkers*, *hooks*, *hipsters*, *maidens*, *spreads*, *gee gees*, and *vigs*. Words as familiar to me now as my walk home from school was then.

"Now can we get on with the gift giving?" Larry said after my father had closed the door behind him and deposited the slip of paper into his back pocket.

He waved Uncle Larry through the house to the porch, where I stood waiting.

"Miss Ruby. Guess what I have for you?" Globules of sweat congregated on the top of Uncle Larry's head. He was big and harmless—occasionally running into things and making noise at inappropriate times. When I was younger, he used to lift me onto his shoulders and spin me around with one deft movement. I remember him moving so quickly that when he finally stopped spinning, the world around me didn't. But Hollis never left my side when we were together.

From behind his back, Uncle Larry pulled a Day-Glo green sack spewing different colors of tissue paper and curled ribbon.

"Open it." I was still wet from my swim, and the tissue paper stuck to my hands like peanut butter. The look on Uncle Larry's face made me want to match his excitement, even if I wasn't that crazy about his gift.

It was a videocassette. There was huge yellow lettering on the case underneath the shrink-wrap: *The entire amazing Dodger season captured. Relive the magic.*

"I thought, this way you could enjoy the season and the Series over and over. Who knows when they'll win it again." This was typical of the gifts that Uncle Larry, Jack, and Hollis usually gave me. They never thought to give me the misproportioned Barbie dolls or toxic makeup kits that other girls my age received. Not that Hollis hadn't tried. There was a period when I was about seven—Darlene had begun her intermittent coming and going, and Hollis signed me up for a distinctly girly activity. Tap dancing.

Every Tuesday afternoon he'd sit in the corner, surrounded by mothers, hiding his boredom as I shuffle stepped through the hour. After a month of watching him suffer, I told him I was happier playing Little League. I think I was. It was enough that he had tried.

Uncle Larry stood there, waiting for me, so I spoke quickly, knowing full well that if we lingered outside for much longer, he might melt into a mustached puddle of green velour and skin in the ninety-degree heat.

"Aw. Thanks, Uncle Larry. Maybe we should play it, huh?" I turned to Hollis. "You got time to watch it now, with us?" Uncle Larry smiled, spreading his combed black mustache out wide across his face.

"I was hoping you'd say that, Ruby."

"I'm gonna dry out here a few minutes," I said. "Then we can watch it together." Uncle Larry and Hollis turned to go inside. I could hear their voices until the screen door banged shut behind them. I plopped down flat next to the Jacuzzi sunk deep in our redwood deck.

Most of the homes in Laguna had an ocean view, and ours was no different. The entire backyard was a pool and wood-planked deck supported by stilts drilled into the slanted earth far beneath it. From the sea, the deck looked disconnected from the house, a giant, lacquered wood raft floating in the breezy coastal air.

One of my favorite activities in the sizzling heat of the summer was dangling my feet from the deck and sticking my head between the wooden posts of the deck railing so that I could no longer see any of the structures supporting me. If I squinted, looking through dark brown lashes, I could pretend that I was sky-scraping above the blue ocean, a cloud sunning itself in warm rays. One afternoon I stayed like this for hours, with the sun hitting my face through the narrow opening between the two posts that framed my cheeks. By the time I went inside, I had a sunburn that ran like a four-inch-thick landing strip down the middle of my face. Hollis called me Redstripe. And after a woeful plea on my own behalf, he let me stay home from school until it faded. He took an entire day off, not venturing into his office once, and by the time we'd finished our take-out burritos that night, the soft area just above my hip ached from laughing.

Rising from the hot wood planks of the deck, I gathered my towel around me and went inside. I resolved to ask Hollis about his business with Uncle Larry after he left, as I had done most every week since Jack's wedding. But my resolve was always tempered by fear of what Hollis might tell me.

As I absently made three pickle sandwiches for us, my mind wandered. It didn't take a wunderkind to realize that the tower of eight dish-outfitted TVs in Hollis's office wasn't decorative. And there was the conspicuous omnipresence of Uncle Larry, who was no one's uncle. And the strange men that came by the house at strange hours. And the fact that my father never went to a real office and was constantly on the phone using the foreign terms documented in my Fort Worth dictionary. Then there were the comments from the mouthiest kids in my class.

I put the sandwiches in the fridge to chill and walked into the den, where Hollis and Uncle Larry waited. The Dodger season-in-review highlight video did not disappoint. The action was set to a soundtrack of high-impact songs that played on our adrenaline release systems and got our hearts beating much faster than TV watching required. My father, Jack, and I had seen game two at Dodger Stadium after Jack's wedding, and it was strange seeing it all replayed faster on our twenty-four-inch television screen. Vin Scully's dramatic narration was enough to evoke doubt about whether the Dodgers would come out on top. They did, of course, in five games—an astounding upset. Hollis and Uncle Larry marveled at Hershiser's mastery in the clincher.

The video was an hour long and, after baking in the sun, I got robin egg-sized goose bumps from the air-conditioning in the house.

"That was great, Uncle Larry." It felt like the Dodgers had just won.

"I knew you'd like it, Ruby. What a Series, eh?" I looked at both Uncle Larry and Hollis on the couch, relaxed and fulfilled. I shivered.

"You mind if we eat out on the deck? It's freezing in here." The odd couple consented to my request. The heat wave had earned a special report on the Channel Seven News every evening for the past two weeks. Jerry Dunphy was keen on highlighting the dangers of dying Christmas trees and living room fires. Patrick Healey interviewed one man who was buying a Christmas cactus instead—each thorn outfitted with its own blinking bulb. Before these reports, Hollis had staunchly refused to acknowledge the Christmas El Niño and kept a fire blazing for most of the afternoon and night. He overcompensated by maintaining the house at a frigid sixty-six degrees, never turning the AC off. My internal thermometer was a mess.

I carried our pickle sandwiches in a stack to the small round table that rested under the shade of a mud-colored awning. Shoreline gusts speckled the ocean below with angry whitecaps. Silence followed; we all chewed happily.

"Is Uncle Larry in the mob, Hollis?"

I still don't know what made the difference. I hadn't asked the thousand odd times I'd thought of it before. I hadn't even asked on days kids had brought it up at school, when it was just Hollis and me on the walk home. Maybe I thought I could get more information if I showed that I had an ace in the hole early on. I was sick of being the only one not in the know. Hollis finished his sandwich in two huge bites, swallowing loudly as the sun pounded us with heat.

"What kind of question is that?" Hollis responded. "Who told you such a thing, Ruby?"

"Well, some of the kids at school. Sandy Lerner said that Mrs. Mazuri told her mom that she knew someone who Uncle Larry threatened—for money. Now, I don't think he's one of the guys that shoots people or anything. I just want to know the score, so I'll know what to say when it comes up." My father put the crust of his sandwich down.

"You want to know the 'score'? Ruby. First off, don't talk like you got a bit part in *The Untouchables*. It's unbecoming. Now," he said, pausing to give me a pensive look, "why in the world would you believe something like that? You and I both know that Mrs. Mazuri is an old coot with too much time on her hands. Uncle Larry is a businessman." I turned my attention to Uncle Larry. He looked down, blushing at the pickle that had escaped his sandwich, so I refocused on Hollis.

"Well, 'member parent-teacher night last year? Howie told me that Miss Bliss was afraid to talk to you because of our 'mob ties.' She didn't want you to send one of your thugs after her. And he says that his dad tells him to stay away from you and Uncle Larry." Howie was my best friend and the kind of kid who everybody's mother seemed to like better than her own child. I'd never known him to lie.

"Oh, Rube. Larry . . . and me for that matter . . . might not be your traditional lawyer or doctor, but we certainly don't do any of the things you've heard. People like to talk about what's different. You know that. We're a little different, that's all. Laguna is a small town full of people itching to blather about anything out of the ordinary."

Hollis was only partly right. Laguna did start out as a small blip on the landscape of Southern California, but what had begun as a colony for artists in search of an endless supply of picturesque nature scenes was now a full-fledged, touristy beach town. Still, it had a main street full of mom and pop shops and, as Darlene liked to say, any town with a main street untouched by chain restaurants was small enough to have a vicious gossip mill. All in all, Laguna was a tough place to grow up if your father didn't have a day job that your mom could brag about at PTA meetings.

"Hollis, I don't think you're doing the kid any good by lying to her." The look my father aimed at Uncle Larry then was fierce—almost wounding me by proxy.

"Larry, this isn't your business. This isn't your family."

"If he isn't family, then why do we call him Uncle Larry? Whose uncle is he, anyway?" We'd gotten this far, and I wasn't about to let the topic wilt in the lunchtime sun. Hollis's brown eyes bounced around like pinballs in their sockets. He searched for an answer.

"I'm not quite sure you're old enough to understand all this, Ruby."

"Why not? If you're not in the mob, then why can't you tell me? What do you do all day in your office? You say it's business. But what kind? Is it something awful?"

"No. It's not that. It's just that you might not understand."

"Do you want me to think the worst? I imagine all these terrible things. Like you burying bodies in the yard and making phone calls to men in your office, telling them which people to kill, talking in code so I—"

"It's nothing like that, Ruby."

"Then *what* is it? What do you do?"

Hollis looked pained. His worried brow formed new creases. "Well, I have a good head for numbers."

"So what does that mean?" There was a slight tremor in my voice—I could tell I was getting close to the truth.

"So are you a gambler then? Like the men from the riverboats?"

"Well, yes, but not exactly. I do some of that, but I'm also a handicapper."

"Then why don't we have special license plates? And what's that got to do with anything?"

"No, I'm a handi*capper*. It's different. When I'm in my office, I'm studying players and figures. I set odds and people bet money against and for those odds. All types of people for all types of sports."

"Well, what does that make Larry?"

"He's a bookie." Bookie. It was a word I had written down and considered before. "He takes down people's bets." Finally, a definition I could add to my dictionary.

"Howie says that Larry probably breaks people's legs and fingers and arms if they don't pay him enough money. And that the men that come around the house sometimes are undercover. Is that true, then? Is that a bookie?" I looked over at Larry. He shifted in his seat uncomfortably.

"That doesn't happen, Ruby," Hollis said, assuredly. "Men who keep bets, or 'bookies' like Uncle Larry here, they don't work that way anymore—it's not like in the movies. It's professional—like a boutique for serious bettors—an upscale store, or something." Nervous sweat beads again dotted Larry's forehead and scalp.

"And we call him Uncle Larry because, yes, I work with him, but he's also like family. He's like an uncle to you."

"That's right, my Ruby. I might as well be your uncle," said Uncle Larry, looking right at me and grabbing my hand with his large paw.

"Isn't all that illegal?" I questioned.

"Well, no one ever gets in trouble for it—the police have bigger things to worry about."

"So it *is* illegal?"

"Not in Vegas and Atlantic City, and a few other places."

"So you could go to jail for it in California?"

"No. Of course not." Uncle Larry had remained conspicuously silent for most of a conversation that heavily involved him, and he left soon after.

Hollis and I spent the rest of the day lounging by the pool. We talked for a long while after that, about whether the Dodgers would pay enough to secure Fernando Valenzuela for another year, about how the deck needed refinishing, about who came up with the idea for the first pickle sandwich. We talked about everything but our earlier conversation. But I knew that what I had suspected since my first dictionary entry was now an absolute certainty, and that certainty began to shade every aspect of my life. What my father was doing in his office, why Uncle Larry visited and gave me presents, why I could walk to Howie's house but he could never walk to mine. Suddenly it all made sense.

Three

Perhaps if Hollis had never made his poolside confession, Flash Gray wouldn't have ended up in the emergency room with his head cut in one place and his arm broken in two. Kids had taunted me before, but I'd never had a reason to believe their bullying was anything more than day-to-day playground cruelty. Now, with my newly expanding vocabulary, I knew that my father was a handicapper who watched sports to make money and "Uncle" Larry was his bookie. Suddenly my family started its slide from *offbeat* to *criminal*. And so began my struggle with the truth.

Flash Gray was this struggle's first unfortunate victim.

It was a "minimum day," which meant we got out of school at noon. And it was also the day before Laguna Heights's Open House—an annual ritual designed to let parents come to school and bask in the glow of their children's creative genius. That genius usually took the form of odd construction paper creations hanging from classroom ceilings and rickety dioramas made from sugar cubes.

Hollis walked me the half mile up Bent Twig Road, to Skyline Drive, and finally to school, as he always did. I had given up trying to convince him that I was old enough to walk to school alone.

"You know you're supposed to come to school tomorrow night and meet my teacher, right?"

"They sent ten reminders in the mail, how could I forget? I'll even wear a nice shirt, if you want." He'd shown up in shorts, a Hang Loose T-shirt, and Rainbow sandals at my piano recital. The other fathers had opted for crisp suits and silk ties.

"Yeah, don't want people thinking you don't have a real job."

It was the first time I ever made a joke about Hollis's sketchy profession. I waited, nervous for him to laugh. It felt like my ears were clogged, and they didn't pop until Hollis finally chuckled.

"I think this whole town has known about me longer than you have, honey." Hollis smirked, patting my head. "So is Miss Sharpe going to tell me about how wonderful she thinks you are?"

"Oh yeah, I paid her off already. She should be absolutely raving 'bout me tomorrow night."

"How much did it cost you?"

"How much does a dime bet cost?" I was desperate to plug more definitions into my Fort Worth dictionary.

"Ruby, I'm flattered that you've taken a keen interest in what I do, but there are details not meant for young girls." He was still smirking. "Who taught you the art of bribery, anyway?"

"Jack," I replied. "How do you think he got through school, Hollis?" My father threw his strong chin up and smiled at me.

"What am I supposed to do with you?"

I knew he didn't want an answer. We reached our stopping point, and I continued on alone toward the redbrick school building.

By eleven, the hyperactivity that minimum days promoted was in full swing. The class was restless and our teacher, Miss Sharpe, was struggling to enforce the daily half-hour period of silent reading. Miss Sharpe had colorless skin that, in combination with her pale blue eyes and mud-colored hair, gave her a wintry look. She wore suits in browns, grays, or tans, and they hugged her curvy figure in a way that made boys in the upper grades scrawl things about her on bathroom walls.

Miss Sharpe always seemed to be sizing people up. And since my first day in her class, I often imagined that she stared at me more than at the other kids.

That particular minimum day, Howie and I were passing a slip of paper back and forth for our usual before-lunch game of dots. Howie was winning. I was letting him.

Miss Sharpe sat at her desk reading something by Nora Roberts with a brawny man on the cover. Every once in a while she'd cast a quick glance in the direction of clusters of stifled whispers and giggles.

She looked up from her book. "Howie? Ruby Tuesday? It's silent reading time, not silent writing time," she said. "What are you passing back and forth?" I palmed the paper and put my hand under my desk, looking down. When I looked up, Miss Sharpe loomed over me. Teachers could move so quickly.

"Well, Ruby Tuesday. Hand me the note."

"It's not a note. It's, er, really nothing," I evaded. Howie had already conceded defeat. He put his head on his desk so all I could see was a dense mat of black curls in front of me.

"I'll be the judge of that." Miss Sharpe's delicate hand hovered in front of me. I reluctantly handed her the telltale paper as a voice resonated from a back corner of the room. It was the customary spite of Flash Gray. Wisecracks and insults often flew from that back corner.

"She's probably making money off of Howie, taking bets like her old man," said Flash.

Flash Gray made two or three visits to Principal Gelson's office each week. He'd been held back, and he was six inches taller than anyone else in my class. I never believed that his real name was Flash, but when Miss Sharpe read roll the first day of class, sure enough, she called out Flash Gray as naturally as Tiffany Brown, Matthew McGraw, and Joshua Emerson. His hair, spiked and peroxided to a yellow hue, played second fiddle to the large safety pin in his left ear. His grubby Slayer T-shirts, coupled with his viciousness, were enough to intimidate most of Laguna Heights into submission.

"Flash, please be quiet," Miss Sharpe snapped.

"Yeah. It runs in the family, alright," Flash continued. "Jo-Jo Fletcher's dad had to sell off property because of Old Man Sweet. The guy's a four-fingered freak. Do they let criminals into Open House?" Kids around Flash snickered. My face felt hot. I turned.

"You're nothing but white trash!"

Without saying a thing, Miss Sharpe crumpled our game and retreated to her desk. Lifting her tortoise shell glasses to her nose, she continued reading. The classroom was like a burial ground until the recess bell sounded.

Calling Flash white trash hadn't packed the wallop I had hoped for. If only I had come up with something more clever. *Do they let criminals into Open House?* Full of boiling fury, as soon as the bell rang signaling the end of the day, I ran out of class toward the playground swing set that no upper grade student would condescend to use. Howie chased dutifully behind me.

"What you up to, R.T.?"

"Howie, you keep out of this. Your stupid game got me into this mess in the first place."

"Hey, you're getting mad at the wrong guy, here. Flash there's the one you want."

"Don't you worry." I turned around and gave Howie a look full of menace.

"What are you gonna do? Go beat him up? Spit on him? Come off it, R.T. It's not worth it. You know the rumors—he's crazy. He tried to burn down his last school." Howie's eyes were as wide as tablespoons.

"Oh, go hang around someone else. My dad's a criminal anyway."

Howie's face was pleading.

"You know I don't think that." He pursed his lips together. He'd always taken my side. "Flash was just trying to get at you."

"Well, he did. I don't care if he kills me, I'm sick of all

of it." It wasn't the first time Flash had mouthed off. This time it was different, though. This time I knew the truth. I looked across the playground at Flash Gray, and hot anger welled up inside me once again. His hangout was behind the storage shed that housed the physical education equipment. Now and again Flash or one of his cronies smoked a cigarette or snuck a nudie magazine behind the shed.

"What are you gonna do?"

"Something I've wanted to do for a long time."

"Like what?" I liked the fact that Howie was curious, and I wanted him to stay that way.

"Meet me out front at school tonight. And be there at midnight. If you tell *anyone*, I'll tell *everyone* about the time you wet your pants in homeroom and said you spilled water." I was as shocked as Howie that I had just threatened him. Perhaps I was a Sweet after all.

"That was three years ago!"

"No one'll care when they're laughing at you."

"Jeez, Ruby, you don't have to get so serious on me."

"Are you going to be there?"

"I'm not sure I can sneak out of my house . . . I've never tried—"

"Fine, it doesn't matter anyway. I don't need you."

Howie must have sensed my desperation.

"I'll be there, alright? I'll be there."

"Good."

I hopped off the swing and walked toward my house alone, planning the night's retaliation, knowing that what I was about to do was risky.

As Hollis and I waited for the Chinese food to arrive for dinner, sitting on our respective stools, I tried to talk to him without any noticeable show of nerves. I took a stab at something mindless.

"At school today Howie was trying to tell me that Fernando is the best pitcher ever to play for the Dodgers. Do you think that's true?"

"Nah. Just because you two grew up during Fernandomania—but if he had been there—if he had seen Koufax or Drysdale, he wouldn't dare utter such things."

"He is one of the best, though, right?" I always deferred to my father's opinion on the Dodgers. And pretty much everything else.

"Well, I think he had one of the two best seasons any Dodger pitcher has ever had in 1981. The other was Koufax in 1966—twenty-seven complete games, 2.04 ERA, 382 strikeouts."

"Well, do you think anyone else will ever win the Rookie of the Year, the Cy Young, and the MVP all in one year like Fernando did?"

"No, I don't." Hollis and I didn't look at each other, remaining so silent I could hear the ocean lapping through the screen door.

"You remembering what I'm remembering, Ruby?"

"What's that?"

"Game three of the '81 series." Hollis's fond memory took me back to the 1981 World Series. Dodgers versus the New York Yankees—the most hated team in the Sweet household.

"Fernando got shelled," I said. "He was only seven years older than I am now. And he was up there on that mound, throwing screwballs to the likes of Mr. October and Dave Winfield. It's almost hard to believe."

"When you put it that way, Ruby, yeah, it is hard to believe." He laughed. "Great game, though. You, me, and Jack could barely hear each other, the crowd was so loud." Hollis shook his head.

I couldn't help but smile. It was a great game. Valenzuela gave up nine hits and seven walks, but still led 5–4, thanks to an RBI by Scioscia in the bottom of the fifth. Jack reminded me once that Hollis had scalped a fourth ticket for Darlene. Up until five minutes before we left for the stadium, he'd paced and looked out the window waiting for her Thunderbird to arrive.

"Your mother probably got caught up in something,"

Hollis had said. "She'd be here if she could. Besides, it's just baseball."

It had never been just baseball, and we all knew it.

After the delivery man arrived with our food, I managed to engage Hollis in talk of the Series and Fernandomania until he devoured the last bite of sesame chicken. He retreated to his office, and I cleaned up the messy soy sauce–drenched Styrofoam and crumpled paper napkins before going to my room.

I knew it would just be a matter of time. Hollis would come to say good night, and then revenge preparation would begin. Sure enough, at about ten, Hollis stuck his head in and told me to sleep well. I was fully clothed, already in bed. My room was dark, and my stomach was alive with butterflies. I tiptoed to my desk and clicked on the light. Underneath my pre-algebra textbook was a slip of paper I had jotted notes on earlier that afternoon. I stared at it.

CONGRATS TO LUCY KRAFT:

LAGUNA UNIFIED TEACHER OF THE YEAR

I had copied down the exact wording of the sign perched on the rooftop of Laguna Heights School. The blank sign itself had been given "proudly" to the school by the class of

1979. It usually announced upcoming holidays or important bulletins; sometimes students who deserved special recognition made the sign. That night I was going to ensure that Flash Gray *made the sign*. In half an hour, I had figured out exactly what I wanted. I began worrying whether Howie would be there—I wasn't sure I would have the courage to follow through without him.

At 11:55 I climbed out my window, dressed in a black hooded sweatshirt and black sweats and carrying a small bag. I started my sprint toward Laguna Heights. The street lamps were on, but my fear made it seem pitch black. Headlights brightened Skyline Drive ahead of me. I tried not to panic. What was someone doing driving around at this hour? More importantly, what would they think of a girl wandering the streets alone? My heart pounded. I looked around. The car approached, and I dove into a cypress bush that lined the sidewalk.

I waited, not knowing whether the driver had seen me. The car slowed down to a crawl as it passed me. I was cold, it was dark, and there were four branches between me and being discovered. Finally the only thing I could hear was the lull of the balmy Laguna night. I brushed soil and twigs off and continued, desperate to ease my desire to run home.

And then I saw Howie, sitting on the curb of the empty school parking lot.

"I thought you might not show up. That you were play-ing a trick on me or something," Howie said as I approached.

"You're early."

"You're late."

"What's this all about, Ruby? Why am I here?" I said nothing and pointed to the sign. Howie stood up and turned around. He spoke the words slowly, straining to read through the darkness: "Congrats to Lucy Kraft: Laguna Unified Teacher of the Year." He paused to glare at me. "Okay, so what does Mrs. Kraft have to do with this?"

"Nothing and everything."

"Quit being weird and tell me what's going on or I'm going home, Ruby. We're out here in the dark at midnight, and you're pointing at signs. This is crazy."

"We're going to change the sign."

"To what?"

"You'll see. I need you to let me climb on your shoul-ders."

"Are you joking me?"

"No." I tried to sound authoritative, both for Howie's sake and my own. "Now bend over and quit wasting time."

I had no idea whether Howie was strong enough to sup-port my weight on his shoulders, and I had no idea whether

I would be able to reach the sign. But I had to try.

Soon I was standing straight on Howie's shoulders, as high as possible, swaying in the cold night air. Howie lumbered and grunted beneath me as we formed an ever-bowing arch. He shuffled his feet toward the roof ledge where the sign was anchored, and I bent forward. We were a leaning tower of human, and I was about to fall from five feet up. Far out in front of me, my hands slammed into the stucco ledge of the roof, which narrowly prevented me from toppling down on my face. Howie groaned.

"We're there, Howie. I can reach the sign. Hold tight."

"I don't have much choice, do I?"

The sign's plastic cover swung open from the bottom with the release of a latch. It was anchored by hinges at the top of the metal frame that enclosed it. Using one arm to lean against the roof and the other to lift and keep the cover propped open, I slipped my head in between the plastic and the actual board that held the letters. I could barely make out which letter was which, because my entire neck and head were inside the sign itself. I tried to work quickly, rearranging the letters, getting anxious each time Howie trembled under the pressure of my weight.

"Jeez, R.T., hurry up. I can't take much more of this." I threw down the extra letters I didn't need, dizzy from trying to hold the plastic and remain balanced. As I threw the placards down, I did my best not to hit Howie with the downpour of vowels and consonants: A, N, D, U, I, I, A, H, and T.

Ducking, I released the plastic cover and it slammed. With the master lock I'd stashed in my bag, I padlocked the latch shut. Not waiting to give Howie notice that I was done, I jumped from his shoulders and we both fell into a crumpled heap on the grass. Howie lay there looking at me.

"You're just as crazy as he is, you know that, R.T.?"

"You saying I should let Flash say awful lies about Hollis and not do a thing about it?" Howie didn't respond, too busy brushing the grass off his pants. I jumped up and ran back so I could take in the whole sign at once:

CONGRATS TO FLATULENCE GRAY:

_____ OF THE YEAR

Only it wasn't a blank. It was something much worse. Something that began with an *f* and ended with an *er*. It shames me now to think about all the kindergartners who would use the word regularly from the next morning on, creating a school-wide "profanity problem" for the rest of the year.

"Whoa." It was Howie's only reaction before his

mouth formed into a wide smile. "You padlocked the sign?"

"You think I was going to let us go to all that work and not make sure that the janitor couldn't take it down with a ladder in five seconds?"

"But a padlock? It's going to take hours." Howie snickered. "Flash Gray may kill you yet, R.T., when he sees this."

"Wait, I'm not done." Backing up farther to get the full effect of the sign in the glow of a nearby streetlight, I pulled my Polaroid camera out of my bag. There was just enough light for a shot.

"Just when I think you can't get any more twisted, R.T., you pull something else out of that bag. Is that really necessary?"

"Howie, this is a story that we will both tell our grandchildren."

"Not if we don't want them to think we were delinquents," he said, laughing.

"Well, I want some photographic evidence."

I snapped the picture and we walked home in the darkness together, full of adrenaline and triumph.

The hoopla that my sign editing caused the next morning far exceeded anything I had imagined (and teachers were always saying that I had a very vivid imagination). I saw more K through eighth graders milling around that sign than I had ever seen assembled at Laguna Heights. Hollis and I were running late, but when we saw the murmuring crowd nearly a block away from the gate, we both stopped in our tracks.

"Is there something special going on at school today?"

"It has to do with Open House, I bet. Maybe an assembly or something."

"Oh yes, Open House."

"Well, I'm late Hollis. I'd better step on it."

"Sure, you'd better. Can't be late the day I'm getting reports from your teacher."

I took off running and immediately began my search for Howie's mat of dark curls. I spotted him among the curb-to-curb crowd.

"R.T. Can you believe this?" Howie said, his mouth wide open.

"What's happening?"

"Don't you see him! Up there!" Howie pointed above the sign. Sure enough, Flash Gray was on the roof.

"He was so mad. He climbed right up there, and he's been shaking the sign, trying to pull it down. He even tried breaking the plastic. And he's been screaming like he's possessed."

"How'd he get up there?"

"I have no idea. But no one can seem to figure out what to do. Judy Park's sister, who's in kindergarten, just told Principal Gelson that he was flatulent! She tried to, anyway."

Flash swung one leg over the sign, kicking it and screaming. I wasn't positive, but his face looked streaked with tears. In two minutes school was to begin, and teachers frantically tried to usher children inside. Concerned parents lined the sidewalk—I had never seen such pandemonium. And all eyes were on Flash Gray, perched on the roof, kicking and screaming. It wasn't long before I heard the solitary voice of Principal Gelson.

"Come down from there immediately. We will fix the sign. You are disrupting school." Principal Gelson had been at Laguna Heights since Jack was a student, and as far as I was concerned, he was as insincere as he was bald. Completely.

I can't say when Flash first spotted me, or how long Principal Gelson had been trying to coax him down before Flash pointed at me. But when he did, there was nowhere to hide.

"You! You did this, Ruby Sweet! I am going to make your life a liv—"

Flash lurched forward, flailing his arms in the air as he tried to keep balanced. But it was no use. The crowd below sensed danger and dispersed, making room for Flash to fall unimpeded. Even Principal Gelson ran for cover under a pepper tree nearby. The sound Flash made when he flew beyond the grass and hit concrete was unlike any I had heard before—it was a thud combined with a crack.

Of course, as Flash Gray fell ten odd feet to the ground, the assembly of onlookers screamed as one. Some of the mothers who had stayed swore that a fall like that would most likely kill someone, especially a boy who wasn't even full grown. Some of the younger children started crying, and many eyes focused on me, the accused. Fortunately everyone was ordered to proceed to their appropriate classrooms. Principal Gelson's fury was enough persuasion for everyone to file in without question. Howie looked panicked.

"Don't worry," I whispered as we headed to Miss Sharpe's room. "There's no way they can prove it was us. Especially you." Flash's howls continued until the blaring sirens of an ambulance drowned him out. I tried to fake a look of indifference. Secretly I wondered how close I'd come to accidentally killing Flash.

Class was torture. Every time Miss Sharpe looked up, I thought she would yell out my name and tell me to go directly to Gelson's office. I figured it was only a matter of time before I was put in shackles. Recess came and went.

Rumors darted across the playground. *Ruby Sweet is going to get suspended. Ruby's been framed. Flash will never walk again. They're going to have to use a crane to remove the padlock.* I couldn't tell if my classmates were scared of me or scared for me. I suppose it didn't make much difference. Lunch came and went; I kept a low profile. When the final bell tolled, I couldn't wait to jump out of my seat and run home.

"Ruby, if you wouldn't mind staying for a few minutes, I'd like to chat with you." Miss Sharpe spoke with a great deal of calm. My classmates quickly cleared out of the room.

About once a week, Miss Sharpe would ask me to stay after and talk about a story I'd written or a book she wanted me to read. The last one was *The Old Man and the Sea*; before that was *Romeo and Juliet*. Now that I knew the basis for my family's reputation, I wondered if she felt sorry for me; I imagined the teachers' lounge after Jack's wedding, abuzz with talk of Hollis's self-amputation.

I had never been nervous before about seeing her. This time, though, I was.

"Miss Sharpe?" I said, gingerly.

"Ruby Tuesday. Pull up a chair at my desk," she said. Last night's butterflies returned to make dizzy circles in my stomach. Miss Sharpe handed me a book—Gabriel Garcia Marquez's *One Hundred Years of Solitude* opened to page ninety-six. The word *flatulence* stood out from the rest of the words on the page. It had been highlighted.

"Didn't you read this at the beginning of the year?"

"I couldn't finish it. Too many big words to get through. You told me to put it aside."

"But wasn't *flatulence* one of the words that you wrote down as unfamiliar before you stopped reading?"

"I don't remember."

"Ruby Tuesday, I'm not here to get you into trouble. Please be honest with me. My guess is that nobody else in your class would be able to spell that word, let alone use it for evil."

After a night of secret ops and a day of worry, I lacked the stamina to lie to Miss Sharpe about my involvement. She simply sat next to me and sighed.

"Are you going to tell Principal Gelson?"

"Mr. Gelson is a pompous old man who can't see the forest of learning through the trees of educational bureaucracy," she said. I didn't quite know what she meant by that, but I felt a unique thrill. It had to be against the Teacher's Creed to bad-mouth the principal in a student's presence.

"I don't know what to say. I'm so sorry about everything."

"Ruby, do you realize that we had a group of six-year-olds trying to pronounce the word *flatulence* today? And as for that *other* word, all day children have been spouting their new favorite profanity? You may have single-handedly perverted an entire age group of children." Fear lumped up in my throat.

"I'm so sorry," I said. "I was trying to defend Hollis. Give Flash what he deserved." I wasn't sure if I believed myself. "Miss Sharpe? I'm afraid I might have killed him." Tears fell down my cheeks in rapid succession. This had been the single worst act of my life.

"You've handled things in the worst possible way. I'm disappointed in you, Ruby Tuesday." After several of my sobs, Miss Sharpe's sternness seemed to melt away.

"Ruby, I don't think that punishing you will do any good. If you're the person I think you are, you'll punish yourself enough. That's why I want to keep this between us." She continued: "The incident earlier today was something that I wish had never happened. But I should have silenced Flash long ago. And if I weren't absolutely certain . . ." She paused here and focused on me. "If I weren't absolutely certain that this will never happen again, I would report my suspicions faster than you can say 'broken arm.' You are to spend a half hour with me after school every day for a month and we will carry on as we usually do. Understood?"

"Understood. Flash only has a broken arm?"

"I think he cut his head pretty badly, but he's going to be absolutely fine."

"Thank goodness."

"And that's the last I ever want to hear about it, then." We were so close I could see the wrinkles beneath her makeup. "Did you finish *The Old Man and the Sea* yet?"

"Yeah, I did."

"And?"

"I thought it stunk."

"Really?"

"Well, it didn't stink—I mean that Hemingway guy is good—but the story . . . it was such a downer." At last Miss Sharpe smiled.

"The vast majority of great literature is not happy, you know," she said.

"I know, but Miss Sharpe, the old man chases a big fish around the ocean for one hundred twenty-six pages, finally catches it, only to have sharks eat it, and then he collapses on page one twenty-seven. I mean, I don't want to read a hundred and twenty-six pages only to find out that the old man doesn't even get to taste what he caught. And don't even get me started on *Romeo and Juliet*, Miss Sharpe. Sure, Shakespeare's a genius, but, I mean, come on. All she had to do was check his pulse."

Miss Sharpe laughed out loud. Her eyes twinkled. "You certainly say what's on your mind. That's a good quality, Ruby. Never water down your opinions."

"Why do books always have to be so depressing? People die, love is lost, characters go crazy."

"We learn more from reading about man perverted than man perfected, I'm afraid," she said. Her smile was sympathetic.

"I guess so."

"It's not depressing if you take something away from it, Ruby Tuesday." Miss Sharpe was the only one besides my mother who ever called me by my first and middle names. Somehow when *she* did it, it never bothered me. "Well, all I can say is keep reading—it's time well spent."

I wanted to jump out of my seat. I had survived. It felt glorious. Until Miss Sharpe spoke again.

"Are you coming with your father to the Open House tonight, Ruby?"

"Uh-huh. I'm going to show him my story." I pointed to a wall papered with student writing.

"Is your mother coming?"

"She's out of town." I had the urge to laugh as I imagined Darlene, in red hot pants and stilettos, mingling with the other mothers in their loafers and designer jeans. "But my father will be there, for sure."

"Well, good, I'm glad to hear it. Do tell your father that I would like a word with him tonight, then. I'll be looking out for him."

My heart sank. I knew she would tell him about the sign. It was hard for me to keep my face under control.

"Sure. I'll let him know."

"I called your house during recess, Ruby. No one was home, so I called your brother and explained to him what went on here today. I didn't think you should walk home alone after the day you've had. He should be waiting out in the parking lot for you."

I ran straight to Jack's yellow jeep and climbed in as he started the engine. I wasted no time.

"Are you mad, Jack?"

"Oh, Ruby, of course not. I'm your brother. You can tell me anything and not worry about getting in trouble. Besides, I don't know if you know this, but I was an absolute terror in school."

"So you're not going to tell Hollis?"

"As far as I'm concerned, he doesn't need to know. Besides, it sounds like that jerk had it coming. You always were a wordsmith." Jack was beaming. "No throwing rocks or punches for you, Ruby. I like your style, little sis."

"I took a Polaroid of it."

"Did you really? Even I wouldn't have thought of that."

Suddenly I had to ask.

"Why didn't you ever tell me about Hollis, Jack?"

" 'About Hollis'? What about him?"

"I mean, why didn't you ever tell me about Larry or the gambling. I know everything now."

"About the ticket on the Series?"

"What?"

"Look, Ruby. This isn't an easy thing. After all, some people in this town have lost big money to Larry's outfit. Losing makes them resentful. They think it's like the movies. Most of them have never seen *The Gambler*. And they act like Dad brought the mob with him to Laguna or something. I know it sounds crazy, but you just have to ignore it."

"The mob? Ignore it?"

"Yup, ignore it. And do me one favor?"

"Yeah?"

"No more creative writing with school signs, okay?"

"Miss Sharpe said she wants to talk to Hollis tonight at Open House, Jack."

"So?"

"What if she tells him about what I did and about what Flash said?"

"I wouldn't worry too much, Ruby. The worst is over."

"But if Hollis finds out . . ."

"If she tells him, he'll handle it. Dad, er, Hollis is tough."

Jack sounded confident. But then again, he wouldn't have to brave Open House, now just hours away.

Four

That afternoon my imagination went into overdrive with all sorts of garish Open House scenarios. I pictured a yelling match between Miss Sharpe and Hollis. Miss Sharpe would slap him across the face and tell him he was a bad parent. Jo-Jo Fletcher's mother would confront Hollis, demanding the return of the money her husband had lost. And the Emerson family would yell at him for bringing the mob to Laguna. Once I'd started, I couldn't stop. Each thought was more ridiculous than the last. Eventually I pictured Hollis with his jacket off, shirtsleeves rolled up, fists clenched, fighting off a circle of ruddy-faced, outraged parents as he defended the Sweet family name.

I took to the deck. Lying on the warm redwood planks, I started Miss Sharpe's latest recommendation, *A Separate Peace*. Concentrating was difficult. I read the first few pages, about a man visiting the prep school he had once attended, willing my thoughts to stop whirling around the night's impending disaster. I had to squint to read the sun-brightened pages. I was on page four when Hollis opened the French doors, carrying two grilled cheese sandwiches. He crouched to set a plate next to me and sat down closeby.

"What are you reading, Ruby?"

"*A Separate Peace*," I said, not looking up, afraid he might ask how my day at school had been.

"Is it any good?"

"I don't know, I just started," I said, only glancing at Hollis for a second.

"Is it for school?"

"No."

"Well, it must be pretty good, huh? You seem captivated." I had no idea why he was being so chatty.

"Not bad so far."

"You know—reading in the sun is a great idea. That way you can read as much as you want and next time your mother's in town, she won't blow up at me about how pale you are." I looked straight at him, losing my place on the page. He hadn't mentioned the events of the wedding since we left the hospital. My eyes shifted to the gauze that covered half his hand—I had stopped noticing it. Now I wondered if its eventual removal would leave a strange tan line.

"Yeah, I guess so," I said awkwardly.

"Ruby, is there something bothering you?" I'd been trying so hard not to look worried.

"No, I think I need to take a nap or something."

"Is this about Open House?" I was about to panic. My fight or flight instincts kicked into high gear. "Is it Darlene? Are you disappointed she's not coming?"

I had long since gotten over any expectation that Darlene would show up for anything. When I was younger, even if I hadn't seen her for weeks, she would come to events having to do with school: shoddy productions of *The Wiz*, Back-to-School Nights. But these visits usually ended with Darlene in an argument. She had a knack for saying inflammatory things to highly flammable people. In fifth grade, the last time Darlene bothered showing up for a parent-teacher conference, she told Mrs. Willis that the Rolling Stones, in the span of a chorus, could teach a class of fifth graders more than Mrs. Willis could in three years' time. She referred to Mrs. Willis's teaching methods as "educational injustice perpetrated on innocent minds." The conference came about because of Mrs. Willis's refusal to let me bring in The Rolling Stones' *Sticky Fingers* for Free Music Day. She said it was profane. Hollis spent the half hour after Darlene stormed out of the conference calming Mrs. Willis.

In any event, Darlene not showing up was the least of my worries.

Hollis continued. "Did you know, Ruby, that when you were four years old you got a serious case of pneumonia? You were shaking and sweating and had a raging fever. It was just Jack and me at the house. I've never been so worried in my life. I was staring at you in your bed looking weak and helpless. I was terrified. Not knowing what else to do, I took you to the emergency room at four in the morning. I hadn't seen or spoken to Darlene in four months. But I called someone—someone who usually knew how to get in touch with her and, I don't know how she did it, but she was here in three hours. She flew in from Austin." I squinted at Hollis as the sun shone behind him on the deck.

"Really?"

"Yes. I don't understand your mother, Ruby, I really don't. But what I'm trying to say is that if you ever needed anything, she'd be the first person by your side, I'm convinced of that."

"Okay."

"Anyway, I've got to go make some phone calls, so I'll let you get back to your reading. You want me to bring you the egg timer so you know when to flip over?"

"That's okay. Thanks for the sandwich."

"Anytime." And with that, he took his half-eaten grilled cheese inside with him. I got to page seven, but my mind kept wandering. I read the same sentence over and over again: "I said a lot of things sarcastically that summer; that was my sarcastic summer; 1942." Maybe this was *my* sarcastic fall. I gave up on reading and went inside to my room. Climbing on my bed, I put *A Separate Peace* in front of me and used it to rest my head.

My head was still on page eight when Hollis came in two hours later ready to leave for Open House.

He looked handsome—practically distinguished—in his brass-buttoned blue sports coat, chinos, and Rockports.

"Hey, you look nice."

"I told you I'd dress up. You ready to go?"

"Sure," I said, burying dread deep beneath my voice.

Hollis and I began our walk toward Laguna Heights beneath shining street lamps.

We walked up Skyline Drive, the hissing beetles in the underbrush our only soundtrack. Benzes, Beamers, and Jags lined the streets approaching the school. The lights were on, and the buildings glowed against the night. Parents of students, kindergarten through eighth grade, in their Sunday best, filed through the courtyard.

We cut through the sycamore-lined quad toward Room 303. The open door cast white light on the pavement as we approached the buzz of parental pride. As Hollis crossed the threshold of Miss Sharpe's class, he took my hand in his tight, clammy grip.

The room was packed with parents—it looked like a cocktail party without the cocktails—and no one noticed our arrival. Blonde mothers with white pearls and tan fathers with suede shoes chatted over and among school desks.

I noticed Howie with his mom and dad across the room staring at a student painting exhibit. Jimmy Jameson, flanked by his parents, looked out of character in a polo shirt and pleated slacks. My stomach churned. Flash appeared with his mother. An Angels hat covered his head, and his arm was in a blue cast. I hid myself behind Hollis's pant leg. Outwardly, Flash's mother resembled the rest of them: Her eyes were lined with black pencil, her lashes were thick, and her eyebrows were arched. Perfectly coiffed hair framed her flawlessly made-up face. She wore a periwinkle cashmere sweater set, flowing black pants, and close-toed heels. How had a woman like this produced someone like Flash? I continued to observe, protected by Hollis, knowing I would be dodging Mrs. Gray all night.

If Open House was a show, then Miss Sharpe was its star. She was holding court in the opposite corner, wearing a black dress with small white polka dots that matched her white skin. Her brown hair was in a French twist, her lips painted burgundy, and her pedicured feet in black strappy sandals. She was surrounded by a group of chatty adults. A long line of fawning parents waited close by for a turn to pay their respects. It would take Hollis at least fifteen minutes to even get face time with the woman. I breathed a sigh of relief. Open House was safe.

We maneuvered about the room and, like dominoes, one set of eyes turned as the rest followed in sequence. Tiffany Brown's parents moved away upon realizing they were next to us. Matthew Roberts's father yanked him by the arm and pointed at us. Andy Karine's mother covered her mouth and whispered something to her husband. Parents near us fled toward the student work that adorned the classroom walls. They were the Red Sea parting to Hollis's Moses. It was as if we were being spotlighted for theater in the round with an audience of scornful parents. He was Laguna's outsider, and we stood alone, together in the middle of my classroom.

Hollis managed to maneuver us toward a corner.

"Well, why don't you show me some of your work, Ruby? Isn't that why we're here?" His voice was calm—oblivious to our showstopping entrance. I took him to a picture of mine on the back wall of the classroom, hiding my horror.

"Mr. Sweet?" Miss Sharpe said, tapping him on the shoulder. Hollis turned from my painting.

"Yes?"

"I'm Miss Sharpe, Ruby's teacher."

"Oh! Well, it's nice to meet you." Hollis stuck out his hand, all friendliness. His smile was white and his demeanor calm. Miss Sharpe looked pleased.

"It's a pleasure to meet you, as well."

"Let me just say how much Ruby has enjoyed your class. She's always talking about the books you've taught."

"Actually, I would love to talk to you alone for a few moments if you wouldn't mind."

"Why, sure," Hollis said, registering concern. "Ruby, I see Howie over there; why don't you keep yourself busy for a minute or two."

"Sure, Hollis."

Does she always call you Hollis, I could hear Miss Sharpe say from their corner as I turned my back and walked toward Howie. Before I reached him, I felt a hand on my shoulder.

"Excuse me," I heard from behind me. "Are you Ruby Sweet?" I turned around, face-to-face with the dreaded Mrs. Gray.

"Are you the girl who defamed my son?" I looked around, panicked. Miss Sharpe and my father were talking.

They stood engrossed in the corner, speaking quietly. Miss Sharpe took both her arms and thrust them emphatically at Hollis. She looked frustrated, his eyebrows bunched up with worry.

"Um, what do you mean? I think that you have the wrong person. . . . " I had no idea what I was saying. Feeling dizzy, I looked over again at Miss Sharpe. Miss Sharpe shook her head, impassioned. She pointed in my direction without looking at me. Hollis raised his eyes and threw his hands up.

"Do you know that he had to be rushed to the emergency room because of what you did?" Her voice was low—she seemed hesitant about scolding a child she didn't know.

"I'm sorry that Flash got hurt. I heard about his fall, but—"

"Did you have anything else you wanted to show me, Ruby?" Hollis was at my side, his cheerful voice showing no signs of confrontation with Miss Sharpe. He soon noticed that I was engaged with the glowering woman in front of us.

"Oh, hi there. I don't believe we've met. I'm Hollis Sweet, Ruby's father." He stuck his hand out assertively.

"I suppose, then, you know about Ruby's attempt to defame my son," Mrs. Gray said haughtily, refusing his handshake.

"I know nothing of the sort, although I did hear

something about your son climbing the roof in a rage and hurting himself," he said, looking down at me.

Miss Sharpe must have told him everything.

"Why, your daughter needs to be controlled—"

"Thank you. But from the look of your son, I'm not sure you should be doling out parenting advice, Mrs. Gray."

"I've heard about you, Mr. Sweet. Don't think I don't know what you do—and I think it's despicable. Your daughter seems to be following in your footsteps."

Hollis was smiling knowingly now, a man in charge.

"Leave my daughter out of this. And you can reprimand me all you like, but I think we both know that your husband has a reputation for welching on bets. If there's one thing worse than a gambler, it's a gambler who doesn't pay up when he loses."

"I beg your pardon?"

"You heard me." Hollis lowered his voice, his smile motionless. "And hear this: Rumor has it, your husband owes about a yacht's worth. Why don't you ask him why he sold your Jag?" With one dismissive movement, he turned us both toward the door and guided us out of the classroom.

We rushed into the darkness.

I had always admired my mother's ability, in the span of

one sentence, to transform a chat into an attack, all the while maintaining a cool reserve. Until that moment, I had not recognized that ability in my father. The fact that he had used it in my defense was something I would not soon forget.

"I'm sorry you had to put up with that, Ruby," Hollis began. "Darlene has always been right about Mrs. Gray. That woman has such a narrow mind, when she walks fast her earrings bang together."

We cleared the parking lot and a block of parked luxury cars before I spoke.

"Hollis?"

"Yes," he said in a what-next tone.

"What did Miss Sharpe talk to you about?"

"She talked about what a brilliant young girl you are." He stopped under the arched light of a street lamp to look at me. "I guess that bribe worked out for you, didn't it. Tomorrow we'll buy you a gallon of Jamocha Almond Fudge as a reward. For all your hard work." I didn't want ice cream.

"You were arguing with her."

"I wasn't arguing with her. We were just talking." He resumed walking. I followed, balancing myself on the narrow curb, one foot after another.

"What else did she say?" I said to the back of his sport

coat through the darkness.

"She said I should get a day job, Ruby." His words sounded like they'd traveled a great distance by the time they reached my ears. "She said that it would be easier for you if I did."

"Flash said you were a criminal, Hollis. So I changed the sign out in front of the school. I changed it to say awful things about him. I'm sorry."

"I know."

By the time Hollis and I had made our way home, the California night had turned cool. It was a relief to be inside.

"Do you want to play some Monopoly, Ruby?" For as long as I could remember, Hollis and I always had a game of Monopoly going. I was the top hat to his thimble. He claimed he didn't need a flashy piece to win. When we last left the board, I had him on the ropes, with four monopolies of my own. Even Mediterranean Avenue was dangerous. That night I knew no part of him wanted to pick up where we had left off, so I let him off the hook.

"Nah, I'm too tired tonight."

"Yeah, it's been a long day; I guess I'll have to wait till tomorrow for you to break ground on four new hotels." We said good night and I went to my room.

I knew that tomorrow, when I woke up, there would be

a gallon of Jamocha Almond Fudge waiting for me in the freezer. What I didn't know was that by Friday afternoon there would be a detective waiting for Hollis on our front porch.

Five

My father was a handicapper and my uncle wasn't my uncle, he was Hollis's bookie. I didn't want knowing the truth to change my life with Hollis, so I tried to convince myself that I'd known since my sixth birthday. Deep down, maybe I'd known all along.

It was on my sixth birthday that Uncle Larry gave me that O. Henry story "The Gift of the Magi." It's the story of a man and woman so in love they buy each other presents they can't afford. He gives her combs for her hair and she gives him a chain for his watch. Wouldn't you know, the lady sells her hair to pay for the chain and the man sells his watch to buy the combs. A real upbeat children's classic. Hollis promised to read it to me that evening in an attempt to get me to fall asleep. I remember it began with a cheerful summation of the couple's fortune: "One dollar and eighty-seven cents. That was all. And sixty cents of it was in pennies."

That's where Hollis stopped reading.

In his flannel pajama pants and faded Hard Rock Café T-shirt, he got up and clamped the book closed.

"This story isn't worth reading," he said.

"Why?"

"Because, honey, you can't make a buck eighty-seven with only sixty cents in pennies, that's why. How do you account for the seven cents?"

"But it's not a real story. Mr. Henry made it up. Anyway, the numbers don't matter."

"The numbers always matter, Ruby."

And so I began inventing a history—a history that involved filtering every memory I had through a sieve with my father's illicit activities.

Now it's hard for me to imagine a time when I didn't know Hollis was a hero when it came to handicapping, a fiend on futures, a success with spreads, a victor over the vigorish. I wasn't born knowing that a football gambler must win 52.38 percent of his bets in order to make money. Nor was I born knowing that the best overlays are found in carefully studied prop bets. Nor that it's wise not to bet the college home dog when the spread is two touchdowns or more. I must have acquired my father's gambling wisdom gradually, but it appeared to come at me as fast as the noisy hooves of eight thoroughbreds pounding down the straight-away of the final furlong. In fact, I remember more about the special report on Christmas tree hydration (one method included wrapping the trunk in damp cloths and replacing electric lights with elaborate foil structures) than I do about how, exactly, Hollis explained the illegal world of sports gambling in terms a young girl could understand.

Despite what Darlene often called his "ability to be content with doing nothing," I never doubted Hollis, even after he cut off his finger. Sure, we lived on a steady dinner diet of takeout and Macs, both Easy and Big. And the house did look rather ragged the day before Maria, our cleaning lady, would come—heaps of soiled laundry and dishes gathered in random piles throughout the kitchen and den. But these were trivial facts. It was the other details that started catching my attention.

Like the way my father watched the eight thirteen-inch televisions in his office on autumnal Sundays. He was tuned in to multiple NFL games, keeping careful tally of his nickel bets, his dime bets, his overs and his unders, as he did for all other televised sports. Each TV sat in its own cubbyhole, in a specially built mahogany tower, four sets by two sets. I would dizzy at the sight of uniformed mobs swirling against the eight backgrounds of carefully manicured fields, glistening ice, or shiny hardwood, depending on the season, while Hollis studied and called in wagers, sometimes even on the halftime lines.

Hollis and I were both transfixed by his wall of TVs when someone rapped on our door late one Friday afternoon. I assumed it was Uncle Larry, coming by to mix a pleasant visit with what I now knew was his usual business—dropping off another thick envelope of cash, the spoils of another solid week. I opened the door. All I could see was the backlit shadow of a looming cheap suit, covering a man who flashed a badge and identified himself as Detective Ernie Sanders. Detective Sanders spoke to me in that slow, deliberate way of adults who assume all children are stupid creatures.

"Now I wonder if I could speak to one of your folks. Are they at home?"

"Let me go get my father."

"I just need to ask him a few questions." I motioned the man in and ran to Hollis's office, where the tower of TVs blazed with instant replays. My short sprint across the house left me panting with excitement.

"Hollis, there's a policeman here, and he needs to speak with you."

"What does he want?"

"Answers to his questions," I said.

As Hollis, barefoot and bathrobed, made his way down the hall to the entryway, I camped out in the den, hoping that the conversation would be charged enough to allow for undetected eavesdropping. The pair sat at our kitchen table.

I often wonder what Hollis would have told me later about the detective and the murder had I not overheard every single thing that was said.

The first overheard word to catch my attention that afternoon was *homicide*. Detective Sanders's visit concerned Uncle Larry. Larry Brenn was dead. He'd been shot twice in the head. His body had been found the previous night in a drainage canal in Tustin, three towns away.

"Was Larry Brenn a friend of yours?" Detective Sanders asked my father.

"He was, yes, sure." Hollis's voice hung in the air, as thin as a soap bubble.

"In what capacity?"

"I've known him for years. He's a friend of the family."

"Your daughter's picture was in his wallet, dated, with her name, and there was a card with your home telephone number and address on it." I imagined my photo with its scribbled date in Larry's now-orphaned wallet.

"Sometimes he baby-sat for Ruby. I trusted him. And he liked coming to see her."

"Look, Mr. Sweet. I know Larry Brenn ran an illegal gambling operation. I'm not interested in all that. Brenn's death looks like a professional hit. Two bullets to the head. Body dumped. I'm just trying to find out who killed him, and I think you can help me. We both know it's in your best interest." Sanders's tone was menacing. My heart pounded.

"What do you mean, 'in my best interest'?"

"How did you hurt your hand, Mr. Sweet?"

"I cut off my finger a couple of months ago," Hollis said defensively. "These things take quite a while to heal."

"I'll be frank. You are not a suspect at this point. We've been following Larry Brenn's activities in connection with the Pickford crime family for quite some time now." Detective Sanders shifted in his seat.

"Our sources in Vegas tell us that Brenn had been calling around, trying to hire a hit man to kill someone the wise guys in Vegas know as 'Middleman.' Someone who masterminded the famous 'middling' of the '79 Super Bowl line. Someone who isn't allowed back in Vegas because of it." Detective Sanders paused expectantly. "It took us a while, but we now know that 'Middleman' is you, Mr. Sweet." I wanted to look up *middleman* in the dictionary that very instant, but I was too astonished to move.

Hollis responded in a quick, agitated voice. This was not the time or place, he told Detective Sanders in a voice that did not sound like my father's. Could he come to the station and sort this out. He had to take care of a few things. Detective Sanders set up an appointment. The weathered creak of the door and Hollis's interminable sigh echoed through the house. He paced down the hall and found me, as cold as an icicle, on the couch.

My father stood in front of me, tired and worn. His tanned face hung from his skull, forming loose pockets where his defined cheeks and chin should have been. His neck sunk into his shoulders—it looked as if he would soon be nothing more than a smallish heap of skin and preshrunk cotton. He was old.

"You heard all that?"

"Uncle Larry's dead?"

"Yes."

"It's gonna be okay?" I said, stuttering, incapable of uttering anything that wasn't in the form of a question. I hadn't gotten the chance to fully digest the idea of my father as the town pariah—and now his bookie, who'd tried to put a hit out on him, was dead. Good old Uncle Larry.

"Of course, Ruby. Look, I have to go make a few phone calls. I'm going to straighten all of this out." His voice was soaked in misery. "Sit tight, and I'll be right back." Hollis backed out of the room nodding his head, as if to say yes, everything will be alright. I don't think either of us really

92

believed him. He got on the phone. His voice hardened. I ran to my room, not wanting to overhear another word.

Once I'd slammed the door to my bedroom, I looked around. I don't remember how my room looked before or after that moment, but then—then it was Hollis and Darlene competing for wall space. A Dodger pennant hung over the closet. A huge Hot Rocks poster, signed, of course, reached clear up to the ceiling over my bed. Jackson Browne hung on the opposite wall, flanked by framed photos of Tommy Lasorda and Fernando. My bed read *Los Angeles Dodgers* again and again. The comforter had been Jack's and was rough with pills. In the corner the unfinished game of Monopoly gathered dust. I longed for the simplicity of my top hat chasing Hollis's thimble around the board. At least I knew the rules of that game. Hollis entered my bedroom.

"I just called your mother. We've both decided that you shouldn't be here during all of this. She's coming for you." My heart fluttered.

"She'll be here in an hour or so to take you to your grandmother's. You should pack enough to last you until the end of winter break."

"Why can't I stay with Jack and Mae?" I asked, apprehensive about what might happen if my mother and I were left to our own devices.

"Because it's best if you're out of town. Besides, newlyweds don't like houseguests." He didn't even attempt to laugh.

"I don't know what else to say, Rube. I'm sorry this has happened." Shutting the door gingerly, he didn't wait for my response.

The things I chose to throw into my pink suitcase were arbitrary: my camera, my favorite pair of holey jeans, a sundress, the Dodger highlight video, my Fort Worth dictionary, underwear. Hollis had been there when nobody else had and now he was leaving too. Nothing I did would make any difference.

The door from my pastel yellow bedroom to the portico outside rested slightly ajar. I first passed my arm through, careful not to touch the door, then I slipped my whole body through the crack. Laguna looked minuscule, the ocean small. I stayed there, silent, staring out on forever, testing my eyes to see if I could pinpoint the exact place where the sea hit the sky.

I crept to the redwood railing, this time climbing on top of the barrier, sitting suspended out over the bluest sky. I didn't bother to wrap my legs around the supporting poles. The slightest push and I would fall into the mat of tumbleweeds and brush below. I would roll down the steep hill until the brown chaparral gave way to an endless supply of ink-tinted ocean. I would be helpless in the current.

I would drown.

"Ruby! Ruby! What on earth is going on? What *are* you doing?" My mother's wiry arms jerked me backward. Bits of unfinished wood left tiny splinters in my calves as they scraped over the weathered railing. I hadn't heard her on the patio.

"Honestly, Ruby! You could have fallen to your death! What were you doing?" Her shock matched my gloom, my face soaked from sobbing. I must have been there, suspended over the Pacific for quite some time. I hadn't noticed my own tears.

"Oh, what a mess. I could kill Hollis—leaving you out here by yourself." Her nails left puffy red trails as she rubbed tears from my cheeks.

Darlene pulled me to my room. I didn't resist. Searching around in the dim light, she found my luggage and zipped it up. She clutched me in one arm, my pink suitcase in the other, and led us through the house. Then she loaded us both into her Thunderbird. Hollis remained stoic as he followed us to the driveway. Bending down, he grabbed my shoulder through the window.

"Ruby, this is going to be fun. Las Vegas is like nothing you've ever seen. Don't worry. Things are going to be A-OK. You'll see—this will all make sense soon enough." The air around me swarmed with platitudes. Hollis continued to stare. Our eyes were locked.

"You have your inhaler, right?" Darlene interrupted. "Because in Vegas everybody has one thing and one thing only in common: They all smoke." I nodded. She shut the door on me and moved to Hollis. Hollis's voice slipped into a whisper.

"Here it is, Darlene." He handed a folded envelope to my mother, who quickly slipped it into her back pocket. "You'll need it to collect the money. Keep it safe. Without it, we'll have no claim. Make sure you wait a few days, though. They'll be watching."

"I know how it works, Hollis, I lived there too, re-member?"

"I just wanted to make sure you understand the impor-tance—"

"I understand that this ticket is worth a heck of a lot more to you than it is to me! I understand that your cohorts, the dirt bags you invite into your home, might tail us to get it. I understand that you have put us all at—"

"Enough." Hollis refocused his attention from Darlene's face to mine. They both realized I was staring at them. Darlene walked around to the driver's side of the car and hopped in, slamming the door. She was furious. I wanted to be furious too, but Hollis was all I had.

My mother peered at him through her cracked window and started the engine. Hollis leaned into the car through the passenger's side window.

"I just need a few days to straighten this out, Dar—have I ever let you down before?"

"Save your voice. You'll need it for the interrogation room." Darlene's tone was drenched in anger.

"Must I remind you that sarcasm ruins families, Darlene. How could you take a cheap shot at a time like this?"

"Believe me Hollis, I'd rather not have had the opportunity."

"Just take care of Ruby."

"Just take care of this."

Her last sentence was punctuated with a peel out of our driveway. And it was exactly what I would have wanted to do in her situation.

Some daughters hope to inherit their mothers' good taste or sharp wit. There were few things I admired about my mother, but right then I desperately hoped to inherit her talent for executing a perfect dramatic exit.

Six

Greyhound buses are pipelines used to disperse the criminally insane around the country. There is more senseless muttering per capita on Greyhounds than any other form of transportation. The greater the distance the buses travel, the more likely the people on them are carrying around secrets no mentally sound man or woman could live with. At least, that's what Nana Sue had said every time she saw a Greyhound on the road.

When, exactly, my mother got it into her head that traveling the 301 miles to Las Vegas along the I-15 on a Greyhound bus would be a good idea is anyone's guess. In retrospect, she may have figured the bus was much safer than her lame T-bird, given what was in her back pocket. The trip was about eight hours, including a thirty-minute stop in Stateline, a little-known Nevada border town where itchy passengers could stretch their legs and make their first legal bet outside Las Vegas.

Darlene wore tight blue jeans that hugged her figure, movie-star sunglasses, and a red tank top with *Valley Girl* stenciled on it. Her equine teeth were worthy of a toothpaste commercial. She was one of those people who look like they couldn't close their mouth completely, even if they tried.

If I hadn't known that she spent most of her life on the road seeking elusive adventures to ward off crow's feet, responsibility, and God knows what, instead of home with Hollis and me, I might have found her fashionable. Her toned, tanned, wiry frame made her look like she spent two hours in the gym every day.

"I don't understand why we have to take the bus, Darlene."

"Don't pull that 'Darlene' garbage with me, sweetie. Your father may think that it's cute, but I sure don't. I'm your mother." When she was angry at me, my stomach churned in a way I had grown to like, almost crave.

"You're a mother twice a year, maybe. For a couple of weekends at a time." Darlene's expression transformed into shame. Hollis would have told me to never disrespect my mother. But Hollis wasn't here. My contrary words hung in the air. I sensed both of us waiting.

"I deserve that. I know I deserve that, Ruby. But I'm here now."

I wanted more.

"Only because you don't have a choice."

"A person always has a choice." She was certainly right about that, I thought. Darlene had made plenty of choices: She had chosen Vegas, life on the road, Mick Jagger, rock and roll.

"Besides, public transportation is good for the soul." Darlene often uttered non sequiturs in such a convincing manner that I sometimes found myself believing her. "My car's transmission is about to go out. I'm pushing my luck just driving us to the station in this jalopy." In truth, there were few things Darlene was prouder of than her immaculate mint-green car. "And God knows we can't take Hollis's car in case he needs to make a quick getaway." She laughed.

"Don't you think it's a little soon to be joking about this?"

"Oh no. Having a father who's done some hard time in the can will only make you a far more interesting person, Ruby Tuesday. Jail time is very 'in' right now."

"We're talking about Hollis here, Darlene."

"When did you get so serious?"

"When Hollis sent me away."

"Jeez, Ruby. Hollis didn't send you away. I'm joking

about all this because I don't know what else to do. You know what," she continued, "all this . . . everything that's happened . . . it's only going to make you stronger. In the long run, it's going to be good for you." She stared straight ahead at the open road. "It's a dangerous, dangerous thing to have too happy a childhood," she said. "Even if your father and I tried to shelter you from everything, you'd grow up and you'd realize life's rough most of the time. A picket fence childhood would only leave you disillusioned and dysfunctional. And you'd end up in one of two places: the nuthouse or the big house." She paused.

"Man perverted," I offered.

"What?" Darlene said, snapping back to attention.

"Never mind."

"Anyway, I'm afraid we don't have any other options." She rolled down the window and took a cigar out of her glove box, leaning over me so close that her tanned skin touched my own.

"Are you going to smoke that in the car?"

"Are you going to be this unpleasant the entire trip?"

"Why don't you just smoke cigarettes like other people?"

"Then I'd have to inhale. Besides, cigarettes are the addiction of the common person; cigars are distinguished." Hollis used to joke that Darlene was like Confucius gone wrong with her endless supply of homemade aphorisms. "If you're that disgusted with me," she continued, "you can take a later bus. I'll smoke another while I wait for you to arrive in Las Vegas." The way my mother blew smoke out of her mouth while she talked was almost artistic. I decided then that there were two things I would have willingly inherited from Darlene Sweet: her flawless dramatic exits and her way with a cigar.

"What if that thing gives me an asthma attack?"

"I told you to bring your inhaler, didn't I?"

"I don't want to be forced to use it this early in the trip."

"If it bothers you that much, stick your head out the window."

"I'm not a dog. I thought you were supposed to be on *my* side."

"I am, Ruby Tuesday, I am."

She certainly had a strange way of showing it.

"Nana Sue says that Greyhounds are moving hotels for the criminally insane."

Darlene squeezed the bottom of the wheel with her legs, letting her knees do the steering as she looked down and struck a match while sucking on her cigar. "Your Nana Sue is a snob in a lot of ways. She's also got an outdated view of things. I mean, she thinks a computer is nothing more than an abacus dressed up in fancy clothes."

"A what?"

My mother sucked and puffed as smoke slithered from the end of her cigar out the window. The scent of rust and wet dress shoes filled the car. "It's the Chinese thing with the beads—my point, Ruby, is that buses have leather seats now. And TVs. We might even get to watch a movie."

"I'll be too distracted by the crazy person foaming next to me to watch a movie."

"Crazy people don't foam."

"So there *will* be crazy people on the bus," I said, defiant.

"Don't be difficult. Even if I had a vehicle that was operational, the Mojave Desert has claimed too many cars. The bus. We are taking the bus. And that is final. I don't want any more arguments out of you."

The Los Angeles bus depot was everything I hoped for. Like much of California, upright palm trees with green featherlike leaves lined the parking lot in front of the art deco depot.

Homeless people clogged the corners and sidewalks of the stucco station. They were the type of homeless people— the craziest kind—who not only shouted strange words, but also yelled them in random order, creating a senseless word salad. Stepping out of the car, I was greeted by the distinctive sight and sound of a transient with an amp, a guitar, and an audience. He was singing "Hotel California," very popular with the hobos in the area, under the orange light of parking lot lamps. His feet were black, bare, and almost entirely covered by the dirtied ends of his powder-blue sweatpants. A shopping cart with his belongings was tied to the amp—the sound echoed through the parking lot with electrical furor. The chill night air made me shiver.

"See? The crazy people hang *outside* the station. They're not actually making the trip. Take notice, Ruby: Bums in California are unlike bums anywhere else in the world. The cold winter weather never turns them sour, so they have a good attitude about it. I wonder if that one's taking requests. A little 'Gotta Get Away' would be a perfect way to start a road trip, don't you think, hon?" I watched my mother. She strutted a few steps, snapped her fingers, and gave her hips a little shake. It was unmistakable—she looked cool. Darlene Sweet stood alone in the middle of the Los Angeles bus depot's near-empty parking lot, in the dark, singing the lyrics to some song no one had heard of. Her voice wasn't half bad. In fact, it was clear and magnificent. The bum continued singing long after Darlene stopped.

"Can we just get inside the station, please. I don't like the look of these people."

"Why, I think you're hobophobic, Ruby Tuesday."

"Darlene?" The amp-infused music had stopped. So had the singing. It was the hobo-guitarist, calling my mother's name. Darlene turned toward the parking lot concert. She looked indignant. I tried to follow suit by looking horrified.

"Darlene, is that you?" he continued. So did our indignation and horror.

"Excuse me, are you speaking to me? I don't have any money for you. And how do you know my name?"

"Darlene Paley? You haven't changed a bit." The transient abandoned his amp and came toward us. His feet got blacker and dirtier as he approached.

"What?" Darlene maintained her innocence and her anonymity.

"I know, everyone says that—but really, twenty years and you're still so sexy. Every Monday? We would eat together? The Frontier ring any bells?" His slimy grin was full of dark holes.

"The only bell that's going to be ringing, you unworthy nothing, is the bell atop the police car that comes to arrest you for bothering me and my daughter." She grabbed my hand and jerked me toward the arching door of the Spanish-tiled depot.

Another dirty man stood in front of us. "You ladies got

a liiiiiiittle change so I can buy a loooooootta beer?"
Darlene rushed past him toward the ticket counter.
Breathless, she looked away from me and spoke.

"I'm glad your father moved south. Los Angeles is
being overrun by these people. Only in LA. Homeless
people with delusions of grandeur. That man thought he
knew me."

"He knew your name."

"He must have seen it somewhere. You've really got to
watch yourself here."

I couldn't believe it. An amp-toting vagrant who
smelled like rotten plums and had holes in his mouth where
teeth should've been seemed to have more of a past with my
mother than I had. If I had been stronger—if I hadn't felt
like tears were about to run down my face—I might have
stood up to Darlene and asked how she could have let that
happen. But with Hollis gone, she was my immediate
future. We hurried into the station.

"Ma'am, you can't smoke that in here." The depot
attendant was young and pimply, clearly intimidated by the
false glamour of my mother's sunglasses and fur-trimmed
suede coat. She didn't acknowledge him, and he turned
away. When I picture my mother now, she doesn't have skin
but suede—she was always wearing that jacket, even when
the California heat hit triple digits.

She threw the last nub of her cigar on the ground and stepped on it with the heel of her pointed boot.

"I'm beginning to think that we fit right in here. I'm not sure you're allowed to just throw your cigar on the floor like that," I said.

"Well, either I smoke it or I stamp it. He asked me not to smoke it." She paused and put her hands on her size six hips. "And don't be so angsty, Ruby. We've already seen a vagabond rock show in the parking lot. Things are looking up, indeed."

"I thought these mother-daughter road trips were supposed to be about riding with the top down and giggling about strange adventures. We're supposed to be painting our toenails and sharing secrets." I should have stopped. "Aren't we supposed to be bonding over cheap pizza in a Motel Six somewhere?"

"Oh, Ruby. That sounds positively horrifying. Do you really want to stay in motels and braid hair over a cold pizza?"

"I want to go home."

My mother peered hard at me, raising her glasses and craning her neck. Her eyes took me in.

"I'll tell you one thing, Miss Ruby Tuesday." She addressed me in this way whenever her flare for histrionics was kicking into high gear. "Successful road trips," she said, "are certainly not about going home when things start getting complicated. They are about perseverance. When you run out of gas, you find a bit of hose and steal someone else's. When you get a flat tire, you wash dishes till you can afford a new one. When you don't have a place to stay, you make friends with someone who does. And when you have to take a bus, you make it an adventure." As she paused, her arm squeezed my opposite shoulder and she kept her acrylic nails there, digging slightly into my flesh. I was flush against her suede jacket. "You keep going," she said, "no matter who hits you, no matter how hard. Do you understand what I'm saying, honey?" I looked away. I had no reply, and she wanted none. "This is going to be good for us. Besides, your grandmother is going to be our Vegas sponsor. I bet you've never lost gobs of someone else's money before, have you?"

I shook my head. The lingering smell of cigar smoke and Darlene's empty promise repulsed me. The depot was bustling with people around us. All passengers were hurried and looking straight ahead. A few stragglers had beached themselves on benches.

"You see, Ruby Tuesday? Not one of these lovely people is foaming." She waved her hands, speaking loudly as she motioned to everyone around us. We were eye magnets; necks twisted in one coordinated snap as people stared at us in unison. "Take note," she finished. "Bus depots are exactly like airports except that people have shabbier luggage."

Darlene stood in line and bought two one-way tickets for the late night bus, which would get us to Vegas sometime Saturday morning. A long day was becoming longer. We left the station, and Darlene led us toward our Greyhound. It looked like a steel box with tinted windows.

As we ascended the three metal stairs onto the bus, I was shocked. Permanents, dentures, white hair, and mounds of withered skin filled every seat. Apparently it was little old ladies from Pasadena looking to play some Keno who took the milk-run bus to Las Vegas. I was both relieved and disappointed. I think I had wanted to see some foaming, a bus fraught with human frailty. Or perhaps an episode of madness revealing that my mother was unfit to accompany me to Vegas. My life since Uncle Larry's murder wasn't filled with the kind of misfortune that was impressive or sympathy-inducing. It was a series of disappointments. And there was something about this busload of white faces flanked by blue hair that saddened me; our Greyhound was a tragic, moving monument to the elderly.

Darlene plopped down in a gum-spotted seat, faded with a pattern of yellow diamonds and lawn-colored diagonal stripes. I don't think I realized how fast things were changing—most people don't when they're in transit.

Seven

"Let the sinning begin!" It came as a distant battle cry from the back of the bus in a voice as thin as tissue paper. Darlene and I both turned our heads.

"You girls going to Sin City to win big like me and Shirley here?" The woman directly behind us took our head movement as an invitation to talk.

"Last time I walked away with three hundred dollars. Most beginners don't quit while they're ahead. That's how they get you." Her seat partner, Shirley I assumed, chimed in. Most everyone else on the bus had taken their Centrum Silver and fallen asleep. "The city that never sleeps, yes ma'am, I suppose that's why everyone's getting their rest in now." Darlene's squint signaled that she was in a combative mood.

"I thought New York was the city that never sleeps."

"You've never been to Vegas before, have you? Almost half the country has been to Vegas." She must have read this in a travel guide. Neither of us responded, but she would not be put off.

"The funny thing about Vegas is, everybody's a guest. It's the only city in the world where tourists come expecting to be completely surrounded by other tourists. Ever met a Las Vegas native? No one comes to stay," Shirley ended.

"Don't you think that's funny?" The other woman chimed in.

"I lived and worked in Vegas for fifteen years at the blackjack tables, honey," Darlene began. "Dealt more cards than Hallmark." She used her gruff Bette Davis voice, talking from the left side of her mouth.

"Ooooeeeee!" The string of vowels that came from Shirley's mouth clanged in my ears. "Are you kidding? Can you teach us how to win?"

Annoyance and conceit merged in Darlene's smile. "Well, the house always wins. So, I guess you'd have to start your own casino." Darlene never once looked back at Shirley.

"There have got to be things you know that we don't." Shirley's friend clapped her withered hands and bobbed her head.

"How 'bout this one: If you're in a card game and you

can't figure out who the patsy is . . . well, then, you're it."
With this Darlene turned her head just enough to give
Shirley and friend a peak at her face, then settling back in
she rested her head against the window and closed her eyes
for a nap.

I watched closely as my mother slept with her sunglasses on. I wondered if she was sleeping at all. Then I
shut my own eyes, intent on controlling my dreams. It was
something I often did when I couldn't fall asleep right away.
I'd start by picturing a scenario and let my mind drift off.
I always pictured the same thing: Darlene, Jack, me, and
Hollis, sitting together around a beach fire pit in Laguna
until the pink light of the setting sun gave way to the flicker
of the fire. Darlene brought her guitar and played silly
songs she made up on the spot. In the half darkness we did
things that happy families do—lounged, barbecued,
laughed. But it wasn't a made-up dream. It was a memory
Jack had given me. Whenever I got up the nerve to ask him
what it was like before Darlene left, Jack would recount
long summer nights with the three of them around a fire.
But it was his memory, not mine. As I looked at my mother,
imagining it made me angry.

Darlene slept until we got to Stateline, where the bor-
ders of the I-15 turned from towering strip mall after strip
mall to a melted mix of dust and dying tire rubber.

"Darlene, we're stopping," I said. Her face almost bounced off the window. The bus had pulled up in a rest stop, home to a twenty-four-hour pizza place, a burger joint, and some sort of Mexican cantina. All of these restaurants were in the same building with tables in the middle, and all were attended by half-awake employees. The cold Freon felt cleaner than the recycled bus air. Darlene and I decided that we would split two pieces of pizza—one sausage and one cheese. It was ready made and heat-lamp hot. The smell of grease-soaked mozzarella would have been nauseating normally, but I was really hungry. I sat across from Darlene, swiveling in my chair as I wolfed down my portion of the first slice.

She laid the thick frames on the table between us and exposed her ivy eyes. My mother's face was beautiful, even with the subtle signs of decades of misuse. People had called me pretty before, but not very often and only lately. Braces, contacts, pimple prevention creams, and cover-ups had helped me out. I couldn't imagine, looking at Darlene, that she had ever needed much help.

"I bet you're starving," Darlene said.

"There's no reason for me to be starving," I said, trying to take the same tone she had with our two overly inquisitive bus companions.

"You're not old enough to be mouthy."

"You don't know how old I am."

"You're thirteen."

"Lucky guess."

"Ruby Tuesday Sweet was born on March tenth, 1975, into the arms of her father. There were no complications. I was there. Were you?"

"I don't remember."

"Aren't you getting tired of talking back?"

"Aren't you getting tired of telling me to stop?" I asked, dangling a slice of cheese into my mouth.

"Ruby, are you trying to get me to yell at you? I'm not going to do it." She let her pizza fall to the table. Grease jumped from the slice, splatter painting the area around her plate. "Why should I? So you can go write in your journal about what terrible things I said to you? You building a case against me for your future memoirs? You're as clever as I'd expect any child of mine to be. But I've been around longer and I'm not taking your bait." She spoke as if she didn't care, and I hadn't the slightest idea whether she did.

"Where'd you get that shirt? It's cute." I hadn't noticed what I was wearing. It was my favorite shirt, purple and red striped.

"I don't know. Hollis picked it out."

"Since when does your father go shopping?"

"He takes me every August, so I have things to wear

when I go back to school."

"Well, you and I should go. I think your wardrobe needs a mother's touch."

"Why do you care? And how would you know?"

"Never mind. Tell me, what do you do outside of school?"

"Nothing."

"Well, then what's your favorite subject?"

"English."

"Any boyfriends?"

"No." I figured if I had to endure her questioning, I was going to do it with as few words as possible.

"I don't live with you full-time, I know that, but you're my daughter. I'm asking because I want to know." I took a huge gobble of pizza. "Do you think I'm going to stop caring, just because you're a little nasty?"

"No." I was running out of weapons against my mother's emotional fortress.

"Ruby, what do you want from me? What am I supposed to do?" My face was hot with pizza steam and anguish. I wanted to remove my tear ducts and the traitorous lump in my throat. I dropped the slice to my plate and crossed my arms.

"I don't care." I wanted both of us to believe me. I'm not sure either of us did.

I could hear Shirley's grating voice behind me. Darlene sopped up the grease on her slice with a brown paper napkin.

"Did you know that I gave birth to you at home, in our bathtub?" Her stare was affectionate.

"What?" I imagined her spread-eagle in the porcelain tub in our guest bathroom.

"You were born in a tub. I convinced your father that a water birth was more natural. There's a lot of research on it. I didn't want the doctors in the hospital pumping me full of drugs that might affect you somehow. I wanted you to be perfect."

"Weren't you scared that something might go wrong? I could have drowned."

Darlene laughed. When my mother laughed, her nostrils flared in and out like little accordions.

"We had a midwife there. She had tons of baby-delivering experience and came highly recommended. But your father," she said. She was at once wistful happiness. "Hollis was so terrified the whole time. He kept his car keys in his pocket, and made Jack sit by the phone with a finger on nine and another on one, ready to dial at any moment," she said, giggling. "His hand was shaking so badly, he could barely steady himself enough to roach clip your umbilical cord. But you came out, and you were just fine, and we were so happy. I don't even remember you crying." I couldn't help smiling with Darlene at the thought of Hollis pacing through my birth, but I stepped with caution.

"When did things start getting bad, then?"

"Things never got bad, Ruby. Your father and I stopped agreeing on things, that's all."

"Why did you leave?"

"Oh jeez, Ruby Tuesday, I didn't leave. It was more gradual than that. When your father and I met, we were both very different."

"What does that mean?"

"You have to understand something—things weren't the same when I met your father. I was young, and as young people have a tendency to do, I irrationally fell in love."

"And then you left."

"It wasn't like that, honey. Things changed, that's all."

"What changed?"

"It's complicated. When I first got to know your father, he told me he was a chef at Caesars Palace. I'd been a waitress at the Frontier for going on five years," my mother continued. "You may not believe this about your old mother, Ruby Tuesday, but I was going to be a singer. I'd had a little success at it too. So I thought I might try my luck in Vegas—in those days every cocktail waitress, casino hostess, and dancer in the city was an aspiring actress.

People go on and on about the debauchery run amok there—Sin City and all that—but I'll tell you what Vegas is: Vegas is life's most spectacular layover. Everyone is on their way to doing something else. Something big. Most don't realize that the wait itself can be something big, and some end up forgetting what they're waiting for." I could have sworn Darlene's face colored with a self-conscious flush as she continued. "After I met Hollis, we moved to Los Angeles—he was going to be a businessman, I was going to make it as a singer like Joan Baez. I had visions of a Malibu mansion, a rock-and-roll lifestyle, posh parties in Beverly Hills where hobnobbing lasted until sunrise . . . but I was too late. Bob Dylan plugged in his guitar at the Newport Folk Festival and everyone moved from Baez to Bowie." My mother lowered her head—I had never seen her look like that before, almost sad.

"So you were never a dealer in Vegas? You told our bus friend Shirley over there that you were." I pointed over at the golden girls' table.

"I tell a lot of people a lot of things, Ruby." This was another of my mother's favorite lines and a clear signal that, for the moment, she was through giving me a family history lesson. She fixed her eyes on something just over my shoulder and stared long and hard before returning her gaze to me.

"Ruby, have those two men been there the whole time?"

The alarm in her voice was barely shrouded. I looked back at two sinister-looking men sitting about five tables away, both in dark trench coats, both glaring at us over sections of the newspaper.

"Oh no."

Darlene took out her wallet and quickly slid a quarter across the table in front of me.

"Go," she urged.

"What am I supposed to do with that? Who are those men?" Darlene's apparent fear fueled my own.

"There's a slot machine in the hallway by the bathroom. Pull it hard—you won't have a chance once we get to Vegas; they police for minors. You can even keep the winnings, sweetie. Then walk straight to the bus. I'll be watching you the whole time. Don't look anyone in the eye. And don't wander off." She was all maternal concern.

A geriatric tidal wave was moving from the food court to the bus. My mother waited for me to exit the restroom and followed behind. The two men walked to a beige Oldsmobile parked in the lot. It wasn't until we were seated on the bus that Darlene spoke again. She talked as if nothing odd had happened.

"I think I'm going to get us two tickets to the Shade Roberts concert at Caesars, Ruby Tuesday. How would you like that?"

"Okay."

"I know that there will probably be nobody there your age, but I think you'll enjoy it. I know the band. How many little girls do you know who get to go hang out with a rock star?" I didn't know if I should let loose more pent-up anger on Darlene or switch to being worried sick.

"I'm not little anymore. In case you didn't notice, I haven't been little for a long time."

"I know that, honey," she said, still seeming preoccupied. "Look, don't worry about the men. Do you want to go?" The sides of the highway were filling up with shoddy roller coasters, out-of-the-way casinos, and other wonders on the fringe of Vegas.

"Do I have any other options?"

"Of course. I could drop you off at your grandmother's beforehand if you don't want to go. Or if I don't want you to go." She had to make sure I knew it was a privilege.

"Who were those men?" I questioned. Darlene looked at me, turning so that her back was flush against the bus window.

"They obviously want to scare us. They want us to know we're being followed. This must have something to do with all of this Hollis stuff. But we will lose *anybody* who might be following us at the concert, don't worry about it."

"How do you know?"

"Because if there's one thing *I* can do that a *goon* can't, Ruby, it's get backstage." She gave me a playful wink.

"Fine. I'll go," I said, casually. "But only if you don't leave me alone."

"At some point, you're going to have to trust me, Ruby Tuesday. You're going to have no choice soon." Darlene deflected my anxiety with a laugh. "I mean, honey, I'm not incompetent."

Eight

The sign marking the border of the city was so dinky it was comical: "Welcome to Fabulous Las Vegas." Darlene explained that it was put up before Vegas became as huge as it is today—when it was just a hiccup on the highway. She said Stateline used to be a much bigger town. Then Bugsy Siegel decided to make Vegas a destination, and he built the Flamingo Hotel. People came from miles around—mobsters and gamblers alike. It wasn't long before the city was bursting with money and crime.

The bus depot at the city line was saturated with more women like Shirley. My mother found us a cab immediately and barked at the driver, "The Strip." If we were still being followed, I couldn't tell.

Seeing Vegas spread before me, I imagined how strange a California tract house would look among the large, towering buildings and strange sparkling pillars. Vegas glowed in a way I thought was only possible against the backdrop of midnight, not in the bright light of early morning.

"There's the Fremont, Rube. That's where your grandma lives."

"She lives there?"

"Yes. She's lived there ever since she stopped handicapping at Santa Anita."

"Permanently? You can do that?"

"Yes."

"But you can't live in a hotel."

"Sure you can. You can get anything in this town if you have enough green paper in your hand when you ask for it."

"Why does she do it?"

"Oh, I don't know. That's a question you should ask her. I'm sure she has her reasons. Lord knows some people can't get enough of this town. I used to be one of 'em." My mother chewed at the end of another cigar.

The cab dropped us at the edge of the Strip, where themed hotels provided a three-lane paved trail leading deeper inside the heart of Vegas. We spent the morning wandering through the weathered tropical scenery of the Tropicana. At the MGM Grand, Darlene pretended to be as excited as I was to follow the yellow brick road around a life-size mock-up of Oz.

By the time we were in the lobby of Caesars Palace, my feet ached.

Darlene whisked me through the casino so fast I couldn't stare nearly as long as I wanted to. Everything was strange and new. I had a hard time deciding which scared me more—the mechanical movements of patrons, putting one coin after another in the machines or the endlessly dinging machines themselves. They glowed with fluorescent color. Red-tinted lights hung from the garish gold-painted ceiling, and the carpet was nauseating. In the casino there was no way to tell whether it was day or night. There were no clocks, no windows, and no one seemed to mind. Human-made pollution filtered up to the high, unnatural ceiling, forming a dense cloud of nicotine and noise.

We quickly arrived at the ticket window for the venue inside the casino. There was no one in line, and Darlene wasn't shy about knocking on the glass to get the attention of the booth worker.

"Max! You don't happen to be able to wrangle up an extra ticket for me tonight, do you?" The window opened. Max was a skinny, pasty-colored man who looked like he had been born with a cigarette in his mouth.

"Well, Darlene Sweet. Nice to see you, too. You got a man you want to bring? I thought we had something special."

Darlene played along. "No, this here's my kid sister, Ruby Tuesday. Her first rock concert." She grabbed at me without turning away from the booth and yanked me toward the glass window.

"Aw. Isn't that cute. Like the song. You don't look very much alike, though. Sure she ain't the milkman's? Look, Darlene, this is kind of the eleventh hour, isn't it? I mean, can't you make a call and get this done?"

"Max, you know I wouldn't be asking if I could avoid it. And don't think you don't owe me."

"Alright, alright. Fine. I think I have some tickets left at will-call I can give you. The doors don't open for a couple of hours, though."

When we arrived at the reservations line later, there were already upward of forty people waiting, looking like they had been standing for days. None of them was as old or as pretty as my mother. She and I leaned against the wall with our legs crossed, and I dozed off. In my sleep I was unable to push away images of Hollis wearing an orange prison jumpsuit. We watched a Dodger game together, and people stared at him as they walked to their seats with armfuls of French fries and hot dogs. I pictured him at my tennis matches and piano recitals in the carrot-colored uniform. Then at my graduation, looking white-haired and terrible with shackles around his ankles.

"C'mon, Ruby. The line's moving." Darlene's blonde hair leaped at me, brushing my face as she whipped her head around to look behind us. I looked where she did. And gasped. My stomach flooded with nerves. Two men in suits stood five people away—the same men from the restaurant, now in slacks and T-shirts that stretched over their paunches. They didn't try to hide the fact that they were following us. My mother noticed the look of terror shadowing my face.

"Never let go of my hand, whatever you do. We're going to get pushed, but we want to be directly in front of the stage. I don't want to lose you."

"I don't want to be lost," I said, scared stupid. The doors opened and the line started moving. Judging by how tightly Darlene gripped my hand, she was as anxious as I was. We rushed into the concert hall toward the festival seating area.

Sure enough, Darlene slithered past one person, then another, and we were soon up front row center, standing flush against the stage. Until the lights went out, I searched for the two men, sifting through thousands of closely packed heads. They had to be lurking close by.

The opening act was somebody I had never heard of. Darlene remained absolutely still through their entire set, like a dormant volcano waiting for the announcement of

Shade Roberts. She seemed to have forgotten all about our pursuers. The applause was explosive when Shade and his band took the stage in the darkened arena. Our bodies quivered from the amplified percussion two feet in front of us. I was full of adrenaline—knowing that the entire building was shaking with the fervor of thousands of people was intoxicating. And I only wanted to share it with the woman next to me.

Darlene moved her arms, closing her eyes, singing every word like she was the one spotlighted. Everyone moved with the music, but what separated the bad dancers from Darlene was proportion—she jerked and swayed in perfect measure. She only stopped and opened her eyes between songs, and all the while she wore a brilliant smile. Darlene looked beautiful, and, although I tried to resist, I was not immune to beautiful things—it was easy for me to imagine that I loved her. Cigarette smoke tangoed above the dancing crowd. There were so many bizarre people to peer at, but I could do little more than stare at my mother. She was pumping her fists in unison with an Egyptian movement of her head and a wicked swivel of her hips, never missing a single rhythm. There was a small circle around us. Some watched her. Some watched me a foot away, watching her. Everyone gave us space. Her tight red tank top was wet with sweat, and damp strands of her hair clung to her face. During the last encore, Shade Roberts, skipping across the front of the stage, looked down and threw his guitar pick. Darlene caught it. Judging from the smoothness of the exchange, she must have been expecting it.

I pulled myself away, wondering if this was the life my mother led during the long stretches between her infrequent visits to Laguna.

"Come on, Ruby!" As soon as the concert ended, Darlene grabbed me by the wrist and we dodged through a maze of dispersing audience members, finally ending up at the front of the line for the woman's restroom. I looked behind us. The men from the pizza joint were a few feet away, leaning against a concrete wall, as if patiently waiting to pounce. Darlene never let go of my wrist. The bathroom was full of excited women, wiping sweat and mascara from their faces. The yellow lights made the room look dingy. We hurried to a door at the end of the row of stalls.

Letting go of my hand, Darlene grabbed the doorknob and with one fierce pull to her left, she kicked the door open. The women around us looked shocked. Darlene yanked me through the now-open door, slamming it behind us. A burly security guard blocked the busy hallway. Darlene flashed her laminated all-access pass and a smile. I was breathless.

"Well, I think that ought to take care of Tweedle dum and Tweedle dumber, don't you? There's no chance they'll find a way back here."

"But how did you . . . how did you know that—"

"Honey, you stick with me, you might learn a few things."

Before long we were backstage, where Darlene mingled with the band and their entourage. It wasn't as glamorous as I had pictured—a battered folding table supported an array of shriveled finger foods, and guests sat on rolled-up carpets. The floor was concrete, spotted with blackened gum.

Every single person in the place knew Darlene. They fawned and glowed like longtime friends. Their adoration was contagious.

"Dar-Dar! I thought you'd left us for a while!" The speaker was a tubby mustached man in shorts and a Hoover Dam T-shirt that was small enough to expose a ring of hairy stomach.

"You know I can't stay away long, Gerry." Her response came smooth and easy, sealed with a syrupy smile. I would learn later that Gerry was part of a strange breed of homeless experts in concert stage assembly and disassembly—the rock-and-roll roadie.

"You were sure something else out there tonight. Me

and the boys had a bet on whether you'd make it through the entire set. You know you're getting older."

"That was a bet you lost the minute you made it." She turned away, steering me by the shoulder as the fat man laughed behind us. A few more gnarled roadies approached and similar conversations played out. Darlene handed me a withered miniquiche on top of a Let's Celebrate napkin. It wasn't supposed to be this way. I felt invisible next to my mother.

"How many other daughters do you have?"

"What's this now?"

"You bring a lot of other girls here? No one has even given me a second look."

"Ruby, don't be melodramatic. That's how these people work. Rock-and-rollers never judge, lest they be judged. I could be carrying a midget strapped to my waist and no one would say a thing."

"Fine. I don't care anyway." No one, including my mother, believed me.

"Well, well, Darlene. I swear, I think you were pulling some moves out there that I've never seen before." The man in front of us had had thousands of people cheering for him just moments before. Shade Roberts. My jaw dropped. We were in the hallway, each band member's name posted above a door. It smelled and looked like a locker room. I couldn't believe rock stars put up with such squalor. Shade's ragged hair and stubbly worn face didn't fit my picture of fame. He was, as I'd heard most famous people turned out to be, shorter than I expected. More wrinkled. Without the spotlight he was somehow less than the person I had watched on stage.

But it wasn't how he looked that was most memorable— it was his smell. A combination of peaches and manly deodorant. It was like walking into a kitchen and smelling motor oil.

"You sounded good."

"You look good." As my mother was flirting with Mr. Rock-and-Roll, I looked on like I was watching a movie.

Darlene flipped her flaxen hair out from behind her ears and hid more of her face. She wasn't a fanatic, or a groupie—as far as I could tell she had some sort of a relationship with Roberts that meant something to both of them. There was a spark. I didn't like it.

"It's been a year or so, hasn't it?" he asked Darlene.

"Yeah, about that. I didn't know you kept track of that sort of thing."

"You been writing any?"

"No, not really, I've been traveling mostly."

"Well, let me know. I could use a hit."

"Can't we all."

"And who's this?" For a moment I had forgotten that I wasn't just a voiceover in my own autobiographical movie.

"Shade, meet Ruby Tuesday, my baby sister."

"She is a baby, ain't she?" I looked away, figuring that is what you were supposed to do when someone who was bigger than, if not Jesus, at least one of his apostles looked at you.

"She's thirteen."

"Ruby Tuesday. Who could hang a name on you. Your parents Stones' fans or something?"

"What, you think she should be called 'Whiskey-eyed Woman'?" Darlene suggested. It was his biggest hit and the song he played to end the concert. Shade grinned.

"Well, look, stick around as long as you like. You talk to Mike and he can get you and Miss Tuesday here into the show tomorrow. I'd love for you to be there." Another wink directed at Darlene.

Shade Roberts, steel-toed boots echoing across the concrete hall, walked away from Darlene and me as the long light cylinders buzzed above us. He turned around and looked at my mother, having to speak a few decibels louder to be heard.

"It's good seeing you. Been way too long, you know?"

He turned and kept walking. Darlene's voice flickered in the hallway.

"Maybe there's more to life than rock and roll, Shade."

Maybe not.

Nine

We were rushing through a casino again. This time the place was oozing with gamblers clutching handfuls of chips and buckets of quarters. One-armed bandits swallowed people's paychecks one pull at a time. And this was the equivalent of Nana Sue's living room.

"Why didn't you tell me that you know someone famous?"

"You never asked, honey." Darlene was happy. I had to hand it to her: As far as I could tell, her interaction with Mr. Rock-and-Roll had been effortless socializing.

"What was all that talk about writing hits?"

"I used to write songs, sometimes."

"For Shade Roberts?"

"He plays a song that I wrote, from time to time."

"Is it anything I've heard, anything they play on the

radio? Did he play it at the concert?"

"No, 'fraid not. He hardly plays it." I had a hard time believing that a man who looked at my mother the way Shade Roberts did wouldn't play her song, knowing full well she was in the front row.

"Do you write anymore?"

"No, I haven't written anything in years—since you were born." Her reply stung. At that moment, I was certain my mother had left to get away from what stood between her and fame and fortune: Hollis, Jack, and me. After all, stories from a Laguna housewife don't make for good rock and roll. Darlene wanted the subject changed. "Anyway, Ruby, we had best find your Nana Sue."

"Do you know which room she's in?"

"No, but we can ask." She took my hand and we went to the front desk, which was a slab of wood with shifty legs and peeling red paint. It had taken us about three minutes to get to downtown Vegas, which looked quaint compared to the mammoth towers of hotels piled up along the strip. The desk clerk looked like most I've seen since in crummy hotels—bored and unkempt. Darlene slapped a smile on as we approached him.

"Yes, I was wondering if you could help us. We are trying to locate Sue Sweet, a relative of ours. She's a permanent resident here at the Fremont."

"A permanent resident?" When he spoke, his teeth appeared like rows of golden corn. This was starting to look nothing like the shimmering oasis that had danced in my mind as we sped along a darkened I-15. The casino floor was an ocean of flickering fluorescent, dressed-up desperation. The only thing more depressing than people in their best clothes gambling their money away was people in their best clothes, pretending not to notice they were gambling their money away.

"I'm afraid we don't have any permanent residents here, ma'am. Folks usually just lose their money and leave, ticked off."

"I'm sure she lives here. She has a special rate—I think she's been here for twenty-some years. How many old ladies with canes do you see walking around?"

"Plenty. Wait. You *must* be talking about Casino Sue. About five-two? Fiery old thing? White hair and a pet iguana?" Things were getting bizarre. Darlene spoke up like she agreed.

"A pet iguana?"

"Yeah. She carries the thing on a leash. Red leash with rhinestones. Twenty-one, I believe is the name. It's an oversized insect, if you ask me." He paused and looked at us with brand-new interest.

"You're telling me you two are Casino Sue's family?"

He chuckled at us. "She's actually a Nana to someone? I can't imagine that woman giving birth to anything that would live more than a day or two."

"Please. I think you've said enough. If you could just tell us where we might be able to find her." Darlene was losing patience.

"You know she's famous around these parts, right? Would have been kicked out long ago if it weren't for certain loyal followers. I think she's been here forever. The story goes she won five bucks on her first bet on a Keno card here and decided to stay. I heard she had iced her husband or something. You two know anything about that?"

My mother's smile hardened into a steel scowl. "I'm not interested in contributing to your misinformation file, sir. I simply need to know where I can find her."

"Alright. But I don't think Mickey has taken Twenty-one for his evening walk yet. Which means Sue hasn't had her nightcap. Which means she might be a bit unpleasant. But hey, she's family, right? Maybe she'll go easy on you." Now Darlene's face was hard as marble.

"You'll find Casino Sue on the seventh floor, room seven-fourteen. Good luck." His chortles echoed behind us as we turned away. I was beginning to realize that Nana Sue, painted in the fluorescence of hot Vegas light, was going to be different from the grandmother I knew from

Christmas visits and Jack's wedding.

"Wait! I forgot something." The desk clerk's voice chased us through the hallway. Darlene turned around.

"What?" she questioned, approaching the table once more.

"Two telegrams arrived for you. I just put it together. Casino Sue Sweet. I'm assuming you are Darlene and Ruby Sweet?"

"That's a good assumption to make."

"They said you'd be coming by. Which one of you is Darlene?"

Darlene raised her hand and then moved it over the counter toward the man. The clerk took two half-sheets of paper from behind the desk and gave the first to her.

"I'll take both of them if you don't mind. Ruby is my daughter." It was the first time she had admitted it since we'd left Laguna.

"I've been given strict instructions to give each message directly to its intended recipient." Darlene rolled her eyes. I stuck my hand over the counter. The desk clerk placed the folded paper directly in my hand. I tried to grab it without touching him. Darlene and I both read eagerly.

Ruby. When you get this, you'll be at
the Fremont. Wish I could be there for

your first Vegas trip. Busy holding down the fort here. House is empty without you. Listen to Nana Sue and your mother. If you're worried about those men following you. Don't. They are only trying to scare you. I have my eye on you. Always. Hollis.

"What does yours say?" Darlene said with affected casualness.

"It's from Hollis." I said, looking up at her. "Wanna read it?" I held out the slip of paper.

"Not especially," Darlene said, grabbing the slip from me and feasting her eyes on it. It was nice having something I could tell she wanted. She polished off the note and passed it back.

"Hmph," she said. "Easy for him to say. He doesn't have obese men breathing down his neck."

"What did yours say? Was it from Hollis too?"

"Yes. More of the same. Told me to make sure you bet small." She gave me a half smile. We left the counter in pursuit of Nana Sue.

Darlene grabbed my hand and funneled me into the casino once more. The floor was tackier than Caesars. Shades of orange struggled for supremacy against bright blues on the carpet checkerboard. The peach hallways lined with guest rooms were not nearly as grim as the casino itself. Darlene's grip on my hand was tight—I felt like I was on a leash the way she dragged me down the hallway.

Room 714.

The door to room 714 resembled all the others with the exception of a small Polaroid of a green reptile and a smiling old woman duct taped above the dusty room number placard. Darlene knocked with little of the authority she had been heaving around Las Vegas since we arrived.

"IT'S ABOUT TIME, MICKEY, YOU IDIOT. MY MOUTH'S DRY AND TWENTY-ONE IS REST-LESS."

"It's not Mickey, Nana Sue. It's Darlene. Darlene and friend." She said it with timidity.

"We are not friends, Darlene," I whispered.

"This could be very unpleasant if you don't let me handle it right," Darlene whispered back, not looking at me. I was getting the feeling my mother was nervous.

"Who?" Nana Sue muttered through the door.

"Your daughter in-law and your granddaughter! Your relations." The door cracked open, and my mother helped it along. Nana Sue's acid voice and sagging body were incongruous. She was in a chair in the corner. Curling streams of cigarette smoke flanked both her sides. I don't know how she got to the door and back to her chair so quickly, but it was intimidating.

The room smelled of some terrible mixture of talcum powder and prunes. She had a few worn dresses in the open closet, a tilting lamp, and on her dresser a glimmering set of crystal glasses and a decanter of bourbon. Her room faced Fremont Street, and the high-voltage Golden Nugget sign directly across the road shaded every item in room 714 a nauseating yellow color.

"It flashes twenty-four hours a day," she said, noticing that I was staring at the fluorescent sign. "It might bother some, but I look at it as my own personal night-light, glowing just for me. I don't know what I'd do without it now." Her behavior was eerie—she was acting as if she had expected us.

"Darlene, always a pleasure. Would you care for a drink? I don't know what you young things are drinking these days, but all I have to offer is bourbon." Nana Sue's voice had a dryness that rose in the room like heat off Vegas's asphalt streets. "Didn't mean to startle you just then, by the way. It's just that Mickey never comes when he's supposed to. The kid has two jobs, take Twenty-one out for a stroll and bring me my ice cubes. My old boy, Harold, was better, but he just got tossed out of here with Marsha—she mostly managed the craps table. He played at her table on his days off and used everything from bevels to electric dice. Robbed the house blind. They caught on to him when he started hittin' every come-out bet he made, the stupid fool."

Nana Sue glanced toward the corner where a blanket covered a small square structure by the glowing window.

"That's what you think it is, Ruby. My iguana. I'm sure they told you about it. It's always the first thing they mention. Good old Twenty-one. I'll be honest with you, though," Nana Sue continued with a snicker, "that's actually Twenty-one V. Sin City hotels aren't the best synthetic jungles for iguanas, I've found." Nana Sue smiled and shook her head, in her element, delighting herself.

She then hobbled toward the dresser. She hit the ground with the stump of her cane, then took two quick steps, creating an artificial syncopated rhythm that echoed off the thin papered walls. Thump . . . step step. Thump . . . step step. I wondered if they rented the room below her. She walked back toward her faded paisley chair, drink in hand.

"Have they told you yet?" Her voice creaked as she said it, the corners of her mouth slowly spreading apart to reveal a set of reflective dentures. Darlene had taken a seat on the edge of the flowered bed. I stood in the middle of the musky room by myself with light sputtering around me.

"Have they told us what?"

"Well, weren't they surprised to find out that you were my family?"

"They gave us grief, but I thought they were just being rude."

Nana Sue cackled; her mossy colored eyes seemed to hang from her face in wrinkled watery sacs.

"Owwwww!" She squealed with delight and tapped the floor appreciatively with her cane. "They did, they did, I can see it in your expression! Darlene, sweetie, I'm disappointed with your poker face," she said, full of condescension. I was surprised Darlene was putting up with it. She looked down at her malt-colored drink, raised the glass to her lips, and took a sizeable gulp.

Nana Sue continued, "Sometime you should try it, girls. Creating your own legend isn't as hard as it looks—all it takes is a few well-picked details." She needed no encouragement to continue. "Did they tell you that I killed my husband? I think this decade the story goes that I stuck his head in the Thermador and left our duplex forever. Last decade it involved an incident with black-eyed peas. I might start a new rumor soon, stir the pot a little. People love a good story, especially here."

"Nana Sue, I never pegged you for the pathological liar type." Darlene fell back into a natural sarcastic rhythm.

"And I'd never have pegged you for the deserting type, Darlene."

The room stood still. Two of the most stubborn women

in Nevada in the same dim hotel room were about to do battle. Nana Sue stopped her glare and laughed, leaving Darlene alone with her anger.

"Oh, don't get all somber on me, Darlene," she said. "I'm simply trying to loosen things up between us, you know. We're going to have to work together on this, so we might as well get everything out in the open." She stopped short as soon as she registered our bewilderment. "By the way," she said, focusing on me, "what do you think of Vegas, Ruby?"

"I don't know. It's the biggest thing I've ever seen." I sounded like an idiot.

"Well, if I can make one suggestion," she said, picking up the cigarette she'd rested in her ashtray, "while you're here, you should definitely pay close attention to everything around you. A one-stop wonderland. Why, there's money, dreams, sights, sounds, shows, risks, rewards—all at the cost of a reasonably priced hotel room. Despite its bad press, Vegas is something special. It's a survivor—the whole city's made out of steel. In thousands of years, Ruby, people aren't going to go visit the Statue of Liberty or the Eiffel Tower," she said with disdain. "They will come in droves to Las Vegas. They'll come to stare and take pictures of things that were built so people could come and stare and take pictures of them. They'll photograph the slots, the strings of dark bulbs, the dry fountains, the three million empty rooms. That plastic volcano at the Mirage Hotel will be more of a draw than the original in Pompeii ever was. Or take that pyramid at the Luxor, for example. The one in Egypt probably won't last through the millennium; after all, it's made out of the cheap stuff—mud and water. Who needs to go to see Roman ruins when you can visit Caesars Palace? See the sights in the comfort of air-conditioning. What could be better?"

Nana Sue ended with, "Mark my words," to punctuate her diatribe. It was nothing new to me. I had heard it annually at the Sweet family Christmas party—once Nana Sue had two bourbons in her stomach. But now I had a firsthand view of this strange place that had always sounded so preposterous before.

Darlene broke the silence.

"Nana Sue, aren't you the least bit curious as to why we're here, in your hotel room? Your home?" I was grateful someone had finally asked the question.

"Not really. You don't get to be my age, Darlene dear, without expecting surprises. I figured the day would come when you two would show up at my door. And that it would have to do with Hollis."

"You mean you know why we're here?" Darlene was puzzled again. "What's all this talk about working together?" Tell her about our mysterious stalkers, I wanted to blurt.

"As long as Hollis is involved with Larry Brenn and the rest of his chiseler friends, trouble won't be far off." Nana Sue had finished an entire tumbler of bourbon.

"Well, they won't be seeing much of each other anymore. Larry's dead. Hollis spent this morning at the police station. We think we were followed here, but I have no idea why. Hollis said he tried calling you, but there was no answer."

"He should have known better. I like to get at least three rounds of Keno in before lunch." Somehow, talk of Keno after talk of murder wasn't inappropriate coming from Nana Sue.

"We came here because we decided that it would be best for Ruby to be out of town while Hollis straightens out the mess his stupidity has made." I sensed that any minute, one of these two combustible women would explode.

"Let's get one thing straight, Darlene. Hollis is not stupid. Too trusting, maybe, but certainly not stupid. Why, his brilliance is what got him into the business in the first place. If he were stupid, he wouldn't have been able to pull off the biggest sports betting coup in the history of Vegas, now would he?" Nana Sue looked at me and stopped dead. Darlene drew back a few paces. "Anyway, it's about time

Ruby gets a flavor of this strange old town." Nana Sue tapped her cane on the floor for emphasis. "A lot of her parents' history is wrapped up in this place."

"Thirteen might be a little young, considering—"

"Nonsense. The sooner she understands, the better. I made that mistake once with Hollis and I don't think I'll ever . . ." She trailed off, motionless for a moment. "Anyway . . . that's another story for another time." Nana Sue spoke quickly now. "I made sure the room next door was made up for you two. The key's inside and the door's open. We'll talk details in the morning." How did she know we would need a room? I could no longer remain silent.

"Is someone going to tell me what's going on soon?"

"Ruby, we know just as much as you know." Darlene was impatient.

Nana Sue looked at me with sympathy. "Darling, we're gonna take this town from the inside out tomorrow. Casino Sue knows all there is to know, ask anyone."

All I could do was shrug my shoulders. The thousand-watt Vegas brilliance of Nana Sue's hotel room home radiated off every wall. And I was in the dark.

Ten

I've learned that gambling isn't like other addictions. Sometimes it's just the result of pure overconfidence. Most people know that the odds are against them, that the odds were set that way on purpose (by men like my father) but, despite prudence and logic, they put money down anyway. Why?

I call it the Quantity Theory of Losing: Somewhere someone is winning, and if you play right, it'll be you. Eventually a person loses the thickness of his wallet, his watch, his checking account at Wells Fargo, the proceeds from his second mortgage. Some stop at the wallet, some not until the mortgage. It's all a matter of degree. The way I figure it, my father never started to lose, so he never had a reason to stop. Ironically, he *was* the someone somewhere who was winning.

Expecting to find my own white ceiling staring back at me, I woke up instead to the brown water-stained ceiling of the Fremont Hotel. The phone's piercing ring popped the artificial bubble of night. Darlene had requested a wake-up call at ten-thirty A.M., at Nana Sue's request, so she could take us to brunch at the Fremont Café. Our night's sleep had been a never-ending battle to determine who was the sultan of the sheets, and I spent half the night uncovered, shivering, with fifty-five-degree air blowing at me from the rattling air-conditioning unit across the room.

I had never shared a bed with my mother before.

Darlene hung up the phone, stretched her body out, and let a pleasurable sigh escape her mouth.

"Ah. Blissful. Hotel sleep is the best kind of sleep for you—switching beds is like switching shampoos—it should be done once every few months. How'd you sleep, honey?"

"Did you put the air-conditioning on fifty-five?" I questioned.

"Yes."

"Well, I'm freezing."

"Oh, come on. How often do you get to sleep with air-conditioning on and not foot the bill?"

"I don't care if it's free. I think you might have made me sick." I was too cold to be groggy.

"Hollis spoils you. You're not as tough as you should be," she said.

"You're right. I'm sure Hollis regrets that he didn't train me for sleeping in the Arctic." I had shivered away any thought of getting along with my mother.

"Did you pack anything nice in that suitcase of yours?" she asked. "I'm not sure how nice this café is, but we best not be taking any chances since your Nana Sue is putting us up."

"Didn't you think that was strange?"

"What was strange?"

"That Nana Sue knew we were coming?"

"Maybe the desk clerk filled her in. Or someone else. That's something you'll learn, Ruby Tuesday. Casinos are accelerated grapevines. The dealers and croupiers talk to the floor managers. The floor managers talk to the bell-hops. The bellhops talk to the cabbies. And the cabbies? They'll talk to anyone who'll listen."

"Doesn't that seem unlikely?" I continued.

"You're looking for things that aren't there. I think those men scared you to the point of paranoia. Just get dressed." I had a gingham sleeveless dress that looked like a bag on my shapeless body and a distressed denim jacket with holes in both elbows. My mother had brought me the jacket, three sizes too big, shoved in a brown paper bag a few years ago. She had called it "my first high-fashion article of clothing." When I wore it, I looked underprivileged.

Darlene had stayed the night at our house in Laguna a handful of times, but always in Hollis's bedroom or the guest bedroom. Our first morning in Vegas was the first time I witnessed my mother's beauty routine. The entire counter in the white-tiled bathroom was covered with a variety of creams, pastes, pencils, mascaras, powders, and ointments. As I lay on the bed, positioning myself so I could lie back and peer into the bathroom, I took note of each step in Darlene's vanity regimen. First she applied the ointments, then the pastes, then the powders, mascaras, and finally pencils to outline her eyes and lips. A face that had been pretty before was now flawless. What I previously had considered her "natural beauty" was actually a carefully orchestrated, creative endeavor.

She changed out of her sweats and tattered Cream T-shirt and into a dark blue tube top that showed off her bronzed shoulders and wavy platinum hair. A stiff black skirt flared at her knees and accentuated her calves and four-inch black heels. A chain with a sterling silver die hung around her neck, hitting just between her protruding collarbones. She was ready.

"Oh, Ruby, you look darling," she said, peering at me from the bathroom.

"You look good too." She always did, but I don't think I'd ever told her before.

"Is it too much?" she asked, still looking in the mirror.

"You're asking me?"

"Ruby, there's a fine line between fashion and hooking." She examined herself in the mirror as she touched up her foundation. "You'll find that the difference between dressing 'edgy chic' and dressing like you're working the corner of Vegas Boulevard and Fremont Street is dubious at best. Sometimes the difference is just a high-priced label."

Perhaps she was right. The thickness of her eyelashes didn't scream Tammy Faye, but it also didn't seem appropriate before noon. It was eleven before we met Nana Sue downstairs in the Fremont Café. She hadn't changed from last evening.

In Vegas I had learned that there were three props Nana Sue was almost never without—a Virginia Slim, her tumbler of bourbon, and Twenty-one. Fortunately, to prevent cheating, the casino rules dictated that players were not to pick up the cards during blackjack. This way, visitors could both tar their lungs and destroy their livers, all the while contributing to the casino's profits. Nana Sue was no exception.

"You girls sure look nice." Smoke followed her words across the table.

"I hope we're dressed appropriately." Darlene's voice hinted at her deference. Nana Sue was the first person Darlene seemed to have a genuine respect for—not the manufactured kind that scored concert tickets, directions, or a place to stay. Nana Sue had disparaged Darlene, we all had, but as they stood facing each other I saw two women who were beginning to realize they had a few things in common—Vegas was one of them.

"It's Vegas, honey. You know nothing's too much. Inappropriate is appropriate." Nana Sue spoke of Vegas like it was her longtime sweetheart. Before long we were seated in the Fremont Café. Nana Sue sat across from Darlene and me. The pinging from the casino drifted in waves through the restaurant. Twenty-one, red leash wrapped around Nana Sue's varicose wrist, appeared narrowly alive in the vinyl booth next to her.

"I thought that we might head on over to Caesars after brunch. Maybe show Ruby her father's old stomping ground?" Nana Sue smiled at me, her skin bunching up in the corners of her face. "I hope you two like eggs and cheese. I've taken the liberty of ordering for you."

The Fremont Café was unlike any café I had been to. With faux wood paneling covering each wall, it resembled a ski lodge. Patrons looked tired and poor. Before long, a skinny waitress in a tight black T-shirt and a mini miniskirt approached with a tray full of steaming omelets.

"Suzy Q. Your guests have arrived just in time. Do I get some introductions or what?" Her mascara put Darlene's to shame. Dark lashes protruded from her eyes like spider legs. Her leather skirt teetered just below the line of indecent exposure, and her Southern voice had a gruff twang laced with kindness.

"This here's my granddaughter, Ruby Tuesday."

"Oh, ain't that adorable. Like the song."

"Yup, like the song," I said, making no attempt to be pleasant. Every one of my introductions was a reminder that Darlene had been more clever than thoughtful when naming me. A child's name was not, I concluded, a means for parents to demonstrate their musical preferences. I suppose it could have been worse. She could have named me Honky Tonk Woman.

"And her mother, Darlene—in for a couple of days from California."

"Aren't they all, Suzy, aren't they all?"

" 'Cept for you and me, Sandy." Nana Sue and the waitress shared an intimate laugh.

"Anyhow, Ruby Tuesday, Darlene: I'm Sandy. Been bringing Suzy here a three-egg omelet with bourbon straight up and taking her first Keno bet of the day for going on twenty years now."

"I stayed because there are no curbs in Vegas. It's easier with my cane—what's your excuse, Sandy?"

"I told myself I'd stay until I actually saw you win some money at Keno, Suzy. I'm still waiting, by the way. Speaking of which, Sue, I've put you down for fourteen, eighteen, ten, forty-three, and three this morning." Sandy paused and gave Nana Sue a conspiratorial glance. Up close, she looked younger than Darlene.

"Well, thanks, Sandy. I'll holler if we need anything else. Let me know how much money I won with the Keno—I'm feeling lucky this morning."

"I wish that were enough, Suzy Q." With that, Sandy turned away, retreating into the kitchen.

"Isn't she a hoot? Sandy's one of my favorites. When she first saw me, I think she thought I was a fink. But she likes me because I tipped well from the beginning. Sometimes I think that's a more honest basis for a friendship than most, Ruby." Nana Sue looked at me with intensity. "You keep that in mind. Always tip well."

"Someday waitresses will inherit the earth," Darlene interjected.

My grandmother looked at Darlene with surprise. "Why, yes, that's very true," she said, shocked at their common view. Nana Sue, for the moment, seemed to have forgotten that this was the woman who had abandoned her grandchildren and only son. "Anyhow, eat up, girls. Best omelet in town. We've got a big day ahead of us."

It wasn't long before I was sandwiched between Nana Sue, Twenty-one, and Darlene in the back of a gypsy cab. We motored along the strip until we pulled into the huge parking lot of Caesars Palace.

The entrance to Caesars made the Fremont look like a poor man's palace. The marble pillars and brimming lucid fountains were intended to wow patrons, and they did. I had more time to look around now that Darlene and I weren't running through the place in search of concert tickets. The clientele at Caesars was all Gucci and Dior. The quarter slot machines of the Fremont were replaced with dollar- and five-dollar slots. Instead of cracked tiling, green marble lined the walls. And every person of authority in the place seemed to know my grandmother.

"Brought some visitors with you for good luck today, Suzy?" said a tuxedoed man who looked to be running things.

"Luck's a myth clung to by people with hope and no skill. I'm going to teach these girls a few things." Because Nana Sue had to travel at a pace consistent with a bum leg and a pet iguana, we walked slowly and stopped often. We were making the rounds through the chandeliered casino. Three dealers waved to Nana Sue from behind their respective tables. A couple of nicely dressed older men at the hundred-dollar minimum blackjack table looked up from their hands long enough to nod at her approvingly. She saluted them respectfully with her wooden cane. I followed behind with Twenty-one.

We approached a room aglow with light from a high wall of about thirty huge TV screens awash with the yammering of colorful commentators giving the play-by-play. Hundreds of panels lit with countless names and numbers spelled out in red, green, and yellow dots surrounded the TV screens. It looked like a wall of millions of tiny haywire traffic lights. A crowd of mostly men was yelling at every screen, sitting in dozens of rows of plush leather swivel chairs that all faced the bank of TVs. One TV as large as any of those that covered the wall would have been a spectacle. Thirty were dizzying.

That's when it struck me.

This was Hollis's office with an unlimited budget—more chairs, larger TVs, sports teams and numbers in bright lights on the wall instead of on a white board in marker. Hollis hadn't quit Vegas; he'd just moved locations.

"Welcome, ladies, to the Olympiad Race and Sports Book, a legend among bookies and gamblers alike." Nana Sue drenched her announcement in triumph. "Business is good, but you should see this place during one of the majors—the Super Bowl, the World Series, the Final Four—it's elbow to elbow. I can't even bring Twenty-one because I'm afraid he'll get trampled." She looked around at the casino adoringly.

"I thought you were into slots and cards now, Nana Sue—didn't you give up the horse handicapping?" Darlene weighed in.

"This is the real thing, always has been. It's a hard habit to break." She focused on me. "Ruby, back when I was raising your father, I was one of the best horse handicappers this town has ever seen. Hollis grew up in that world—he probably should have hated spending holidays at the track while I studied the maidens and exactas. No world for a child—but he loved it."

Nana Sue's eyes glowed with the intoxication of a fond memory. "Why, I bet he was the world's youngest stooper. I can remember his tiny towhead bobbing up and down through the aisles, hunting for discarded winning tickets at the racetrack. Sometimes he'd find one. We went to Santa Anita and Del Mar from Reno. That was before my rheumatism, though." She clicked her tongue and nodded her head with resignation. "You know there's a saying about all this: You bet you can make three spades, it's entertainment. You bet IBM is on an up move, that's business. You bet on a horse or a football team, that's gambling."

A slender mustached man, chewing on a cigar and wearing a flat-brimmed hat, approached Nana Sue. He stood out in his suspenders and bright orange trousers.

"Sue. I was wondering when you'd be back—haven't seen you in a week or two. Where have you been?"

"Danny Boy! What, you worried I was shopping odds down the street?"

"I thought you might have taken a vacation from your extended vacation. You haven't been placing your exotics with another sports book, have you?"

"Nah, I was just resting up, actually. The boundless energy of youth seems to have slipped through my fingers, Danny." Nana Sue extended her arm to us.

"Meet the family. Darlene and Ruby Tuesday, this is Danny Glass." The entire day was shaping up to be an endless meet-and-greet.

"Like the song." Danny concentrated on Nana Sue. "Look, I hate to break this to you, Sue, but the kid's got to go play someplace else. You know the rules. We can't risk our license, even for your kin."

Nana Sue turned on her sweetness.

"What if I sit her down over there and she just watches? Besides, I spent my whole life inspecting for

Pinks. First sign of trouble we'll leave." Nana Sue was so natural, I know I'd have let her do anything.

"Just don't cause one of your scenes, Mrs. Sweet." Danny turned toward his station on the other side of the huge room. Then spun back to face us.

"Wait a second, I almost forgot—what in the heck is this business with Larry Brenn I've been hearing about? It's been on the news."

"I just heard about it for the first time yesterday, from Darlene here. They took Hollis in for questioning. I'm looking after Ruby." Danny studied me for the first time.

"Ruby . . . Ruby Sweet? Middleman's kid, huh? Another Sweet in Vegas. Well, I'll be . . ." His words floated over me. I was afraid to look directly into his eyes. "What does Hollis have to do with Larry, anyway?" Danny looked genuinely concerned.

"Hollis and Larry, they've been doing business together for some time."

"Hollis and Larry Brenn? Why would Hollis still deal with that slicker? I thought he wanted a fresh start."

"I don't know, Danny Boy, I just don't know." Nana spoke in a chipper tone. Giving his hand a tight squeeze, she looked up at Danny with a skillful arch of her eyebrow. "We'll have one of our talks later, alright, sweetie?"

"Sure, sure. Make sure the kid stays out of sight." Nana Sue nodded.

Darlene was puzzled.

"What was that about, Nana Sue?"

"Danny's an old friend of Hollis's. They used to handicap together back in the sixties."

"I was here then too, Nana Sue. I know."

"Of course you do, sweetie." Nana Sue turned away from Darlene. "Of course you do," she repeated.

"I was living with Hollis then, when he was setting lines for the Santa Anita Sports Book." Darlene's unfiltered defensiveness was brand-new to me. It seemed the two most stubborn women in my life were about to face off.

"I suppose you can tell me, then, what Danny Glass does here at Caesars, right?" Nana Sue's smile reminded me of Hollis's during his showdown with Mrs. Gray. Darlene's teeth were clenched. Her voice was iron.

"I wasn't claiming to know more about Vegas Sports—"

"I know, dearie. I'm teasing." Nana Sue melted. The Knicks versus the Pistons, the Jets versus the Oilers, and the excitement of what looked like a quarter-horse race interrupted the spirit of competition rising between Nana Sue and Darlene.

"Anyhow," Nana Sue began again, "Danny Glass was one of the original members of the line-making brain trust that set the odds for all the sports books in Vegas. Now he signs checks and approves credit lines here at Caesars—has what they call the power of the pencil."

"Oh yes, of course."

Darlene nodded her head and looked away. Even I could tell that my mother felt foolish. Maybe she'd been feeling that way ever since we arrived at Nana Sue's seventh-floor room at the Fremont. It was something I took note of. When Nana Sue spoke of Hollis's past, Darlene wasn't as clear about it all as she should have been. For once my mother and I were on equal footing, and I wanted to bathe in it, if only for a moment.

Eleven

"I'm pretty good at getting what I want, but I have to hand it to you: I couldn't convince a floor manager to let a child stay in the Sports Book." Darlene gave Nana Sue a look of sincere respect.

"Oh, Danny and I have an understanding. He used to raise a fuss every time I brought Twenty-one here. Animals weren't allowed in casinos, he said. No exceptions. Someone might be allergic. Someone might be offended. On and on it went. I told him that if he found someone who was allergic or offended by iguanas, he would never see Twenty-one's scaly face in here again." Nana Sue looked up at the quarter-horse race in progress on one of the thirty screens. She stomped her foot on the industrial red carpet.

"Crimany. I meant to bet that race. Dontcallmeshirley was a shoo-in at seven to one." She swiveled her chair back toward Darlene and me. "Anyway, I would bring Twenty-one every day, and every day we'd have the same argument. After about a month, Danny stopped arguing. He probably got tired of the whole thing. Either that or he couldn't find a single person with a reptile allergy." Nana Sue cracked a grin. "Being a harmless old lady does have its advantages." Darlene and I were speechless.

Danny stood a football field away, on a platform that overlooked the vast room. From the huge molded entryway that opened out to the casino, a fleet of cocktail waitresses mounted an attack. All of them wore simple black dresses, had long fishnet-covered legs, and walked confidently in four-inch heels. While some delivered platters full of drinks, the rest took patrons' orders. Their movements were deliberate—each bettor's alcoholic inclinations were encouraged. Danny's organization of the Sports Book was flawless.

"It looks like Danny's up to old tricks. People are being a little too cautious with their bets, I'm sure. Nothing like a little booze to loosen wallets." She turned to us. "This town is full of things you may think are free, Ruby. Like the cocktails they bring you on command, for instance." Nana Sue signaled with her raised hand at the cavalry of drink carriers. "It's one of the many Vegas paradoxes. They're only free if you're spending money."

I looked at Nana Sue and Darlene next to me and wondered what Hollis would think of the three women in (and out of) his life, sitting together in this smoky parlor.

"What do you say, girls—maybe we should try our luck! I think the New England-Detroit game is about to start. It'll be fun, and we've got nothing else to do." Nana Sue stared at the maze of red, green, and yellow diodes. "It looks like the Pats are the chalk at seven." Vegas was full of the words I'd recorded in my Fort Worth Dictionary, and some I'd never even heard. This place was the home of my father's language.

I had no idea how Nana Sue could glean any helpful information from the rows and rows of team names and numbers that were lit on the faraway panels in the front of the room. Darlene swiveled toward Nana Sue, looking past me.

"Are you sure Ruby should be here—"

"Hold on, I'll be right back." Nana Sue ignored my mother's objection. She clicked her tongue, bringing Twenty-one to attention, and took off toward the four-sided counter in the middle of the room where two bow-tied employees in short-sleeved collared shirts were waiting to take bets.

Thump . . . step step. Watching Nana Sue hobble through the labyrinth of chairs and tables with free drinks resting on scarlet casino napkins made me question exactly how she got along day-to-day. It looked like one accidental bump from any number of distracted casino patrons might topple her over. Lacquered cane in one hand, patent red-leather leash in the other, she arrived at the island of desks. My grandmother was greeted respectfully by the two casino employees; one of them grabbed Twenty-one's leash while Nana Sue sifted through the pocket in her pleated pants. A wad of cash was tendered, and she received a white ticket and the leash back in return. It had the clean and easy feel of a daily ritual.

Nana Sue made her way back toward us. "Well, Ruby, you just witnessed your first *legal* sports bet." She huffed, aware that I'd probably overheard Hollis on the phone to Uncle Larry a time or two. She plopped down in her chair. The three of us sat in our row: me in the middle, Nana Sue on the left, and Darlene by the wall.

"What's the ticket for?" I asked, seizing on the white stub Nana Sue clutched in her hand.

"Oh, just a record of my bet so I can cash in if I win. Look," she said, flattening it on the maple cocktail table between our chairs. "It shows that I put a nickel on the dog plus the points." She pointed to "Detroit +7 $550 to win $500" on the ticket.

"A *what* on the *who*?"

"Ruby, haven't you been paying attention to what your father does all day?" Nana Sue shook her head. "The dog is the underdog, the team that isn't favored. I took Detroit plus seven, which means if Detroit wins outright, or loses by six points or less, I win. A nickel is just short for $500. Easy, right?" It was easy. If you knew the language of nickels, dimes, spreads, chalks, dogs, and touts. My mind dizzied with the thought of all the terms I would soon be defining in my dictionary.

Darlene looked at me and then raised a well-tweezed eyebrow at Nana Sue.

"Maybe we should get out of here, Sue," Darlene said. "This place makes me nervous."

"What do you mean?"

"I just don't think Ruby should be here. Let's forget the game and the bet and go to the Thunderdome," she said. Thunderdome was an adventure land at Circus Circus where parents tried to preserve their children's innocence amongst the hustling greed of Vegas. But Darlene wasn't concerned with my innocence. The same men who had followed us before lurked in the far corner of the casino. She was scared, and so was I. Nana Sue didn't notice.

"You think she doesn't know anything—that she's going to learn something she didn't already know?" Nana Sue demanded. They were each a head taller than me, and as they talked, they leaned in closer, almost near enough to rest their chins on the top of my head. Nana Sue continued. "Hollis isn't discreet. He invited that slime-bag of a bookie into his home for brunch, for pete's sake. That boy always was too trusting for this world."

"I just thought that this may not be the healthiest atmosphere for your granddaughter, that's all."

"Oh, balderdash," Nana Sue said, moving her cane toward Darlene. "I want to give the child an education and that's what I'm going to do. Someday she's gonna wonder what this is all about, what you did, what I did, what Hollis did. Me hiding it is what got Hollis into trouble in the first place."

"She's a kid." Darlene was trying to protect me.

"Why don't you tell Nana Sue about the ticket?" I offered. "Hollis acted like it was important. Or the men following us. Maybe she can help with that."

Darlene looked at me, her jaw slacked agape like an opening cash register. Nana Sue drew in a slow breath and dropped her cane against the table as I slid down into the base of my chair. It was easy to forget that we were in the midst of a bustling Vegas sports book.

"I know all about the bet, and I know that Hollis probably gave you the ticket to collect," Nana Sue said, smiling Cheshirelike at Darlene. "It's all anyone's been talking about since the Series. An unidentified man places a fifty-thousand dollar future in the winter book on the Dodgers at forty to one odds. When it wins, it creates its own buzz. Danny's been crazy over who bet the gosh-darned thing." I calculated forty to one odds in my head. *Could Hollis really have won two million dollars?*

"Didn't Hollis place the bet himself?" Darlene questioned. Huddled together, the pair literally talked over me.

"Of course not, sweetie. It was one of Larry's runners—on behalf of Larry on behalf of Hollis. If Hollis has learned anything from his dear old mother, it's that one should always try to remain three degrees removed from these types of things. Besides, you do realize that ever since the seventy-nine Super Bowl, he's been told not to show his face in Vegas." Nana Sue squinted so that her watery pouches almost covered her mossy eyes.

My mind wobbled in reflection. I thought of Larry and Hollis's heated last conversation, of the detective's comments about the Middleman's ban from Vegas, and then there was the intimidating man who always waited in Uncle Larry's car. There were memories of Hollis yelling "bad beat" at the television tower from his recliner on game-losing weekends, and the elated mood that pervaded the Sweet dinner table when his teams won.

"I had a hunch it was Hollis's score ever since Jack's

wedding. I mean, Hollis wouldn't amputate his own finger over a couple of dimes. And I knew he wouldn't tell me about it—afraid of what I might say. I know it may not seem like it, girls, but I can be quite disapproving from time to time." Nana Sue's speech concluded with a triumphant pound of her cane against the floor. Thump. *Two million dollars.*

Darlene looked down at me—the unintended audience for their enlightening conversation. When I moved, the leather seat squished under me.

"Do you really think we should be talking about all this?" My mother was still in protective mode.

"The child saw her father interrogated by the police and found out that her uncle, who wasn't really her uncle but a crooked bookie who used her dad to predict the outcomes of games, is dead. You're being followed. And now she's in Vegas, keeping court with her rock-and-roll mother, her over-the-hill grandmother, and the only pet iguana allowed in Caesars Palace. Let's give the child a break for once and own up to the fact that this whole thing isn't going to turn up as a plot on some sitcom. If we feed her a diet of poppycock, Darlene, it's only going to be worse in the end."

If my father had spoken to Darlene the way Nana Sue just had, Darlene would have yelled back, tossing her hair, eventually silencing him. This time, however, my mother said nothing. Closing her eyes for a moment, Nana Sue took two lung-capacity breaths. She searched through her pocket coolly and pulled out and opened a slim silver cigarette case monogrammed with interlocking *s*'s. She rolled a single cigarette between her thumb and index finger and raised it to her mouth.

"Darlene, you do as Hollis told you—collect the cash," she said, her cigarette half finished between her thumb and finger. "Did he say anything else about the ticket or the money?"

"Well . . . he told me to just give the ticket to Danny and tell him it was his 'old friend Hollis's.' He said Danny would know what to do." Darlene paused and looked at me once again. Her eyes drooped with self-consciousness. "Hollis said there might be a few goons looking for someone to cash the ticket. But that they wouldn't hurt us. Those two men sitting in front of the five-dollar slots have been tailing us since Stateline."

Nana Sue raised her voice, her face tightening into a shriveled prune. "I can't believe this. I can't believe this. What in heaven's name was Hollis thinking? Last time he hit these guys big he was lucky to get out of town in one piece." Almost as soon as her eyes sank despondently to her own lap, they snapped up. "Don't worry about those thugs. They're just Pickford's muscle looking for their cut of a bet they have no right to. They'll be taken care of soon enough, I'm sure." She looked around the Sports Book, examining each corner. "Those people can only smell two things—blood and money. Most everyone here associates me with Hollis, not you. Go on and take care of it now— I'll be with Ruby at the blackjack tables, making sure everyone knows I'm there." Nana Sue reached her sun-spotted arm around me and grabbed Darlene's hand. Maybe she expected an enthusiastic reply to her galvanizing speech, but she was met with silence.

"Does that sound alright?"

"Yeah, sure, it definitely does. I'll get right to it." Darlene bounced off her chair and strutted toward the desk like a seasoned cocktail waitress who'd mastered walking in heels. Her calves were flexed and golden under the bright casino chandeliers. Nana Sue grabbed both my arms and put Twenty-one's leash in one hand. She led me slowly out of the Sports Book, gently pulling me on. I felt as tethered as Twenty-one. My grandmother hunched over her cane, not much taller than I was upright. We walked in the aisle past the hundred-, twenty-, and ten-dollar minimum tables, Nana Sue staring straight ahead even as every dealer motioned greetings to her. She nodded her head without looking directly at any of them. Twenty-one scampered close behind, and we formed an unlikely train of two humans and a reptile. I wondered how different things might have been if Nana Sue had a cat named Fluffy like most grandmothers.

"Good mornin', Suzie," a dealer behind the five-dollar table said slyly. Nana Sue stopped and turned. She maneuvered around a stool and motioned for me to sit down by pulling my hand toward the stool next to her. With one deft movement, Nana Sue was seated, her feet dangling slightly above the floor. Reaching far inside her blouse, she pulled out a green poker visor and placed it on top of her matted white hair.

"It's always good to see you at your favorite third-base spot," the young dealer said, looking at her more directly than I'd seen anyone else dare.

"Who's the little lady? Does she have a permission slip to be here?" I grimaced at the thought of what a little lady was supposed to look like. Nana Sue snapped her fingers and gave a quick response.

"I've already had a chat with Danny. Don't worry about it." Nana Sue threw VIP status around with the ease of a celebrity. And got what she wanted.

"Sammy, this is my friend Ruby Tuesday."

"I love that song."

"How are you doing, Sammy?" Reaching into her

pocket, she took out eight blue chips and made a careless toss onto the green felt.

"Not too bad today, Miss Sue. Not too bad at all." He held a card perpendicular to the table, facing away from us. Released from his grip, the card fell toward us in a perfect arc, finally exposing the seven of clubs. Sammy had the ace of spades to Nana Sue's seven and a Jack.

"Insurance?" Sammy questioned.

"Nah. I don't believe in that stuff. A spot and paint? You know I'll stay." He flipped over his own card, revealing a seven of spades. Nana Sue shouted, looking down at her feet.

"TWENTY-ONE!" Everyone within ten tables turned and stared at the pair of us, shocked. "TWENTY-ONE!"

"Miss Sue, I think you miscounted. You have seventeen. I just beat you out, I'm afraid." Sammy spoke tentatively, acting as if Nana Sue's mind was as brittle as her old bones.

"I know that, you fool. I've been playing blackjack at this stool longer than you've been alive! I was speaking to my iguana. He was meandering. And we can't have him disturbing other players."

"Sorry, Miss Sue. I didn't realize—"

"TWENTY-ONE, I SWEAR IF YOU DON'T BEHAVE YOURSELF YOU'LL BE EATING A DIET

OF SLUGS FOR DAYS. NOTHING TASTY FOR YOU." Nana Sue glared down at Twenty-one and started banging her cane on the dizzying yellow and orange carpet next to him. The pounding produced a series of thump tremors I could feel through my padded stool. Twenty-one's large glazed eyes and frozen body revealed the look of a terrified iguana. A swarm of security guards, recognizable by their tight suits, bulging limbs, and conspicuous earpieces, soon hovered around us like circling carnivores.

"What's with the iguana?" casino tourists whispered to each other. "Why is that child sitting at the table?" the others questioned.

"OH MY!" a blue-haired lady shouted as she approached the crowd, which had now reached double figures. "Ruby? Ruby Tuesday? Is that you? My word, it *is*!" Under the casino fluorescence, her face was a paler shade than her hair, but it wasn't long before I recognized the lady as one of our chatty bus companions: Shirley. She was determined to annoy wherever she went.

"Well, I thought I might see you here! Where's your card-shark mother? I have a few questions—"

"Excuse me, but I don't appreciate strangers approaching my granddaughter." Nana Sue said it with sturdy anger, swiveling around her stool away from the table toward Shirley. Her feet still dangled; her teeth were clenched the whole time. Nana Sue raised the black rubber base of her cane and placed it firmly where Shirley's protruding collarbone met her fleshy neck. Shirley gasped. Nana Sue snarled.

An earpiece-outfitted man stepped forward and grasped the cane, forcing it down to the ground. Shirley retreated quickly.

"Sue Sweet! Come on, now! What have I told you about raising your cane in the casino!" The man stood before us, brown hair nicely combed, face frustrated.

"Oh, Bob, this young lady and I were just having a bit of a chat. You know how excitable women from my generation can be. I really do apologize for any inconvenience this may have caused."

"Sue, don't play your B.S. charm games with me." The man stepped closer to Nana Sue. "We've talked about this before."

I tried to shrink down on my stool, behind my grandmother's hunched body, but the security guard's gaze seized me.

"What's the kid doing here, Sue? You trying to break every rule in the casino at once?" He seemed to be playing up this confrontation with my grandmother for the sake of the expanding audience, many of whom were dressed in Hard Rock T-shirts, cutoff jean shorts, and flip-flops.

"The kid, Bob, is my granddaughter, Ruby. And I've gotten permission from Danny himself for her to be here. She's not doing anything illegal."

The man threw his hands in the air, toward the ceiling, exasperated. "I don't know why I even question anything with you anymore. You've got all the right people wrapped around your wrinkled little finger." The irritation in his voice caused the casino patrons to fan out in a wider circle around us. On his forehead, now reddened from the passion of his speech, I could see tiny sweat drops.

"Fine. Fine. One day, Ms. Sweet, you are going to do something bad enough for me to kick you out of here. And when that day comes," Bob said, stopping long enough to cross his arms and raise his finger, "I'll be the one celebrating."

The casino hushed. Curious patrons playing slot machines around us suspended quarters in midair, straining to hear.

"You know, I feel sorry for you, Bobby," Nana Sue remarked, full of pity. "Looking to the expulsion of an old woman from a casino for your own jollies—it's pathetic." She turned away from him and swiveled back toward Sammy and the table. "The day I leave this place unwillingly will be the day I stop breathing and they carry me out horizontally, dearie." She slung two blue chips from her pile on the table and stared ahead. I wanted to be that quick-witted, that casual.

The pit boss walked away, waving his hands at the crowd to disperse, pretending not to hear Nana Sue's comment or the few spectators bold enough to chuckle at it.

Sammy addressed Nana Sue. "I apologize. I don't know why I would think a seasoned gambler like yourself wouldn't know your own count. That was foolish of me, Sue."

"It's quite alright. I know you're a newbie. I like you, Sammy." Nana Sue smiled at the young man, and her eyes closed halfway. "You have the perfect mix of swagger and deference. That's hard to come by. And, besides, some-times this casino needs a good distraction." Nana Sue turned slightly toward me and winked. Sharing something, even a facial tic, with this Vegas marvel, suddenly filled me with pride.

"Have you and Twenty-one been properly acquainted, Sammy?"

"No, not formally, Miss Sue. But I've heard a whole lot about him."

Nana Sue paused long enough to produce an awkward moment before she let out an exploding hoot. "I'm sure you have, sonny, I'm sure you have." I thought I might get another wink, but she just focused her dancing eyes on Sammy. The crowds around us stopped staring.

"Ruby Tuesday, do you want to give it a go? I'll play dummy for a turn. You just tell me what to do, and I'll tell Sammy here. That's alright with you, isn't it, Sammy?"

Sammy nodded in agreement.

"Alright, let's start out small. Two blue chips okay to start with, Ruby?"

I looked at Nana Sue. I had played blackjack with her every time she came to visit Hollis and me in Laguna, as long as I could remember. Every Christmas and Thanksgiving dinner, after the dining table had been cleared of dishes and debris, the entire Sweet extended family would settle in for an evening of low-stakes high-drama poker—Texas Hold 'Em, Twin Beds, High-Low Seven-Card Stud, Draw—cards sliding across the slippery varnish until well into the early morning, voices tensing as the evening eroded. But there was something intimidating about being under the watch of a professional. I was play-ing with chips that meant real money now, underneath intense lights that had seen many before me lose sizable sums.

"How about three chips to start?" I said, attempting to mimic Nana Sue's own bravado. Nana Sue's reaction—a broad dentured smile—was the response I had wanted. My excitement grew. Sammy dealt my first card up, his own down. Then one more up for each of us. I had an eight and a three to his six.

"Hope you have some beginner's luck with you somewhere," Sammy said, looking at me amused.

"Are you kidding? She's been playing blackjack all her life. Why, her first words were 'hit me'—speaking of which, Ruby, I think you're going to want to hit that."

"I'll double down."

"Good girl, Ruby Tuesday!" Nana Sue patted my head and threw three more chips on the felt.

Next card: a queen of spades. Twenty-one. I stayed. Sammy turned over his card—a nine of hearts. Sammy pulled paint and busted.

"Good heavens, Ruby! You knew that was coming. Well done. What a natural." Sammy smiled. He had two teeth where one should have been on his left side, creating a jumbled mess of canines and incisors. It was a simple hand. Anyone who knew anything about blackjack would have played it the same way. But Nana Sue acted as if I'd turned water to wine. She scooped up the chips that Sammy stacked on the table, shoving them inside her blouse. A voice boomed behind us like a megaphone.

"Suzie Sweet, I knew you'd be here." Nana Sue swiveled around on her chair, crossing her legs and arms.

A slender man in a black suit and black tie stood in front of us, with streaky hair slicked back in a way that made his head shinier than his polished shoes. His eyes were dark and his eyebrows formed thin black arches above them. His hair ended in a point at the top of his forehead.

"You giving lessons now? How much you charge?" he said.

"I keep the winnings." Nana Sue turned back around swiftly, showing restrained civility toward the man. "Ruby here just doubled down with an eleven and pulled a picture."

"Gutsy. I like it," he said. He moved Twenty-one from his seat to the floor and tied the iguana's leash to the back of the chair so that he could sit down next to Nana Sue. His cologne smelled like week-old flowers. "The kid's a natural, Suzie."

"What do you want with us, Pickford? If you're not going to play, you can't sit there and loiter. Sammy here won't allow it." Sammy was in no condition to disallow anything—it was as if a leech had sucked all the blood out of his face.

"It's fine, Miss Sue. Really, I'm sure Sam doesn't object. The casino is practically empty."

"He might not, but his pit boss will. Trying to get the kid in trouble?"

"You're the one with the minor at the low-stakes table, Sue." He smacked a piece of gum in his mouth between words. "I'm not bothering anyone. By the way, I'm Ty Pickford," he said as he stuck out his hand at Sammy. "I'm a consultant on the board at a couple other casinos down the street."

"Sam Petrillo. Nice to meet you."

"You've been working here long, Sammy?" Pickford's confidence made him seem invincible. Sammy refused to make eye contact with the man.

"About three months." A bell chattered in front of us. A fat lady with a midwestern accent in thick, black-rimmed glasses and a flowered housedress had just won a jackpot from a nearby slot. She jumped up and down with excessive howls.

"Only been working here three months, Sammy, and you've got the gall to let a minor play? That's pretty cocky."

"Well, no, actually, it's not her that's—"

"Oh, calm down, kid," Pickford said, laughing, as if he'd delivered a punch line. His teeth were straight and clean. "I'm not going to report you. Besides, I know that no one says no to Casino Sue. Las Vegas's least successful prostitute and most successful gambler, don't you know it." His jovial tone gave the impression that he and my grandmother were old friends.

"Look, Pickford, we're trying to play some blackjack here, uninterrupted. What do you want? We have no *unfinished* business with each other." She leaned both arms on the table and turned toward him.

"What makes you think I want something?"

Nana Sue let out a high-pitched scoff.

"You're nothing more than a mangy dog who feeds off other people's table scraps. If I threw a stick, would you leave?"

"Fine. Throw decency and civility out the window, Miss Sue." He folded his arms across his chest and sighed loudly. "I was going to offer my help—I've heard that Hollis is in deep."

"He's not *in* anything." Her tone was both crusty and toxic.

"Larry had a lot of enemies. It doesn't have to be Hollis that takes the fall." As Ty Pickford spoke, Sammy's eyes darted around the room in a panic.

"Hollis didn't do anything." Nana Sue's tone was unadulterated venom. She swiveled and faced Pickford with an eye-locking stare.

"Well, Larry owed a lot of money to a lot of people, including me—you know that, Sue. And I haven't received a penny of what I had coming." From across the casino, one might think Pickford was sharing an amusing anecdote, but the threatening content of his message ran counter to his upbeat smile and his pleasant tone. "If you would just tell Hollis to give me a call—I can help. We can straighten all this out." Pickford slapped a glossy business card on the table.

"Hollis isn't involved with any of this. There is nothing you can do for him."

"Right. So he has no idea about Larry's future on the Dodgers, then?"

"What future?"

"Don't play dumb, Sue. I can't help you if I don't know what I'm dealing with." Pickford shook his head with frustration.

"I don't know anything," Nana Sue said, gingerly bending over to scoop Twenty-one off the ground. She turned away, mindless of Pickford, and began stroking the iguana's wattle with tenderness.

Pickford put his hands on the table, displaying two polished golden rings on each hand. "You Sweets never know when to take someone's help," he said, his voice showing the first signs of agitation. "Others aren't going to be as understanding as I am. I hope your luck in life is as good as it is on the table." He stood up and slid behind us once more. He placed a hand on my shoulder. It felt cold and mysterious. I was paralyzed. "Teach 'em young and they'll never forget it, that's what I always say," he said, nodding at me. Nana Sue swiveled around sharply.

Lifting her cane over her shoulder with surprising quickness, she swung it like a baseball bat. The rubber tipped end of her cane hit Pickford on the right cheek. What followed was the sound of rubber kissing bone. He stumbled backward, grasping his cheek, cringing. The bulky men who had been lurking in the corner just beyond the spinning roulette wheel dashed toward us from across the casino. Nana Sue's cane hovered horizontally near Pickford's face.

"You put your hand on my granddaughter again, I swear, you'll get worse than the end of my cane, sonny."

The large men were upon us.

The one closest to Nana Sue jerked her cane out of her hand, pulling her out of her chair and sending her plummeting toward the carpet. The other rushed to catch her, cradling her by the legs and lower back. She didn't make a sound, looking like a leathery infant in the man's burly arms. He set her roughly back on her stool like she weighed nothing. Pickford was in Nana Sue's face, surrounded by hundreds of pounds of angry henchmen on each side.

"You *ever* do that again, Sue, and you can count your days in this casino over. I'll excuse it this time," he said, hissing his syllables like a snake and rubbing his red-marked cheek with the back of his hand, "because I know you're upset that your kid's in jail."

"You tell these slimy goons of yours to stop following us. We don't know anything about this, you imbecile. You're wasting your time."

Bobby, the pit boss, now back on the scene, rushed over to separate Nana Sue from Pickford. "Oh, Sue, I knew you were going to cause trouble today. Is she bothering you, Mr. Pickford?"

Pickford's angry expression faded. "Oh no, Bobby, thanks. Casino Sue and me were just having a few words between old friends." Without another sound, he turned and retreated with his men. I watched him walk away, his expensive suit swishing with each step.

"Sue Sweet, that will be the last time you ever raise your cane in here again. I'm not kidding this time. I think you should leave."

"I was on my way out anyway, Bobby. You know what they say—a proper lady shouldn't have more than three drinks before noon. It's simply that nothing goes better with a cheese omelet than cold bourbon. I'm afraid it must have gone straight to my head."

Bobby turned and left us with Sammy, glancing back as he got farther away. Sammy bore the look of a starstruck fan.

"Was that gray-haired man who I thought he was?" Sammy smiled.

"Who?"

"Was that Ty Pickford of the Pickford crime family? *The* Ty Pickford?"

"It's Ty Pickford."

"No offense, Suzy Q. But are you sure you should be having words with a man like that?"

"Are you asking me if he scares me?"

Sammy hesitated. His eyes focused on her cane. I guessed he was figuring how to tiptoe around Nana Sue without upsetting her.

"Well, yeah, I guess. Pickford's a dangerous criminal."

"Ty Pickford is nothing more than a silver tongue from a crime family that, aside from him, doesn't even perpetrate crimes anymore. He's a dying breed. I wouldn't pay him too much mind."

"Maybe, but his bodyguards seemed pretty serious."

"Those two brainless sacks of fat follow him around because no one else in this town would hire them." Nana Sue's eyes darted past Sammy's concerned face. She had positioned us exactly across from the arched entrance to the Sports Book. If you peered hard enough, you could see Darlene, her flaxen hair now tied back with a leopard print scarf. She stood next to Danny and three other bow-tied employees at the sports desk. Through the mob of casino patrons, I couldn't make out much more than the huddle.

"Nana Sue?" I questioned.

"Yes?"

"Have you been spying on Darlene this whole time?" Her face loosened with relief. I believe she thought I was going to follow up Sammy's line of questioning about Ty Pickford.

Nana Sue's bourbon had arrived. She reached into her blouse and dropped four blue chips into the hand of the waitress who towered above us.

"Must be having a good day, huh? Because when you have a good day, I have a good day." She curled up her shiny red lips into a pout and looked kindly at Nana Sue.

"I smoke a pack a day and make my liver work harder at seventy-four than it ever has. Every day I can ante up is a good day, honey pie." Nana Sue closed her eyes and took a deep breath. "By the way, Ginger, this is my granddaughter, Ruby Tuesday."

"Oh, like the song," Ginger said.

"Yes ma'am. She just doubled down and pulled paint for twenty-one. How's that for a first hand?" Nana Sue's pride gave my hands a slight tremor. With a swirl of her cup and one gulp, she made the entire beverage disappear.

"Nice to meet you, Ginger." As I said it, I grinned,

having always suspected that Vegas would be full of girls named Ginger. Her hand was soft and pale and, when I shook it, it felt as cold as glass. Between my first Ginger encounter and my first win at the blackjack table, I figured I was halfway to having a real Vegas experience. My grandmother peered hard at the entrance to the sports book, absently hitting with a ten and a three showing. From our vantage point a row of tables and a room away, it looked as if the huddle surrounding my mother had not moved, all parties still captivated by the glass countertop of the sports desk.

"Ginger may look like she dances the go-go on her nights off; heck, she probably does. But she takes good care of me."

"Tip me twenty bucks and I'll go get your bourbon for you anytime you want, sweetheart," Sammy said. His was the same tone the ticket guy had used with Darlene. Men in Vegas, it seemed, would even flirt with a grandmother.

"You really do have quite a mouth on you for one so young, Sammy Boy." A family of five walked by; their heads swiveled 180 degrees so they could fully take in the sight of Nana Sue with her green poker visor and her lap full of green reptile. She saw me watching them watching her.

"Oh, don't worry about them, Ruby Tuesday. They're just passing through and a little curious. Someone will fill 'em in about me, and they'll go home with a story to tell, free of charge."

Darlene, a droll speck of tanned skin and blonde hair against the dinging and blinking backdrop of the slots, was now moving farther away from us, toward the back of the Sports Book. I could no longer see her among the legions of waving arms and raised voices as one of the TVs broadcast the final gun of Detroit's 20–17 upset. The latest in a long line of Sweet gamblers, I was in Vegas, I had played my first hand—and I was ahead of the house.

Twelve

Nana Sue swung her legs around, sliding off the stool with the help of her cane. I trailed her, behind Twenty-one, in a line moving in bursts through the casino. Nana Sue would lurch, about to fall over as she stuck her cane as far out in front as she could, then took a step to catch up to it. Twenty-one, jerked by Nana Sue's grip on the leash, would scurry behind. I followed this pattern of acceleration and stoppage, not wanting to fall too far back or step on Twenty-one. We walked through three rooms of clanging slots, spinning wheels, half-empty card tables, and padded walls with faux mosaics of proud two-dimensional Romans and their horses. In front of us a mammoth sign announced the Forum Shops in scripted letters atop opaque sliding doors.

"We'll cut through the mall, Ruby; it'll be faster to get a cab."

"What about Darlene?"

"Darlene knows to meet us back at the Fremont. Don't worry about your mother so much." She paused and turned around to face me. "Children who worry about their parents end up with psychiatric bills they can't afford to pay later in life." Perhaps worried kids grew up to be the foaming crazies at bus stations.

"Wait until you see this."

A cool rush of air came at us as we walked close enough to the doors for the motion censors to activate them. We stepped through the retreating glass, greeted by a long marble walkway with swirling black and white marble walls. The marble tunnel funneled us into a picturesque sunny Roman marketplace, complete with wood-paneled storefronts, large marble fountains, and perfect clouds that moved above us in the stratospheric breeze. Water trickled and birds tweeted in surround sound. Fake plastic trees in real dirt planters provided boundaries on each side of the mall.

"Something else, eh? It must be sunset. It cycles every hour. The fountain sculptures even move." I bent my neck back, dazzled by a soft, pale orange sky that appeared to be miles away, cumulus clouds moving slowly overhead. It was so flawless it was eerie.

We must have looked silly as we stood transfixed in the

middle of the marble path, with my grandmother's arm around me and Twenty-one pulling on the leash in pursuit of the strong smell of pizza. All around us signs of nightfall's approach emerged. The sky above was turning darker hues of pink, until dim stars were shining against the dusky sky. Romantic blue light filtered through the entire mall as faint candles lit the dinner tables of people in restaurants off the main avenue. The fountains gurgled to a stop to signal the end of the day. High-pitched crickets replaced the melodious chirping birds.

A few minutes into the night, I saw a smoke detector's stabbing red light among the stars above. I then made out the edge of the ceiling. It made me inexplicably sad.

"Wouldn't you just love to see this place without all the smoke and mirrors turned on?" Nana Sue said, pushing me forward.

"No," I said. "It would take all the magic away."

"I s'pose you're right. It's an inside market that looks like an outside market, too beautiful to actually *exist* anywhere naturally." We walked slowly, looking at all the trendy clothing stores that lined the way—the somber mood of the new night seemed to warrant a strolling pace.

"Nana?"

"Yes?" My grandmother seemed to know from my tone that my question would be probing.

"Why do you stay here?"

"What do you mean? In Vegas?"

"Doesn't it ever wear you down? I'm tired already, and I've only been here a day."

"Ah. The million-dollar question. Everybody, sooner or later, asks me. My answer: I like not having to worry about curbs and having fresh sheets every day."

"I know that's what you tell Sammy and the ladies who bring you drinks, but that's it?"

Nana Sue rolled her eyes back. Her head soon followed, and she let out a laugh that exploded like a geyser of sound from her mouth. "Is my answer unacceptable?"

"No, I didn't mean that. I just wondered if there was something else—I wondered if those were the only reasons."

"Of course not. They don't have curbs at Leisure World, either. And if I paid someone enough, they would change my sheets every day. I suppose you're the first person to reject my answer." She paused. "I guess it comes down to the fact that I like the life of this city—and when I couldn't handicap horses at the track anymore because of my leg, I thought this would be the best place to be—I wouldn't have to give up the hustle of it all. When you get old, everybody expects you to slow down, accept your fate, bide your time. Maybe I've lost something to Vegas. I stick around because I want to get it back, because I can't imagine going anywhere else. Not now."

"Don't you ever want to be surrounded by real trees, by real things?"

"Oh, sweetie. Who's to say all this isn't as real as anything else? I'm not uncomfortable with the idea that the artificial may be more beautiful than something natural. Perhaps this is natural." She tapped me on the back lightly, ushering me forward. Her hand felt warm in the faux night air. We had almost reached the end of the Forum Shops, and two more opaque sliding doors stood directly in front of us. My grandmother stopped in the middle of the pathway and moved her face close to mine.

"Something about you, Ruby Tuesday, makes me want to philosophize. Or confess. Never stop asking questions, sweetheart."

The doors opened into an afternoon heat that radiated from every surface. The hot wind blasting in from outside dried my eyeballs. The cold inside air churned as it met the hot outside air. My limbs didn't know whether to shiver or sweat. The line of cabs was far longer than the line of people waiting to get them. A brawny man in a toga, with a wreath of olive branches around his head, was in control of the parade of tourists waiting for cabs. As soon as someone reached the front of the line, he barked their destination to the cabbie.

"Fremont Hotel," he said, poking his head in before shutting the door on Nana Sue and me.

"That poor man must swallow his pride every morning before he puts that garb on. I think his shoes were made of rattan!"

The drive took us ten minutes. The farther down Vegas Boulevard we went, the more the buildings shrank, until we arrived at the fifteen-story Fremont. After the splendor of Caesars, it looked decrepit.

As we walked through the lobby, Nana Sue began her parade of waves and salutations. I fell behind—part of her entourage. There were no pit stops before we reached her floor. Exhibiting a sense of urgency that I had never seen before, Nana Sue knocked on the door next to hers, removing her green visor and hanging it on her doorknob. Darlene greeted us.

My mother pressed a red-nail-polished fingertip to her lips, asking for our silence. Nana Sue looked pensive as she entered the room, shoving Twenty-one in with her foot as the door closed behind us. She sat in a chair by the desk and I plopped down in another. The heat and stale air of the room were exhausting. Gone were the cheers, yelps, and dings that had assaulted our ears all afternoon. There was a sharp slap of metal hitting metal as Nana Sue closed her cigarette case. Darlene's feet swooshed against the shag carpet as she hurried across the room to the bed, where the phone receiver rested.

"I'm back," Darlene said into the mouthpiece, picking up a cigar from the ashtray next to the bed and puffing frequently. "They just got here."

Nana Sue sat still, closing her watery eyes as she took a drag, opening them to ash her cigarette and look across the room at Darlene. My mother continued to listen on the phone, repeating *uh-huhs*, *of courses*, and *yeses* in a somber tone. Before long the sinuous trails of Nana Sue's smoke had reached Darlene's own, merging together in the middle of the room against the yellow light of neon and day.

"Of course. Of course. You want to talk to her? Yes. She's right here." Darlene removed the phone from her ear, holding it out to the middle of the room. "Ruby, your father wants to talk to you." I hurried to the bed, sprawling on my stomach next to my mother.

"Hollis?" I said, trying to mask my excitement.

"Ruby! It's so good to hear your voice. How do you like Las Vegas? It's pretty wild, isn't it?" The feedback gave his voice a strange echo.

"Yeah, it is. I got your telegram," I said, imagining Hollis smile on the other end of the phone.

"I thought Vegas might scare you at first—I thought

you could use a friendly note." He spoke hesitantly.

"Look, your mother is going to bring you home now. She might stay with us awhile too."

"It's okay to come home now? It's all over?"

"It's not over, but I think it's time for you to come home."

"You sound weird, Hollis. What's going on?"

"Rube, when you get back, things are going to be different."

"Whaddya mean different? I wish you would just tell me what's happening. I don't understand why I'm here and you aren't."

Darlene put her palm on me and traced circles on the small of my back as I talked.

"I'm at home. Ruby, I haven't been formally charged, but I am the prime suspect . . . do you know what that means?" Hollis's voice sounded distant.

"It means that you're on your way to being a criminal."

"Not a criminal. Look, Rube, I'm just mixed up in this whole murder thing—but it's only because they have nothing else to go on. I've got good people helping me. Don't worry about that. But this thing—"

"This thing?" I interrupted.

"This whole Larry thing. It's all over the news. I don't want you to be here, but you're going to hear about it regardless." My father had never pleaded with me before. He had never had the need. "You're going to have to hold your head up high, no matter what people say to you, okay? Can you do that without reconfiguring any school signs?"

I tried to sound fearless.

"Sure. You bet." I turned my head and looked at Darlene, still rubbing my back. Her makeup looked slightly melted at such close range. She now had three distinct parallel wrinkles running across her forehead and a crow's-foot in the corner of each eye. Vegas heat had undone all her careful face sculpting.

"Well, you hang tough, kiddo. And listen to your mother. I'll see you when you get home."

"Alright."

"Put your mother back on the phone." Hearing both Darlene and Hollis refer to each other as "mother" and "father" was unusual. I handed the receiver to Darlene and remained by her side, intent on listening to her every word.

"Yes. I did that. Sure." She paused for his answers.

"I went unnoticed."

"We're taking the evening bus."

"My car's not working so we couldn't."

"I thought it would be safer."

"You're right." She seemed, by her responses, to be taking orders.

"Yes. I know. We'll be home tonight. Stay safe."

"You too." She hung up the phone, and her face relaxed. The apparent affection of their conversation surprised me.

I looked at Nana Sue, who had just begun to finger her second cigarette. It took her three attempts before her knobby arthritic thumb got the lighter to catch.

"Did Hollis say he'd speak to me later?"

"Yes. He said he'd talk to you after you sent us off."

"Sure, sure. He likes it when *I* call *him*—makes him feel loved." Nana Sue shook her head. "What time is your bus?" We were to leave on a 5:45, which left us three hours to kill.

Darlene gave Nana Sue a sharp look, her eyes broadening to the size of half dollars.

"I have to take care of a few things," she said.

"I wanted to take Ruby for a late lunch anyway. Give us girls a chance to talk and unwind," Nana Sue quipped. "Gambling can be a stressful hobby."

"Hobby? It's a way of life," Darlene chimed in.

"How about Ruby and I meet you at the bus station a few minutes after five, Darlene?"

"Sounds good." Without another word, Darlene kicked off her shoes and headed for the bathroom. Nana Sue motioned me over to help her up out of the chair. The spritely woman who had bounded on and off high stools at the blackjack tables with ease now seemed stiff and feeble.

With her arm around my waist, we jointly limped toward the door. Twenty-one followed, urged on by Nana Sue's persistent tug. When we were safely in Nana Sue's room, she closed the door behind us and kicked off her own shoes, revealing perfectly manicured toenails accentuated with hot pink nail polish. Perhaps the Vegas life she had carved out here wasn't so bad. She hooked her cane on the doorknob and hobbled toward her bottle of Knob Creek. As slow as she was getting to that bottle, she turned over the cup, dropped in some ice cubes, and poured herself a drink as if it were a timed Olympic event. I suppose, in a way, it was an event to Nana Sue. She then limped her way over to the table by her chair, placed the drink on a worn coaster, and called Twenty-one to his terrarium.

I couldn't help but notice how different she seemed. Frailty ruled her body as she labored to navigate her room. Someone had removed the cap from her valve and the air streamed from her body as if from a deflating balloon. She stood hunched over the tank and I could see her shrink. She panted and leaned her bony hand with all her weight against the terrarium. Sighing with pain, she lifted the iguana and placed him in the glass case. On a shelf above the enclosed habitat sat a clear jar containing an army of small insects.

Twenty-one caught sight of the jar, now in Nana Sue's hand, and scratched against the glass.

With one arthritic hand on the lid, Nana Sue clenched her teeth and willed the jar open. I watched her eyes enlarge as she playfully dangled a single grasshopper by the leg above the terrarium. She licked her lips, breathing heavily as she teased Twenty-one. Weak laughter escaped from her. She must have done this every day for the last twenty years. The only thing that changed every so often was a new Twenty-one.

Nana Sue shuffled back to her paisley chair and simultaneously grabbed for her drink and cigarette without looking at either. She had possession of both by the time her back hit the worn upholstery. Swirling her bourbon so the ice cubes clinked against the crystal tumbler, she turned to me.

"How hungry are you, Ruby?"

"I'm starving."

The bright glare of the window in back of Nana Sue made it difficult to recognize her wry smile.

"Vegas'll do that to you, honey. It focuses you in on one human need at a time, I'm afraid. I thought we might have some room service. Sound good?"

"Sounds great." I didn't have to feign enthusiasm. It did sound great. Nana Sue reached over her drink to the phone and punched in a few numbers.

"Yes." There was a pause. "I'll have the usual. But make it for two." Another pause. "No, I'm not extra hungry today. I've got company. Sure. And send up Sandy, please." She hung up the phone and turned to me.

"You don't mind another omelet, do you? This time with ham and peppers—a lunch omelet?"

"No, not at all. Do you always eat two omelets a day?" The room wasn't large, but we sat on opposite sides. This was the first time we had been completely alone, and I was afraid I might say the wrong thing. And where was Darlene, anyway?

"Well, yes, I guess. People say you can have too much of a good thing." She paused, letting a large gulp of bourbon slip down her throat. "But what I love about omelets are the options. You just change what you put inside and bingo, you have yourself a brand-new food. They're never boring." I searched for a response in kind. Nana Sue took another drink just as the air-conditioning unit that hung halfway out the window started up with a roar.

"Your father used to love omelets. He actually got me started on them." She released a nostalgic sigh. "Darlene didn't like them much so he stopped eating them—why, I think that's the worst thing about her. I've little patience for omelet haters."

"Nana Sue," I timidly began, "why is Hollis called Middleman? Why can't he come to Vegas?"

"What?"

"It's what the detective said when he came to question Hollis. Did he kill someone?"

"Oh dear, child. The amount of misinformation in your head—I'm surprised it doesn't combust."

"What do you mean?"

"Sure, some people around here call your father Middleman, but it has nothing to do with any murder or crime. You understand what Hollis does, right?"

"He decides how much better one team is than another and sets odds. Then people bet on them."

"That's right. And he did that for a while here in Vegas."

Questions flooded my mind. "How did it begin, then?"

Nana Sue stared at me, puzzled. "Well, Ruby, that's a long story."

"We have three hours." Nana Sue's white dentures shone wide, making way for a cackle.

"You won't be put off, will you?" It seemed like an accusation, but her eyes shone with pleasure. I didn't respond, knowing she would take the conversation where she wanted.

"Hollis was living with me in Reno, a couple hours from

here. It had been just the two of us for a long, long time—I raised him by myself. I wasn't a good mother, Ruby, anyone you ask can attest to that. You know now that I handicapped horses for a living. I handicapped here, Hollywood Park, Santa Anita, Del Mar, Bay Meadows. And for a while, I was the best. When Hollis wasn't in school, I would take him with me wherever I went. People in the game knew us." Nana Sue started laughing, but she kept on talking. "Why, the only reason I knew the child needed glasses was because he couldn't read the odds on the tote board at Santa Anita. He was about your age.

"Anyway, at that time, the gambling world, I'm talking sports, casinos, horses—you name it—was run by organized crime. You couldn't clear any decent amount of money without skimming some off the top for the Syndicate, men you may have heard about before, like Siegel and Lansky in Vegas—a bunch of hoods out to make their own fortune any way they could. They had the FBI handled, the local cops under thumb, and enough politicians in pocket to prevent any meaningful laws from curbing their activity. It was a different time, Ruby—before the movement to make Vegas a family place. These guys—you'd probably call them mobsters—were less involved in horses, but they were still interested, and they all knew me. The creeps, they liked me fine because they piggybacked my picks and made money.

"Hollis was eighteen when I found out he'd been making secret trips to Vegas on his own for upward of two years." She stopped and peered at me.

"How are you at math, Ruby?"

"I don't know. I get As."

"That's good. I'm sure you're just like your father. He had such a head for numbers—it was almost frightening."

"I can tell. He helps me with my homework sometimes."

"He came up with a mathematical rating system—it was legendary. And worst of all, he loved it. He was making bucket loads of money for the four sports books in Vegas— before there were sports books in the actual casinos. I couldn't stop him—lost him to it before I even knew about it." She stopped, her watery eyes waltzing around the room with delight. "Can you imagine it, Ruby? Your father setting odds at all the sports books in Vegas, and him not old enough to legally place a bet when he started. He was heavy in it before he could understand what that meant.

"When he moved to the west coast with Darlene, he thought he was going to stop all this and work nine-to-five. But once the Stardust opened up its very own sports book in its casino in seventy-nine, things changed—legal sports betting became big business, and soon every casino had their own sports book. Hollis's partner, Danny, the one you met, moved from the Santa Anita Sports Book to Caesars. So many people sought Hollis out—his expertise became indispensable. I knew he wouldn't stop. It's too easy for him." Nana's mood turned gray against the golden window. She creaked upright and hobbled over to the corner to fix herself another cocktail. Up until that point in her monologue, Nana Sue had set her gaze right above me, as if she had to concentrate hard in order to reach far enough back into her mind to produce her memories. When she shifted her sights to me and saw that I was anxiously waiting for more, her eyes sagged with watery sadness.

"I didn't mean to ramble on like that, Ruby," she said, her voice growing weaker and softer as she looked down at the shag carpet.

"I have no one to be proud of," I said.

There was a long pause.

"You have plenty to be proud of, Ruby Tuesday. It is true, to some extent—all this isn't something that you're going to want to bring up at your school's show and tell day—but that's just because it's a bit unorthodox." Nana Sue took a long sip from her bourbon, with an audible slurp. I leaned forward in my chair anxious, excited. "It's not your typical story. If everyone's father was a dentist, Ruby, we'd live in a boring world filled with clean teeth. Sometimes the cavities are the most interesting part."

"Is Hollis a cavity?"

"That's not what I mean, Ruby. Don't be silly."

"Why is Hollis called Middleman?" I wouldn't be deterred.

"That's something you should ask your father. Speaking of your parents, how are you getting on with your mother after all this time, Ruby?"

"Fine, I guess."

"Oh, don't beat around the bush. I'm too old, Ruby, I don't have enough time for that."

"I mean, it's fine. . . . Can I ask you a question, Nana Sue?"

"Sure."

"You know when you said that Darlene 'abandoned' us? Do you think that's true?"

"Oh, I don't know, sweetie."

"Do you hate Darlene?"

"No, of course not. But it doesn't really matter if I do. Do you?"

"No, well. Well, sometimes, when she's away, I think that I do."

"I see a little of myself in your mother, Ruby. Don't give up on her, not quite yet. She got mixed up with musicians and rock and roll, got a taste and never could quite shake it—that's something I can relate to."

Nana Sue had confirmed that my mother left me for rock and roll. I was angry all over again.

"What about all that? What has Darlene done?"

"Again, Ruby, these are all questions you are going to have to ask your parents. It's not for me to say."

I wanted desperately to hear more, but I knew Nana Sue wouldn't respond to pushing. So, I answered my own questions with worst-case scenarios: Neither parent had wanted me. I was an unfortunate accident. Hollis's past was murderous and too slimy to talk about. Darlene had given up something wonderful to have me. She resented me for it. Jack and I had made them both unhappy.

As she took another drink, Nana Sue seemed to recover. Her voice crackled with its usual resolve.

"Well, I guess it's true then, what they say. That the only thing history has taught us is that we don't learn from it. Because here you are, just like Hollis, being exposed to a world that you're way too young for—without a choice." Nana Sue rubbed her rheumatic leg and pressed at her eyelids as if she was in pain. "But at least it's with your eyes open. You won't have to rely on this city, like your father, or me, or Darlene. Not if I can help it." She paused.

"I don't know where our food is, but I think that it's about time for me to wave the red flag, don't you?" She had switched out of storyteller mode, cranking her crotchety woman persona up a notch. She dialed.

"Yes, this is Sue. We've been waiting for our food for far too long. Can you check with Sandy? There is nothing worse than a cold omelet. If they're cold, you just tell her to have them make new ones. DO YOU HEAR ME?" She hung up the phone with a resounding thump.

"Nana Sue?"

"Yes, sweetie?"

"Why do you stay in this hotel when everyone knows you at Caesars? It's so much nicer there."

"That is a worthy question, my dear," Nana Sue said, pointing her finger at the ceiling. "This hotel may not be as nice, but my money carries more weight here. At Caesars people put up with me because I know the bosses and I've been around for so long, but I wouldn't want to wear out my welcome. There, punters lose more money in one evening at the baccarat table than I ever have. Understand?"

"Uh-huh." Sure enough, there was a knock at the door and Nana Sue motioned for me to answer it from my chair next to the door. I was careful not to knock her cane from its hanging place atop the doorknob.

"Hiya, Sandy," I said, making way for her to set a large platter on the desk next to the door. She greeted me by mussing my hair and immediately took a plate with a steaming omelet over to Nana Sue. She apologized for the delay.

"They couldn't find me—my shift just ended," she said, smiling at my grandmother.

"Oh, you know you didn't have to come up here. They could have sent someone else. I wouldn't have been mad."

"Aw. Suzy Q. You're cute when you lie."

"I'm just particular. I like who I like, you know?"

"Sure, I know all too well." It was a successful tactic with Nana Sue. One part lip mixed with three parts respect. Sandy had changed out of her mini mini and into jeans and a faded baby blue Bruce Springsteen Pink Cadillac T-shirt. She looked older, lit up by the afternoon sun flooding in through the window. A small web of veins ran across each of her temples; her cheeks didn't have any healthy color. She had been in Vegas for fifteen years, but Sandy looked road weary. Hurriedly, she said good-bye to each of us.

"Ruby," Nana Sue said, holding out a bill she had pulled from her bra, "run over here and give this to Sandy for me." Sandy turned from the door, propping it open.

"It's alright, Nana Sue. You've tipped me enough for one day. I don't want you robbing young Ruby's trust fund—*or* thinking you own me."

"Nah, I insist. You and Joe Citizen are paying for my social security. It's the least I can do." Not knowing whose urging to defer to, I slipped the twenty-dollar bill into the purse Sandy had left by the door. We hugged good-bye like old friends. She didn't notice the money and the door slammed behind her.

"Sly girl. Thatta way." Nana Sue beamed. I ate my omelet quickly; Nana Sue ate hers quicker. The mixture of peppers, ham, and fluffy egg was delicious. Vegas did indeed have a way of making you hungry. In the corner of the room, Twenty-one had almost completely devoured the grasshopper, shooting his tongue out in rapid bursts at the insect's remaining appendages. Nana Sue smoked three cigarettes in succession, speaking sporadically while we sat moving the remaining parsley and French fries around our plates. The silence came as a relief. After an hour Nana Sue stirred from her chair, shifting her body and looking at her watch.

"I guess we should get into a cab and take you to the depot. I think we have time for one stop." Nana Sue gathered her purse and her cane. The three bourbons had little noticeable effect on her besides a slight flush in her drooping cheeks. We were going to the top of the Mirage, Nana Sue told me, where she promised we'd get the best view of Vegas.

From the Strip, the Mirage looked like a cross-shaped tower. It offered majestic man-made fountains, and pools, and a genuine false volcano that erupted precisely on a pre-programmed schedule. Inside, a huge aquarium filled the wall behind the concierge. Brightly colored, well-lit tropical fish swam around a series of bottom-dwelling plants that swayed with the current. The carpet was intense, but tasteful, and every piece of wood that lined the entrance looked newly lacquered.

Nana Sue had a brief conversation with the French concierge at the desk, who disappeared behind the glass aquarium only to emerge a few seconds later with someone who was to be our guide.

"So sorry for the mix-up, madam—I just wanted to make sure the penthouse was unoccupied, you see," he said, almost bowing his head. His French accent had strange dignity amidst the garish opulence of the Mirage.

"This is Frank. He will take you straight up." Nana Sue responded with a small huff and turned to walk toward the elevator, relying heavily on her cane. The elevator zipped up the twenty-five stories quickly. I thought I felt blood pooling in my head by the time we reached the top story. There were two doors in the hallway, both as far apart as could be. The pimpled bellhop led us to the right and opened the door to a pristine and luxurious sitting room. I couldn't imagine actually sitting in it and risking the chance of squashing the perfectly fluffed pillows and cushions.

Windows that reached from the ceiling to the floor, from wall to wall, glowed on each side. Three white leather couches on soft gray Berber carpet surrounded a TV that looked like it belonged in Caesars' sports book. A large basket of fruit and candy in yellow cellophane sat atop the oversized translucent coffee table. I followed Nana Sue to the left wall of plate glass windows.

Fake-looking mountains complemented the fake-looking city—I quickly realized that neither of them were. This was real. The sun had already set behind the high Nevada range. Against the cherry sky, the mountains rose like jagged brown cardboard cutouts, forming a sharp line where they ended and the sky began. The way the sunset lit the sky reminded me of countless smoggy sunsets I had seen from our balcony in Laguna. A few hotels along the strip towered high to the right and left of us, but beyond that were hundreds of thousands of cookie-cutter houses. There was no gradual transition between the populated neighborhoods and the desert. Beyond the lights of the city, development simply stopped, making way for the brown desolation of pure desert. Vegas was like a formless amoeba of light and life that spread out in all directions. But only I-15, glowing with headlights, extended beyond the engulfing desert.

"Pretty incredible, huh? Must have been the ultimate challenge to build a city here. A metropolis in the most impossible of places." Nana Sue pressed her head against the window, brushing her permed hair against the spotless glass. Her voice reverberated off the windowpane. Las Vegas was like the American Dream in fast-forward. Get rich, fall in love, pursue your destiny, all in the span of a card game, a lap dance, a pull of the handle. "You sad to be leaving it?"

No. I definitely wasn't. The majesty of Las Vegas was lost on me.

"I think I'm ready to go home."

"Of course you are." Her weathered voice crackled. "Well, I just wanted you to get one last look at the place before you went. I bet you'll be back. I'm afraid the fate of this family and Vegas are intertwined—for better or worse."

She took my hand and we moved away from the window, past the bellhop who stood in the doorway. As we passed through the lobby, it was clear that no one working on the floor here knew Nana Sue. To the dealers, croupiers, and pit bosses, she was exactly the same as the legions of other bored old ladies who swarmed around the quarter slot machines most afternoons.

When Nana Sue got me to the bus depot, the place was frantic with people running around. It was huge compared to the Los Angeles depot.

Darlene faced us on a bench, blonde hair tied neatly

into a ponytail with a red scarf. Again, she was wearing her large glamour glasses inside the terminal. With her head in *People*, Darlene didn't spot us until we were close enough to touch her.

"So, girls, how was your lunch?"

"It was nice. Ruby here had a bit of a history lesson about the family," Nana Sue said. I looked at my mother's face. Her mouth jerked into a grimace of uneasiness. I wished I could see her eyes beneath the reflective lenses of her sunglasses.

"Oh, that old boring story . . . I bet that put her to sleep." Her words matched the unnatural laugh she followed with. Nana Sue gracefully changed the subject.

"Did you tie up all the loose ends you needed to?"

"I sure did. I got our tickets, too, Ruby." She pulled two tickets to Los Angeles out of the magazine she was reading. "In fact," she said checking her watch, "we should probably board the bus soon—no way I'm sitting next to a stranger."

"You know how I feel about public transportation, Darlene. But if you had to do it, you had to do it." Nana Sue reached to give her a hug as she stood up. Darlene slipped an envelope out of her magazine and handed it to Nana Sue. Something about the transaction made my stomach turn queasy.

Nana Sue tucked the envelope securely in her blouse, and the two embraced briefly. Then my grandmother turned to me. She bent down slightly until our heads were at the same level and put her knuckle gently under my chin. We were so close, Nana Sue's face was in front of me like a skin-colored sea of wrinkles. I could feel her hot smoky breath on my face. "Ruby, remember, you hold your head up."

"Of course, Nana Sue." I wondered how many more times I would hear this.

"Good people do bad things. Larry Brenn was a cancer for this family."

"What?"

"I just mean to say I loved having you around. I'm glad we got the chance to spend some time gambling and laughing together, Ruby Tuesday. There's hope for you yet. You're leaving town a winner," she said triumphantly. She didn't pause for my reaction; she just squeezed me tightly with her bony arms.

"Good-bye, Ruby. Good luck in everything you do. And remember: Always split aces and eights." Bus stations seemed to inspire stirring speeches. We boarded the bus to find a more diverse group than we'd traveled to Vegas with. They weren't all geriatric, and there were still no foaming crazies.

Darlene and I didn't say a word after watching Nana Sue limp off. The loud thump of her cane echoed against the high ceiling and cement tile of the bus depot as she walked toward the exit. My mother let me have the window seat. The sun had faded completely, allowing Vegas's trillion-watt glow to shine unrivaled. As we sped away from the lights along I-15, we were met by blank darkness.

Thirteen

The evening news is one story after another about bad things that happen to people just like you. Someone gets robbed, someone gets shot. You may even feel that it is happening to you for the span of a two-minute news clip.

I used to imagine myself on the news a lot, usually as the heroine in a vivid tale of daring and bravery. I envisioned people recognizing me in the streets later and wanting to shake my hand and talk to me about what an inspiration I was. Being the daughter of the subject of one of these two-minute clips was not quite as glamorous.

The first time I saw Hollis's picture on television, we hadn't even made it home from Vegas. He was staring out from a TV screen in the bus terminal in Los Angeles. Darlene saw him first. She dropped her bag, and the sound of makeup mirrors and foundation bottles shattering spun me around. I saw her mouth form the words "Oh no."

Her glasses slid down her nose; her face registered shock. I looked where she looked. Newscaster Jerry Dunphy spoke as a picture of Hollis and Uncle Larry flashed in the corner. They were smiling, each holding up a large bass with their arms around each other's shoulders. It was one of the many fishing trips the two had taken to Baja. I tried to remember if I was the one that had taken that particular photo, as if it would make any difference. I wondered how the news channel had gotten the picture. I ran over to get within earshot of the broadcast. Torn between watching the newscast and the emotional earthquake shaking Darlene's face, I only caught bits and pieces of what the newscaster said. It was enough.

"Murder rocks the Southland. The first murder in the exclusive beach town in over a decade. Hollis Sweet, local businessman, is said to be the only suspect. The murder, it is believed, resulted from a dispute over a two-million-dollar payoff from a bet made on the World Series. The slain man, Larry Brenn, was an active member of the Laguna community and had contributed money to both the Laguna Playhouse and Laguna Schools Foundation. Sweet has been released on bail while the investigation continues."

It didn't take Darlene long to refocus. She spent our car ride home trying to convince me that none of this would affect our lives permanently. It wasn't until I asked about the description of Uncle Larry as a pillar of the Laguna community that Darlene raged.

"Are you kidding? The only money he gave away was money he couldn't launder—money Hollis probably earned for him—so he used it to get himself a tax write-off. School kids and plays? The only 'plays' that interested Larry were the ones he made on the Lakers. It's bull—it's nonsense."

"If Hollis didn't do it, how did they have enough evidence to arrest him?"

"They throw warrants out like candy canes at Christmas these days, honey. It doesn't mean a thing. Not a blessed thing!" Darlene defending Hollis instead of criticizing him was a small comfort. She answered each of my questions emphatically, sprinkled with expletives. Hollis's mob ties? *He never had any.* The bet? *Hollis has made those criminals money for years.* The trial? *No way there'll be a trial.* I wanted to believe her. Of course, the alternative was pretty grim—my father the murderer.

When we arrived home, up the steep hill and onto Bent Twig Road, I half expected the whole place to be lit up with news media and towering satellite feeds. By the orange light of the street lamps, though, everything was quiet. Darlene opened the garage. I had forgotten that she still had an opener like a regular member of the household. She pulled her vintage Thunderbird into Hollis's empty space.

"Where's Hollis's car?"

"The police took it as evidence."

"Evidence of what?"

"Someone saw Uncle Larry in Hollis's car hours before he died. So they took it. To see if they could find anything."

"But Hollis and Larry always drove around in his car."

"I know that, honey. But the investigators don't. Don't worry, they aren't going to find anything." As we pulled into the garage, the headlights of the car shone directly on Hollis, who stood in the doorway that led to our kitchen. He looked ragged in a hooded sweatshirt and sweatpants. He tried to appear happy waving at us, but his smile was short-lived.

"It's already started," Hollis said, as soon as we exited the car.

"We know," Darlene said, not looking at Hollis. "We saw the news clip at the bus depot. What are you going to do?"

"I unplugged the phone."

"Oh, great. Problem solved, then." She threw her suitcase out of the car.

"Being angry at me isn't going to make this any easier, Dar." Hollis's voice filled with sympathy.

"I know." Her voice quavered. I imagined tears

beneath her dark lenses. Hollis pushed the button, and the garage door cranked shut behind us. Darlene pointed her finger at Hollis.

"Hollis—do you understand that this is why I left in the first place. It's happening, Hollis, maybe not the way I thought, but it's happening." Darlene spoke between emotion-ridden stutters. "I knew I wasn't cut out for this, and I *dreaded* the day when I was going to have to do this without you because you got shot or killed or *whatever* by those sleazeballs. And here we are with all this awful stuff to deal with and Jack's gone and I'm going to have this kid—" As she waved her hand toward me, she turned, sobbing loudly and breathing like she had something caught in her throat. Darlene cowered in the corner for a few seconds and went into the house, slamming the door. We heard her sobs as she shut the door to Jack's old bedroom off the garage. Hollis came to me and took me in his arms.

"She's just upset, you know that, right, Rube?" His embrace comforted me. His chin hit the top of my head as he moved his mouth. "It'll get worse before it gets better . . . but it will get better, alright?"

"Yeah. I know." The thought that Monday, a school day, was just two days away haunted me. The thought that the one dependable thing in my life, Hollis Sweet, might be taken away from me terrified me.

Hollis and I retreated to our kitchen stools and ate Frosted Flakes in silence. When he said good night an hour later, we both went through the motions of our normal routine with deliberate accuracy, careful not to change a single movement. Then we saw the Monopoly board. It hadn't been touched in days. A tiny spider had taken up residency between Marvin Gardens and Water Works. Neither of us said a word about it, and it was too much for me. My eyes brimmed over with tears.

When Hollis poked his head in to whisper his final "sleep well," I wondered what else about our lives would change. I waited a half hour before I snuck out of my room to call Jack. The house was completely dark, and in the kitchen not much light shone through the large-paned window. I struggled to find the cord of the phone and fingered the wall until I found the jack, reminding myself to unplug the phone again when I was done. In a way, I felt like I was breaching Hollis's confidence. My hand trembled as I dialed my brother's new phone number.

"Hello?" Mae's voice sounded like I imagined it would on the phone.

"May I speak to Jack, please?" I was nervous. My voice showed it.

"Is that you, Ruby?" It was one of those moments when I was surprised that a person remembered my name.

"Yes. It's Ruby. I'm sorry it's so late."

"Oh, sweetheart. We were up anyway. Don't worry about it. I know he wants to talk to you." She was sympathetic.

"Ruby! I've been trying to get you people all day. It just kept ringing."

"Hollis unplugged the phone." I tried to hold it together.

"I guess a lot of people were probably trying to get in touch with him."

"I don't know."

"How are you doing?" I felt like crying. Or running. Or being anywhere but Bent Twig Road.

"I'm fine. We're all fine. I don't know why I called."

"I'm glad you did." I wasn't sure I was.

"Did you see it on the news?"

"It was hard not to. Ruby, do you want to come stay here for a while? You and Mae could spend some time with each other. I have work, but it might be better for you."

"No, I should probably stay here." All I had wanted was for him to offer—it was enough. I wanted to stay with Darlene and Hollis. "We got home from Vegas tonight."

"Hollis said you might be there for a while."

"He wanted us to come home."

"Look, Ruby, it's okay to be upset about this. It's an

awful thing. But it's going to work out. Trust Hollis. He is not a murderer." I believed him because I had to.

"I know. I have to go, Jack. I'll talk to you later. Good night." His voice continued to trail through the receiver until I put it back on the hook. I pulled the cord out of the wall quickly, knowing full well that he might try to call back. When I reached my bed through the darkness, I collapsed.

The next morning my father's picture—the one with Uncle Larry and the fish, the one I was now certain I had taken, was on both the front page of the *Orange County Register* and the *Los Angeles Times*. The *Register* called it the biggest scandal to hit Laguna since 1967, when Timothy Leary and his sons were picked up and arrested on Main Beach and charged with possession of LSD. The *Times* said that the police were moving on important leads in making a case against Hollis. In the last paragraph of the article, continued on page five, it mentioned me. *Sweet has two children, ages 13 and 22.* There were other stories about consumer spending and some huge fire in Chicago. They seemed trivial next to the picture of my father.

Darlene emerged from Jack's old room shortly after I woke, with puffy sacs under her eyes, still in her clothes from the day before. Grabbing a Diet Coke, she plopped next to me at the kitchen table and lit a Tiparillo.

"You know why this story is so big, Ruby?"

"Because it's ours?"

"No. I'm talking about two of the three big Gs. Gambling and guns. All we need is gangsters and this could blow up to Tom Brokaw proportions. People get falsely accused of murder all the time, but it's never like this." Hollis had left a note for us, buried underneath all the papers. We only discovered it after each of us had read both news articles twice.

Girls,

Had to go meet with the lawyers and for more questioning—DON'T GO OUTSIDE! There are reporters in front of the house. If they come onto the driveway, call the police. Darlene, don't smoke in the house—it upsets Ruby's lungs. I love you both. Hang in there!

Hollis

Hollis had assumed the role of head cheerleader. I rushed up to the living room to peer out at the driveway, leaving Darlene with the papers, her Diet Coke, and her prohibited Tiparillo. Through the venetian blinds, I could identify a small news truck and a solitary car behind it. The van had "Action News" written across it in huge red letters, and in the car sat Jody Larch, who I recognized because she was the sole reporter, photographer, and editor of the *Laguna Ledger*. She had shown up at Laguna Heights a few times to take photos of events like the Chili Cook-off. Darlene had plugged in the phone and was now talking in the kitchen. It sounded like she was trying to convince someone to deliver a pizza. It was 10:45 in the morning.

"Kiddo, I've convinced Domino's to make us their first delivery at eleven—Hollis doesn't have any food and it appears that he's borrowed my car, so we're going to be stranded here for the day."

"Is pizza all you eat?" I said, craving one of Nana Sue's omelets.

"I thought you liked pizza."

"For breakfast?"

Darlene walked to the window and pulled a curtain back. "Jeez. Are we already a second-page story? I was expecting at least some rolling video cameras or some photographers. Pathetic. What kind of mixture of public humiliation and tragedy is this, anyway?" I knew Darlene was making light of the situation for my benefit, but it didn't mask her swollen eyes, her half smile, or her unmistakable restlessness. Hollis was on the front page of both local newspapers. Our family name had been publicly vilified. It was easier for both of us to focus on the relative scope of the story than think about the details. Like what the police were asking Hollis. Like when he was coming home. Like *if* he was coming home. By noon, after snapping a few pictures of the house, both reporters had disappeared. When the pizza arrived, we devoured it. Our nerves had amplified a normal appetite. We clutched our stomachs and looked at each other.

"I ate too much. I feel sick."

"Me too, Ruby."

"I think it must be the stress," Darlene said, her first slight acknowledgment that we were both scared senseless.

"Is it a little warm in here? What do you say I turn up the AC a little?"

"It's sixty-eight degrees outside, Darlene. It's winter."

"Hah. A California winter is like summer, really." Darlene had changed into huge backless flannel slippers and one of Hollis's oversized dress shirts—the kind of deliberately casual outfit you see women wearing in commercials, extolling the smoothness of their legs to hawk some new and improved feminine razor. Darlene could have been one of these women. I had noticed that men who looked her up and down often slowed when their gaze reached her legs. She sauntered over to the thermostat in the living room and flipped it to its lowest setting: fifty-five.

"Great. We should be able to see our breath soon," I said.

"We can get blankets and curl up on the couch all day.

I love lazy days." She put her arms up over her head and yawned. Her casualness was all an act. I kept remembering the things she said in the garage. I wanted to scream out to her to stop pretending. It was only making me feel worse.

Darlene and I situated ourselves on the couch, gathering all the blankets and quilts we could find and wrapping ourselves in them. She kept the TV controller and didn't stay on a channel for more than four minutes at a time. She was roaming for more news clips, but we didn't catch a single mention of Hollis or the murder the entire day. From time to time, she would stroke my hair, casually, as if we had spent days all throughout my childhood together. I remember the newness of her touch. It shouldn't have made any difference in my mood, but in the smallest of ways, I felt better having her there. We watched part of *The Young and the Restless*, *The Bold and the Beautiful*, *General Hospital*, a replay of some pairs ice-skating competition, and the last half of a made-for-TV movie about a girl who kills her best friend in order to steal the deceased's boyfriend. Everything we watched was stupid. Nothing helped. The phone rang six times. Neither of us picked it up or even acknowledged that it was ringing. No one left a message. It could have been Hollis, or Jack, or Howie, or Nana Sue. It could have been the police. We didn't want to know, so we stayed curled up on the couch in the same position until darkness descended over the Pacific. I had never spent this much quality time with my mother.

When Hollis returned, Darlene and I were still in the TV room buried in the same couch in a sea of blankets; the whole room was awash in flickering blue-gray light from the television.

"Girls, I'm ho—is this what you two have been doing all day?"

"No. Of course not. We stopped for twenty minutes to eat," Darlene responded. Hollis let his body fall limply onto the couch next to ours and curled up.

None of us spoke.

We were all at the mercy of Darlene's fickle TV viewing habits. When the six o'clock news came on, Darlene and Hollis turned to each other.

"Do you want me to change the channel? I'm sure we can find an *I Love Lucy* rerun to watch." Darlene was all sympathy.

"Aren't you supposed to watch your own press?" Hollis questioned. "I mean, people try their whole lives to make the news—and here I've done it without even trying."

Uncle Larry's murder was the third story on *Channel Seven Eyewitness News*. There was a tease for it during the first and second commercial breaks. Jerry Dunphy was calling it the Dodger Murder. The story hadn't changed since yesterday's rendition—with one addition. Authorities had now linked Hollis to the Pickford crime family and other organized crime groups in Las Vegas.

Darlene funneled air out through her pursed lips in a depressed sigh. The triumvirate of *Gs* had been completed—gunfire, gambling, and now gangsters.

Anyone having information about the murder should call the police hotline. A number flashed across the bottom of the screen. This time they flashed a picture of Hollis, his head lowered, entering the police station.

Seeing Hollis staring out at me from inside the television was creepier than it had been the first time, namely because now he was right next to me. The same man wearing the same clothes was lying on the couch, and his khaki pants and blue button-down shirt somehow seemed inappropriate in our living room. They were the clothes of a suspected killer.

The next news story was about a dog that had been stuck in a drainage pipe for three days. It included interviews with the valiant animal control officer and an off-duty policeman who constructed a pulley system to lift the canine out. We all watched, faking interest. When the news was over, Darlene flipped to a *Bonanza* rerun on a cable station. Hollis rose and went to the kitchen briefly. Darlene and I pretended not to notice that he had made a phone call.

"I thought you might be hungry after scavenging for food all day, huh? So I just ordered us Domino's." The laughter that followed was a big relief. Stress had made Darlene and me an easy audience.

"What? What's so funny?"

"Oh, nothing," Darlene said, pulling a bronzed leg out from beneath the blankets and stretching it out on top of the empty pizza box that lay on the coffee table.

"Oh. Oh. I see. I should have known. You always default to pizza in any situation, Darlene. Well, how about we declare today pizza day?"

"Why not," she countered.

"It's an icebox in here."

Hollis bent over the fireplace. With one turn of the gas key, he created a blazing flame that lit our three faces orange. Darlene looked at me and pinched my arm with quiet amusement. Neither of us moved to turn the air-conditioning off.

The pizza came and quickly disappeared. So did seven, eight, nine, and ten o'clock. The phone had stopped ringing at nine. We watched two movies on television—one was some old black and white thing where everyone talked too quickly and out of the sides of their mouths. The other was *Back to the Future*, which always made me yearn for a car with doors that opened straight up instead of sideways. It was strange because it all felt so normal, even with all that had happened, and it was the first time I could remember us all huddled together. When we got up to go to our separate rooms, we hugged each other as if it were a well-practiced routine. If I wasn't worried about my father's arrest, it might have spurred the hope that my parents would "get back together," "find love again"—phrases that predicted happy endings. But I knew that Darlene and Hollis would never be together in any conventional sense. Now was no time to start believing in fairy tales. I focused instead on avoiding images of my father in a jail cell. I thought about how long things might go on like this.

The media blitz Darlene had jokingly wished for arrived early Sunday. While sipping his coffee in the fog and mist of the early morning, Hollis had caught a paparazzi lurking in the bushes of our sloping backyard, beneath the overhang of our patio. When reporting this to the police from the kitchen phone, he looked out toward the driveway and counted five news vans—one with a long satellite tower on its roof. Our narrow stretch of Bent Twig had become even narrower—only one car could slowly pass through the line of parked cars and vans. Rows of photographers and reporters lined our driveway like it was a red carpet, with their respective microphones, tape recorders, and cameras in hand. Neighbors on both sides had come out sleepy eyed to stare at us in the center ring of the media circus. Hollis rushed outside toward the press corps and waved his hands, demanding that they all leave.

"This is a private drive. I've called the police. You can't be here," he yelled, in words muted by the pane of glass in the living room that separated me from him. Instantly manmade lightning from bright photo bulbs and camera lights flashed, blinding my eyes. Hollis was assaulted by a deafening chorus of *who* and *what* and *when*, *where*, and *why* questions. A mob of about thirty surged, swarming around him. I could no longer see any part of my father through the huddle of journalists.

At first only Hollis's arms emerged out of the throng. It was as if he was performing the breaststroke through the reporting blob. As he shot out of the pack, he stumbled onto our lawn, landing on his stomach, rolling toward our mailbox. Dazed and with grass skid marks on both knees, Hollis jumped up and ran toward our front door. The entire front of the house was radiant with the strobe lighting of flashbulbs capturing a fleeing suspect. As he arrived inside, door slammed tight, gasping for breath, I ran toward him.

"You alright?"

He grabbed his chest. My heart pounded too.

"Jeez, Hollis, those people are crazy."

"I know, Rube. I know." Hollis reached his arm out,

signaling for me to come to him as he leaned against the door. He tucked his arm around me, and we walked into the kitchen. Darlene was now up and on the phone, sitting on a metallic stool, smooth legs crossed, in another of Hollis's dress shirts. As soon as Hollis caught his breath, he stood upright and spoke to Darlene.

"Ordering your morning pizza?" Something about being a murder suspect had released a glib sense of humor in Hollis. Darlene put her index finger to her lips, eyes bulging.

"What was the number again? Sure, I understand. Thank you for the warning. Uh-huh. I understand. I'll give him the message." Darlene hung up the phone. Her face looked as ghostly as the backdrop of the overcast coastal sky behind her.

"That was Ty Pickford," she said in a robotic tone to my father. "He wanted you to know that a lot of Larry's Vegas contacts want to be paid, and Pickford thought they might come looking for you to settle some of Larry's debts."

"How did he get our home phone number?"

"I don't know. He didn't offer up that information, Hollis." She was fuming. "He went on to say that the men who might come looking for you to square up Larry's debts were dangerous, and we should give them what they want.

"He asked if I knew anything about Larry's winning future bet on the Series. He says he wants to help us."

"Did you say anything to him?"

"No, of course not. But, honestly Hollis, maybe we could use the help."

"Pickford is sending those men for his own benefit, Darlene. He doesn't want to help us." Hollis threw his hands to his head and paced about the kitchen. "You did exactly what I told you to do with the ticket, right?"

"Right. I placed your new bet, making sure that Danny saw me. Later I slipped Danny the ticket with your note, just like you said. He wrote the check out to Nana Sue." Neither of my parents knew what to say. Darlene spoke again.

"What did the note say, Hollis? What does Danny have to do with this?"

"The note told Danny to keep quiet about the winnings and to tell no one about it for as long as he could. If Pickford thinks that future ticket died with Larry, he'll have no reason to come after us. He's just looking for the ticket."

"How do you know Danny'll do what you asked?"

"He will."

"And if he doesn't? If Pickford thinks we have the money? What's your plan then, Hollis? Or are you not

237

worried because all this will happen while you're safely tucked away in your jail cell?" She was borderline hysterical. My father took two steps toward her and forced her into his arms. Darlene rested her chin on the gradual dip of Hollis's shoulder and closed her eyes. I could have stared at them like that forever, but Darlene opened her eyes and pushed herself away. Hollis was still close to her when he spoke.

"It's nothing to worry about. Pickford is a dinosaur. He's only running on the fumes of the Pickford family reputation. You didn't tell him anything else, did you?"

"Of all people, Hollis, you should know better than anyone how good I am at playing dumb."

"You always did know when to act the ditz, Darlene."

"Guys tipped better when I acted stupid. You would have done the same thing." My mother took a strand of her hair and twisted it around her index finger until it was entirely covered in blonde.

With the fire lit, we watched TV until past midnight. As we huddled on the couch, the murmur of the TV seemed to soothe us into numbness. The madness and worry of the day almost made it easier to pretend that we'd spent countless nights before like a real family, together in the blue glow.

Fourteen

The morning my father was arrested on charges of first-degree murder, I didn't even have to beg Darlene to let me stay home from school. Winter break had ended and it was supposed to be my first day back since the news cameras had begun stalking us. The knock on the door came at seven-thirty in the morning. I was finishing my bowl of Frosted Flakes at Darlene's urging. She didn't want me to be late. My father was greeted by two men in suits asking for Hollis Sweet. Both investigators wore sunglasses, though the sun had not yet peeked through the coastal fog. Hollis identified himself at the door. Ironically, the driveway was empty of all reporters. Up the coast in Malibu, a few houses had fallen off their cliffside perches, and every news vehicle had sped up the coast to cover the story.

When the two tight-lipped men arrested Hollis, they did

everything like I'd seen it on television. They flashed their badges, read him his rights before they handcuffed him, and then made sure he didn't hit his head as they loaded him into the backseat of their black sedan. The fact that he didn't say good-bye didn't surprise me. What was there to say? Darlene and I ran out to the driveway and watched them take my father away. She grabbed my shoulder and we stayed on the porch for several minutes after the unmarked police car disappeared into the morning fog. The sedan looked like countless other cars on the road. Only we knew that it carried a suspected criminal.

Shuffling into the kitchen, Darlene grabbed a bag of tortilla chips and continued to the family room. Something about a corn chip without anything to dip it into seemed sad. Last night's fire still glowed as the hazy morning light seeped in through the window. Not knowing what else to do, I followed Darlene to the couch, laying my head on her thigh as she threw blankets over both of us.

I tried to think what might be happening to Hollis at that moment but came up blank. After all, they never showed that part on TV. There was always the arrest and then an immediate cut to the good-cop bad-cop part, where they offered the suspect coffee and then grilled him in a tiny, beat-up room. They never showed the car ride to the police station. Was there dead silence in the car or did they chat about the weather?

The TV was on, of course, and this time Darlene had opted for cartoons. It was the episode where Tom and Jerry stowed away on a pirate ship. Tom saved Jerry in the end, though they despised each other until right before the last commercial break. Darlene opened her bag of chips and laughed in all the wrong places. Morning was rapidly brightening into afternoon. We deliberately misled ourselves, acting as if nothing had changed. Our TV would broadcast the same formulaic cartoons whether Hollis was thrown in jail for the next thirty years or released tomorrow.

By noon the air in the family room was beginning to stale from the heat of our bodies and the smoldering fire. Darlene's leg was probably asleep. Neither of us had moved at all since we first plopped down on the couch. From my vantage point below her, I could see that she wasn't wearing any makeup. She was still beautiful. She looked older, sure, but her eyes shone fiercely, even if they did seem slightly sunken from the toll of stress and tears.

The first non-TV sound of the day was the guttural growl of Darlene's stomach, which came at two P.M. We both ignored it. I thought if I left my imagination to its own devices a moment longer, I might drive myself crazy, so I struck up some conversation.

"Darlene?"

"Yes, honey?" she said, rubbing my head once again.

"How do you know Shade Roberts?"

"I've known him for a long time, Ruby Tuesday. I met him in Vegas when I was with your father."

"Are you in love with him?"

My mother was flabbergasted. She took a moment to recover.

"In love with who?"

"Shade Roberts."

"That's absurd. Where on earth would you get an idea like that?"

"Well, Nana Sue told me that you got mixed up in rock and roll. That's why you left us."

"Oh." Darlene exhaled. "I was afraid she might tell you something like that."

"Is it true?"

"No. I met a lot of musicians back then. I traveled in that circle."

"Do you know the Rolling Stones?"

The phone rang. We ignored it. I sensed I was running out of time.

"Did you leave because you couldn't write songs any-more?"

"A person can write songs anywhere."

I didn't know when else I would have my mother like

this, too wounded to divert any question. So I held nothing back.

"Well, what was it? Were you mad that we kept you from being a famous singer?" Darlene shook her head. The answering machine had picked up after the phone's fourth ring. She waited for the machine to finish. Hollis's recorded voice echoed through the house: "Hi, this is the Sweets. Leave us a message and odds are, we might call you back." I could hear myself giggling in the background. It's never the things you expect to affect you that do. Salty tears filled my eyes even before the beep sounded. I let grief sink in.

This was just a phase, I thought. I much preferred the sadness of tears to the anger of resentment, hatred, or heaven-knows-what. A male voice began talking after the sound of the beep. Darlene hopped over the back of the couch into the kitchen. It was Hollis. He was probably calling from the police station.

"Hello? Hello? Hollis, it's me. I'm here." The answering machine had not stopped, and I heard my father begin to answer.

"Darlene. It's so good to hear your voice. Has Ruby be—" Darlene cut the machine off. There was a pause as Hollis finished the rest of his question.

"We're fine. We've been vegging out all day, watching

cartoons. How are you?" Another pause as Hollis answered. Darlene began again.

"How is that possible? Couldn't it have been from anything? He was always riding around in that car. What is going on, Hollis? What are you not telling me? What am I supposed to tell *your* thirteen-year-old daughter?" The string of questions stopped. Darlene waited for Hollis's response, audible only to her. "Of course, that's enough evidence to arrest you. Your lawyer thinks *what*?" Darlene got more irate, grinding her teeth while she listened. A feeble powerlessness took hold of me.

"Alright. Alright. I understand. I'll talk to you soon. Stay safe." Hollis was probably safer in jail than anyplace else. As soon as Darlene put the phone down, I flopped back onto the couch and flipped the channel to a music video featuring hard bodies and harder chords.

"That was your father," Darlene said in a very formal tone. "He's with his lawyer at the police station. They're just working out some details. They found blood in the Corvette. We don't know much yet." She rattled out sentences, answering questions I hadn't gotten around to asking.

"There was blood in his car?"

"That's what they're telling him. But they say all sorts of things to get people to confess. Who knows if it's true."

Her voice gave nothing away—she might very well have believed it herself. As she walked around to sit next to me, the leather still warm from where her body had just been, the phone clamored once again.

"I thought you were only allowed one phone call, Hollis." Darlene's impatience had grown since the last conversation. "Oh, Sandy! I'm sorry, I thought you were my husband calling." Hearing Darlene call Hollis her husband was strange—but it was stranger still hearing the everyday tone she used with the Vegas waitress. For all Sandy knew, Darlene had thought it was Hollis calling back from work, to ask what he should pick up for dinner. Then Darlene fell silent. I muted the TV, leaning over the back of the couch to eavesdrop.

"No. Oh. Oh no." It was as soft a voice as I had ever heard from Darlene. Through the doorway, I could see her lean over the counter and cradle the phone between her ear and neck. She ran her fingers through her hair.

"Was it natural causes?" She paused. That was it. I had reached my limit for dealing with only one side of important conversations.

I leaped up and went out the French doors that led to our deck.

It was breezy and bright; clouds filled the sky. I shivered as the warmth of the house escaped through the door.

There was Hollis's coffee cup, stained with congealed coffee from days before, on our round picnic table. The cup's Caesars Palace logo was imposed over a black-outlined decal of the Parthenon. I took it with me to the edge of the balcony. Thick coffee jiggled in the cup with each step. My stomach was now flush against the wood railing.

Beneath my bare feet the wood planks of the patio felt slimy with morning dew. I looked down. Little new grass blades the color of lime peels covered almost every inch of the earthen slope until it met the ocean. The thirsty hillsides of Southern California were like chameleons—they shifted from muddy brown to verdant green in the span of one rainfall.

Taking a step back, I heaved Hollis's mug over the ledge and folded myself over the railing in a U-shape. My head and arms dangled toward the ocean. For a brief moment I could see my own feet on the other side. When I looked up, the moment played out before me in slow motion—coffee spilled out of the mug, making an arc as it plummeted toward the sea. I closed my eyes and barely heard the cup splash, but I imagined it forming an exploding foam ripple when it hit the water. If I stood on top of the rail, I might just be able to fling myself far enough to follow the cup and hit the cold blue water.

I bent over the railing once more, my face parallel with

the sea. I could see that the white mug hadn't sunk and I was disappointed as I watched it float away. I could no longer make out its shape or the imprint of Caesars Palace. The tide sucked it out to sea until it was just a white fleck mired in vast blueness. I watched the mug until it disappeared completely.

"Ruby? Ruby, come away from there and come inside. We have things to talk about." Normally Darlene would have yelled at me for standing so close to the railing. She would have told me I was a foolish child. This time she waited by the door and shepherded me into the house. I sat down on one couch and she chose the other one. There was barely time for me to catch my breath before she spoke.

"Nana Sue passed away. Early this morning." Her hands covered her mouth and nose in a tepee shape. "I'm so sorry, Ruby."

Nana Sue passed away. The phrase hung in the air like a colorful balloon at a wake. It didn't belong in my life.

A person was supposed to get signals for this type of thing: a cough, a corroded artery, a coronary bypass, a cancer. I had seen her yesterday, and she was old, but I thought she would stay that way forever. Death was not in keeping with Nana Sue's enduring old age.

I imagined her alone in her hotel room. Perhaps the maid had come in to change her sheets. Perhaps she lay on the floor, a pile of white hair and wrinkled skin, a mournful Twenty-one, escaped and unleashed, timidly exploring her corpse. Her uncovered face and limbs would be a colorless canvas bathed in the yellow light from the Golden Nugget across the street. Maybe there was blood. Maybe she wasn't in room 714 at all. Maybe she was in a ditch like Uncle Larry. Nana Sue seemed to be the one person whose role in my life was unchanging. And now she was gone. Bad things weren't supposed to come in pairs; I was angry.

"Was she murdered?" A week ago, I wouldn't have thought to ask such a question.

"Of course not."

"How do you know? How do you know someone didn't want her dead? How do you know it wasn't Danny or Ty Pickford, or . . . or . . . maybe she won too much money. Maybe she's playing one of her tricks or she—"

"That's enough, Ruby." I shut my eyes tightly, willing tears down my cheeks, but this time none would come.

Darlene's eyes shifted around the room. Uncertain, she went on. "I don't know what to say about any of this. I know I'm supposed to look you in the eye and explain it to you, tell you we're going to handle this and it will all work out. But I can't say that. You'd see through me. I can't say anything."

"What are we supposed to do?"

"Well, Sandy said she would take care of the arrangements for us—I explained what was going on. She was happy to do it. She cared for Nana Sue."

"Why, because Nana Sue tipped her enough to care?"

"That's not true, Ruby." Flashes of my grandmother parading through a casino of waving employees played like a slide show in my head. "Don't say things like that."

"Nana Sue was the one that got Hollis into gambling. She told me." Getting mad felt good.

"Don't misplace your grief. Nana Sue would have done anything for you. And Hollis." Darlene's defense of Nana Sue was a surprising show of respect.

"I know."

"She was at the blackjack table. She fell off her stool."

"What did she die of?"

"They think it was a heart attack. She smoked and drank every day. It's not exactly the best plan for longevity."

"Who found her?"

"Some dealer named Sammy called the paramedics. She was dead on arrival."

"Why didn't the hospital call?"

"Nana Sue always insisted that Sandy be the one to call Hollis if something ever happened to her."

Nana Sue's death may have been the only shock great

enough to release us from thoughts of orange jumpsuits, visitation rights, and parole. Her passing was a less complicated misfortune for Darlene and me—a woman we had both come to respect, maybe love, had died. Of old age. And my sadness had an easy simplicity.

Until the phone rang again.

"Hello?"

"Yes. Uh-huh." There was a pause while Darlene listened. "Yes. I understand," she said passively. "No, he's not here, but when he calls I will give him the message." She was trying to please whoever she was talking to. "Of course, yes. Of course. No, I think I understand. Yeah. Thanks." Darlene hung up the phone. Her face was white with fear. She ran to the window, hiding herself behind the frame. With one calculated move of her head she peered out into the front yard so as not to be seen. I followed her into the kitchen.

"What's going on?"

"Nothing. Ruby, go get a sweatshirt and your shoes. We're taking a trip."

"Where are we going?" I refused to leave the kitchen and moved in front of the window. Then I saw what had scared my mother. Two men in a black car sat in plain view of the house, staring, almost waiting for us to stir. I had wanted them to be the men who had followed us the first time—a familiar terror—but they were not. They were clean shaven, better dressed, and more menacing. Darlene grabbed my waist and pushed me to the floor, slamming my knees against the tile. She wanted me to crawl below the window.

"Go. Go now. And come straight back here." When I returned from my room, Darlene was standing by the door to the garage with her keys and her purse in hand.

"Who are they, Darlene? And who was that on the phone?"

"It's just some people making threats to scare us. We're going to get out of here just in case."

"Won't they follow us?" We moved together into her Thunderbird. Darlene started the engine without opening the garage door.

"They'll try. Don't worry, honey." She clicked the garage door open, gripping the steering wheel, her knuckles white and her knees shaking.

"I'm going to throw it in reverse down the hill. Don't look back at the men. And hold on." She registered my concern. "Look, I've done this a million times before—if there's one thing I know, it's the Laguna Hills." The garage door was creaking up slowly. It was halfway up when Darlene put the car in reverse and slammed on the gas. My head jerked forward into my lap.

"Keep your head down, Ruby. This is going to be an E-ticket ride," my mother yelled over the roaring engine. She stared intently in the rearview mirror. We gained speed. To our right, the men had started up their car and moved to block the road. Darlene only pushed the accelerator harder against the floor, swerving and skidding, continuing backward down Bent Twig Road. I felt as if the body of the car might fly off the wheels, and I bit my lip to keep from screaming. Once we hit the fork in the road, we turned up toward the maze of streets that wound through the hills. As Darlene shifted into forward gear, the car lurched and made such a clamor I thought the transmission had dropped right out onto the road. The approaching black car made no attempt to slow down as it followed us. Her Thunderbird squealed up Skyline Drive to the left. The road was a switchback trail winding above Bent Twig and our house. I could see the determined faces of the men who followed us making the sharp turn onto the road Darlene and I were already speeding along. Darlene took possession of both lanes, swerving around a Mercedes in front of us, swerving back when a Nissan came at us. I gasped as the side-view mirror swiped a eucalyptus tree branch, then one of the orange trees that overhung the road.

We climbed higher and higher as we traveled faster and faster. The look of concentration on Darlene's face made it clear that she had no intention of slowing down. When we had covered roughly a mile, we reached the ridge at the top of the hill. From it I could see speed-drenched views of the blurred canyon on one side and the ocean on the other. I rarely got up this high. It would have been beautiful, had I not been afraid of dying at every railless curve and hairpin turn.

We descended into Laguna Canyon, and our increasing speed made my stomach feel as if it were wedged in my throat. I was both terrified and nauseous. The distance between the black car and us increased with every turn. By the time we reached Laguna Canyon Road, we had far outdistanced our pursuers. We traveled for several miles down the road, inland, away from the ocean. Darlene ran the first two red stoplights we came to. At the third, she finally stopped.

"Well, it looks like we lost them, Ruby." Her sense of calm shocked me.

"How in the he—"

"Don't swear, Ruby. You shouldn't swear until you're old enough to vote."

Normally I would have argued, but I wanted an answer. "Sorry. But where did you learn to drive like that?"

"Hollis used to chase me up and down these hills practically every time I left. I guess he thought I wanted to be chased and it would convince me to stay. Or maybe he just wanted to chase after someone. I don't know. It was *To Catch a Thief* and I was Grace Kelly to his Cary Grant."

"Why didn't you just talk like normal people? That's crazy."

"No crazier than what a lot of people do to each other."

"So where are we going now?"

"To a place where no one will look for us."

"Who were those men?"

"I'm sure they were sent by Pickford to watch us—that was him on the phone, trying to intimidate me. I don't think we should take any chances, so I'm taking us to my friend Peggy's place."

"When can we go home again?"

"I don't know, Ruby, we'll see. You'll like Peggy. She's a hoot." I could think of nothing to say. We remained silent for the rest of the ride. The first thing I recognized was the shabby parking lot and shacklike appearance of Woody's Wharf—we had made our way to Newport Beach via Pacific Coast Highway. Restaurants and bars lined both sides of the highway, which was congested with shirtless men in convertibles and soccer moms in expensive German cars. Darlene turned on her blinker. Across from the ocean side of the highway stood fenced rows of trailers advertised as "Newport Mobile Home Park, A Community for Nice

People" on a large, faded sign. We turned into the gravel driveway. Dust rose up behind us as we moved deeper into the park. The trailers came in all shapes and sizes: Some were blue, some were brick red, some had strange colorful paintings on them, some had awnings, some were dull and faded. There were rows and rows of them. We pulled up to a cream-colored one with orange detailing. Brown-striped cloth awnings stuck out, shading the front side of the mobile home.

"We're here," Darlene said, killing the engine and opening the door.

"Does Peggy live here?"

"She's an old friend of mine."

"Does she know we're coming?"

"She never knows when I'm coming. And it never seems to matter." The Community for Nice People was a hot pocket on the cool Newport coast; all the cluttered trailers, separated by tiny gravel roads, retained the warmth of the afternoon. We walked on one of the many roads to a unit toward the back. When Darlene knocked, it sounded as if she was tapping on a tin can. Peggy appeared behind the screen door.

"Darlene! Holy—"

"Please, not in front of the kid."

"Oh, of course. What are you doing here?"

"Peggy. Didn't think I'd be back so soon, did you?" Darlene's trailer friend was wearing a yellow tube top and tight stonewashed jeans. Her face was worn with eyes so dark I couldn't see her pupils, and silver streaks spread evenly through her long black hair. The coffee mug she clutched looked like a natural outgrowth of her hand.

"And who's the little one?"

"Ruby Tuesday. Ruby, this is Peggy."

"So this is the infamous daughter, huh? Well, I know a lot of people who would give their right arm to look like your mother—and you, Ruby Tuesday, are her spitting image." I couldn't help but swell with pride. Up close, Peggy's face was full of subtle wrinkles; even the small flap of skin under her nose had soft lines. It was strange to me that a friend Darlene's age would have gray hair. I had always thought of my mother as much too young for gray-haired friends.

"So what's the news? I thought you were going to Vegas and then Tempe to see Shade and the Stones?" Her voice sounded like it had traveled through gravel before exiting her mouth—like she might cough up phlegm at any moment.

"I wish my life were that simple."

"You look terrible."

"I feel terrible."

"Oh, honey. Come on in." Darlene talked as we made our way in.

"Hollis has been arrested for his bookie's murder. We went to Vegas to visit his mother and take care of a few things, were followed there, and now have a couple of creeps still following us. And Hollis's mother just died."

Inside, shaggy carpet covered every square inch of floor. The kitchen was part of the living room and the living room was part of the bedroom. Things were orderly, but dust covered every surface. Even the dust looked dusty. Knickknacks had overtaken the place. One table was chock full of Pez dispensers. Another table had clay whale creations, and on the TV were buttons of all shapes and sizes, strewn artfully about. The entire back wall was a magazine cutout shrine dedicated to David Letterman with a huge mock-up of his gap tooth as its focal point. Forest-green wallpaper bubbled out in places, and crammed into the kitchen were an oven, a table, two chairs, a fridge and a small sink. It was dark and musty; the only two windows in the entire place had their shades drawn. I could stretch and reach the living room couch from the kitchen table. Darlene's association with all this depressed me.

"Well, you two take a seat. You must be worn out." She pointed to the couch, and Darlene and I sank into it, exhausted. Tube top resting dangerously low, Peggy took three paces to the kitchen, retrieved three assorted glasses, a dirty ashtray, and a bottle of Johnny Walker Red and placed them on the card table in front of us.

"Look, your life's in shambles—why don't we get wrecked? I mean totally smashed." Peggy seemed to be the antimom.

"Not in front of Ruby. She's too young."

"Oh, like she doesn't know that things are a disaster right now. A drink might help—if she does it when she's young, she'll have less of an urge to do it later. I read that in a parenting magazine."

"You don't read parenting magazines."

"True, but it sounds pretty right on, doesn't it?" Peggy's laughter was coy. "Besides," she said, "I already brought her a glass." I liked Peggy's no-nonsense attitude. She treated me like my mother's equal.

"I don't want to do that now," Darlene replied with reluctance. "She's barely thirteen. I just thought maybe we could relax and watch some TV." Without a word, Peggy picked up the controller and the TV hummed.

"Fine. But have one yourself. It'll take the edge off, Dar." She took the bottle and poured two generous servings. They each grabbed a glass and pressed liquid to lip, smiling.

"What the heck, huh? I've had a pretty bad day."

Watching both of them attack the liquor with the same determination made me want to join in the event. Instead, I just watched. Both finished in two gulps. They sighed with an equal mix of comfort and discomfort. I wondered if this was why people liked alcohol. Peggy poured two more glasses. This time Darlene didn't object. Their cheeks reddened from alcohol as they looked at each other and brought full glasses to their lips once again. It went down easier the second time. I watched, waiting for the effects to settle in.

"Dar, I should have been watching the news, checking out what's been going on."

"Nah, it's just too depressing." Darlene took the bottle and filled her glass again. Peggy followed.

"Ruby." Darlene was gesturing more than normal and speaking in a loud voice. "Peggy and I. We used . . . we used to work at the Frontier together—although I, you know, was a much better performer." They both laughed. I wondered how many drinks it would take for them to be drunk and what would happen once they were.

"I gave Peggy the benefit of the doubt when I found out she thought the Beatles were better than the Stones. It's a sore subject between us. How can you respect a person after something like that? The whole thing almost ended our friendship before it began."

Darlene moved over to the TV and muted it. She grabbed a record, slipped it onto Peggy's record player, and set the needle down. She flopped back down on the couch.

"Pound for pound the best album ever, Ruby," she said, speaking slowly and hitting me on the thigh with each word she spoke. She was talking to me as if she had something to prove. Her eyes shimmered, half closed. She was drunk. By the look of Peggy's ruddy face, she was too. Light seeped in through the corners of the blinds. It wasn't close to dark yet.

"What is it?" I asked.

"The Rolling Stones, Ruby. The Rockin' Rolling Stones, of course. *Let It Bleed. Let It Bleed.*" Darlene fell back into the couch and closed her eyes, singing to herself as "Gimme Shelter" played.

"Can I try some?" I questioned, clutching the half-gone handle of Johnny Walker.

"*Absolutely* not. It'll make you sick," Darlene said, pointing her finger at me. She shut her eyes once more. Her smile made her look goofy. I wanted to feel the numbness I saw on her face. Taking the bottle, I poured my glass half full. Lifting the glass to my nose, I took a sniff and nearly gagged. It smelled like rust. I drank it anyway.

Right then, I learned you've got to be practiced in the art of masking your own pain to pour hard alcohol down your throat. The Johnny Walker not only burned like I had poured hot liquid metal down my esophagus, but it turned my throat inside out, making me hack and choke.

"Jeez, Ruby," my mother said, hitting me on the back. "If you're going to do it, don't drink it all at once like that."

"But," I said, pausing to gasp and wheeze, "that's how you did it. That's how Nana Sue did it." Saying Nana Sue's name out loud now felt unnatural and gloomy. I didn't want to have to think about her.

"Yeah, well, we've had years of practice."

I poured another half a glass, trying to forget how much it hurt the first time and the awful taste of oxidation it left in my mouth. Peggy and Darlene, both drowning out Mick Jagger with their own drunken yodeling, poured themselves two more glasses. Darlene danced, swiveling her head, her hair flying out like a fan in all directions. She moved wildly toward the record player and turned it up so loud the music became scratchy and distorted. Peggy commanded us to take our glasses and raise them. We did so, standing up, Peggy whooping as our glasses hit each other with a clink. She counted. One, two, three. I watched them as I gulped my own cupful down. I closed my eyes to try to dull the pain. They shouted more than they sang. Their out-of-tune voices echoed off the tin walls of the mobile home.

"Yeah, that's what I'm talking about," Peggy shouted.

My head began to feel so light it might float away. The words they sang entered my head and seemed like they would bounce around there forever until they were just dull noise. Peggy handed me a cigarette.

"Just SUCK," she shouted. "I'll light it for you." I put it in my mouth and sucked as she held the lighter up to the end. I could see it extend out from my mouth as I looked down. "If you're gonna get totally screwed up, honey, you might as well do it right." Her laughter was reckless. Her screaming was hard to hear through the fog of alcohol, smoke, and the Rolling Stones. Holding a cigarette in my hand gave me the urge to pose. I wanted my cheeks to sink into my face as I sucked in and I wanted to blow the smoke out of my mouth in one hard burst, effortlessly, like Nana Sue. Instead, I coughed. And coughed some more. I could feel my heart pounding in my head.

Darlene spun around, mirthfully taking Peggy's hand. I couldn't tell if they were spinning or if it was the room. They clapped and hollered and jumped—each time they did, the entire trailer would shake with a good-sized tremor.

"I feel sick," I said, barely able to hear myself. They sang with boozy zest. "I feel sick, Darlene. I think I might throw up."

They only gazed at each other, arms slung around one

another as they faced me on the couch. They continued to sing, jumping up on the couch and swiveling with bent knees. I felt like I was at a strange sort of slumber party. This was the Sweet version of mother-daughter bonding.

I grabbed my cup, opened my mouth, and vomited into it, dropping the cigarette to the floor. The Johnny Walker had not altered much from time spent in my stomach. It looked about the same. I fell over onto the couch, exhausted, tears welling up in my eyes. Below me, a small stream of thick black smoke rose from the dark green shag carpet. It smelled like burning plastic. Darlene shrieked, cut the music, and stomped on the carpet until the smoke stopped. She sat next to me and put my head in her lap, grabbing hunks of my hair and running them through her fingers.

"Oh no," Peggy said, looking at me. "Her face looks green." The atmosphere of the tin room had instantly changed.

"You think you might be sick again, Ruby?"

"No. I feel okay." But I didn't. My mouth tasted like smoke and acid and my throat burned all over again. "I just need to sit here for a while."

"Absolutely, baby. You take as much time as you need." Peggy switched the volume of the TV on again.

"Oh, Ruby, I'm so sorry about all this," Darlene said, her voice drenched with dishonor.

"It's okay, Darlene. It seemed like it was making you forget all of it. I wanted to forget it too."

I wondered if the alcohol was making me as maudlin as I had seen it make Nana Sue.

"I've been trying so hard these couple of days, you know?"

"Are you going to leave again?" I said without apology.

"What do you mean?"

"Are you going to leave again, so you can chase your rock-and-roll fantasy?"

"My 'rock-and-roll fantasy'?" She was emphatic now. She grabbed me by my shoulders. "Let me let you in on a little secret. I'm no songwriter. I wrote one song, years ago—I got lucky. The royalties are enough to live on, but honestly, I'm nothing. The rock-and-roll thing, it's just something I've always loved. I leave because I don't know what else to do. I couldn't control Jack. And Hollis was a natural—he was always so good with you."

She paused, and just when I thought she wasn't going to say anymore, she did. "That's why I leave, Ruby Tuesday. If I'm not here. If I'm not around . . ." Her words came to her slowly. "If I'm not here, then I know I can't screw you up." I tried not to let my eyes brim over with intoxicated tears as my mother tried to read my face.

Darlene gave me her hand and a compassionate smile.

I hung on to both.

She stopped talking altogether as we all settled into fatigue. We watched the television, but I can't remember what was on. We must have sat there for hours, dazed, letting the alcohol seep into and out of our bloodstreams—it was dark outside when news cameras showed Hollis walking out of the jailhouse, his face bright with flashbulbs.

"The investigation of The Dodger Murder has shifted focus to organized crime boss Ty Pickford, who has his hand in many of the grand hotels of Las Vegas and is now believed to be the prime suspect."

I couldn't make myself believe it. It was too much. Darlene's face gave away nothing.

"C'mon, Ruby. We're leaving." She peeled me off the couch and faced Peggy.

"Peggy. I'm sorry about all this. Let me know what it costs to fix the carpet and I'll send you a check." A week before I wouldn't have believed my mother even had a checkbook.

"Consider it on the house this time, Darlene."

"Don't you mean trailer?" We laughed.

Maybe Hollis was in the clear. There was none of the howling and crying and joy making I had imagined. Peggy smiled and walked us to the door.

"Ruby, it was nice to meet you. Dar, when she gets

home, feed her some tomato juice. I swear, it's kept me alive and functioning this long."

"Will do. Thanks for everything." We got into the car. My mother didn't even look back at Peggy, who stood watching us drive away from her retractable porch, waving. We were in Laguna again before my mother spoke.

"Ruby, your father is going to be exhausted and, well, I just don't think he needs to know about—"

"I won't tell him about any of it, I promise. Except, maybe, for the car chase. I think he'd like that part, don't you?"

Darlene's expression was so earnest, I couldn't help but smile back. When she looked at me, her eyes beamed with appreciation. For the first time, I was certain I had made my mother happy.

Darlene and I made it to the living room before either of us noticed Hollis on the couch.

"I hope I didn't miss anything fun, girls." He stood up to greet us, arms out wide, his smile overshadowing every feature on his face.

"Hollis!" Darlene and I exclaimed in unison. I fell silent, letting them decide where to begin. Darlene ran over and threw her arms around his neck. My parents' affection filled me with warmth. She was small in his arms.

"The charges were dropped." He said it calmly, as if he had practiced delivering the line during the car ride home. He let his words wash over us; then he came and sat next to me on the couch.

"That's incredible. We saw it on the news. Why? How?" Darlene let out a high-pitched yell and did a spontaneous little leap. I jumped on Hollis's lap, messing his unstyled hair until it stuck straight up. None of us thought it strange to celebrate over something to do with a murder.

"They found the murder weapon yesterday morning in a Dumpster on an anonymous tip from somebody on a pay phone in Vegas. When the prints were a match with Ty Pickford's, they picked him up at his penthouse at the Frontier to bring him in for questioning. They found blood on one of his suits and scrawled directions from Vegas to Larry's house in Laguna."

"It's almost too good to be true."

"What about the blood they found in your car?" I questioned.

"Larry probably had a bloody nose one day or something. It could have been anything. Who knows. To think it almost did me in, though."

"But why? Why would Pickford do it? I know Larry had debts"—Darlene paused—"but nothing worth killing him for."

"The only thing I can think of is that Pickford thought Larry had the ticket for the two million and got greedy. But that doesn't add up, somehow. There's no way Pickford could have known that the bet was Larry's."

Darlene and I exchanged glances. For the past few hours, we had forgotten. *Nana Sue had passed away.* Darlene reached over and took Hollis's hand in hers.

"Hollis, something happened while you were gone."

"What else could *possibly* have happened while I was gone?" Darlene's somber tone hadn't deterred his glib enthusiasm.

"Sandy from the Fremont called."

"The waitress?"

"Yes." Darlene paused. I dreaded the effect her next sentence might have on my father.

"Your mother passed away this morning."

Neither Darlene nor I spoke. Hollis turned away, but his head lowered and raised, his chest convulsed, and he sniffed.

"I'm so sorry, Hollis," Darlene said. I wished they would hug again. They didn't. "This has been a miserable day." As I studied Hollis, there was almost that eeriness of watching a stranger cry. It took him a long time to respond.

"Did they say how she died?"

"Sandy said she fell right off her stool at the blackjack

table. She was dead before she hit the floor." Darlene looked painfully at Hollis and stopped. She didn't add what she had told me earlier—that Nana Sue had just pulled five cards to a soft twenty-one. Or that Sandy said it was the first time in all her years at the Fremont that not a single card was dealt on the casino floor for over five minutes. I knew she would tell him later.

Fifteen

After Nana Sue's death, we Sweets developed a routine that, for the first time, involved Darlene. Each morning she started the fire in the living room and cleared the remains from the previous meal. Sure, this meant turning the gas key and trashing a pizza box with a few mangled pieces inside, but still, it was more consistent work than anything I had seen my mother do in the past.

The three of us kept to the couch, ordering in both lunch and dinner. We were on vacation together in our own house. Our days all had the same feeling to them—we were greeted by the heat of day, followed by the coolness of night, with little else in between. The mood rested precariously between celebration and mourning. Sometimes we would joke about a television show, Hollis's brush with the criminal justice system, or one of Darlene's misadventures.

Then something would pop up, in conversation or on TV, reminding us of Nana Sue, and we would remain silent for long periods of time. A broadcast of *Viva Las Vegas*, with Elvis dancing around in Nana Sue's city, turned the room somber. Darlene and I watched transfixed until Hollis abruptly changed the channel.

Nana Sue's funeral was to be on Saturday in Las Vegas and, by Darlene's edict, I had to attend school the Friday before. It couldn't be put off any longer, she said; it was the first mandate my mother had ever issued. Hollis had left us to tie up some loose ends at the police station.

"I've already missed four out of five days. Why can't I just miss the whole week?" I pleaded.

"Because you can't."

"The funeral is tomorrow."

"We shouldn't have let you stay home this long, but with Nana Sue's passing and the murder, well, it was a momentary weakness on our part."

"I don't see how one day makes a difference."

"After all this, Ruby? You can't tell me after everything that has happened in the last week that you have no appreciation for how much difference a day can make?" My mother in the authoritative parenting role was a reality I wasn't quite prepared for.

"You're right." She was—but every time I thought

about school, I felt a sharp pain in my stomach.

"You'll go to school, Ruby, because it's important." She grabbed her keys off the counter and made her way to the front door. "It's going to be rough if you go back today. It's going to be rough if you go back in three weeks. You might as well get on with it."

"Hollis usually walks me to school."

"Walks? Up the hill?"

"Yeah. It's only a few blocks."

"Why, that's . . . that's uncivilized. That's unladylike. As long as you're with me, Ruby, you will be driven. In style." She reached in her purse and produced a pair of Jackie Os just like hers. "Here. Put these on."

"Thanks." We drove the two minutes to school. Being next to my mother gave me a feeling of cool maturity. I had been to Vegas and back—and seen and done things that the kids in Miss Sharpe's class couldn't imagine. Before long we were in front of Laguna Heights.

Darlene pushed me out of the car.

"Everything is going to be fine. You'll see. I'll be waiting across the parking lot. School ends at two, right?" I thought about lying to her, but decided against it.

"No, two-thirty. I have to serve detention."

"What? How on earth could you have gotten detention?" She questioned me through the car, the door still open.

"I changed the sign in the front of the school to be about Flash Gray. I guess it was vandalism. He was mouthing off about Hollis."

"Jeez, Ruby. You're walking to school, you have to serve detention, you're vandalizing school property. You're as bad as Jack was at your age. They probably think you've been truant for the last four days."

"I doubt that. People do watch the news here, you know." Darlene smiled. Her sunglasses slipped down to the tip of her nose, and I could see her eyes dancing with warmth, exactly as I had imagined them.

"Well, go on. We can't have tardiness tacked on to your list of offenses." I shut the door and did not look back.

It had been foggy all morning. I walked into the center of campus, an open-air quad with lockers for the older grades lining the clusters of classrooms. I noticed the stares first thing as I approached my locker. Kids gazed at me, not with fear or pity, but as if they were witnessing some curious oddity. By the time I reached Room 312, I was convinced that every pair of eyes in the place had given me a once-over. A couple of students from the lower grades had the audacity to point at me. It was as awful as I'd imagined it would be.

I entered Miss Sharpe's classroom and was shocked to find a room full of kids my age. Maybe I was half expecting a room full of slot machines and gaming tables. When Howie first spoke to me, it almost came as a surprise to be talked to instead of stared at. Halfway through first period, he whispered from behind me.

"For a while there, I thought you might not be coming back, R.T."

Hearing his voice comforted me. I couldn't answer without alerting Miss Sharpe, who seemed determined to carry on class as usual, despite the furor created by my return.

"I kept calling you," he whispered. "There was never any answer at your house."

Miss Sharpe was approaching.

"I wanted to make sure you were okay."

I couldn't tell what I was more afraid of: Flash's saying something explosive from the back corner or Miss Sharpe closing in on Howie and me.

"We kept watching it on TV. I didn't know where you were." His whispers grew louder—he had no idea that Miss Sharpe stood a meager foot away.

"Ruby Tuesday. Howie. I'm sure you two have a lot of catching up to do. But I'd prefer you do it on your own time. Not mine." With that, she walked away, leaving us to our assignments. "Welcome back, Ruby," she said as she reached the front of the classroom. "I'll expect to see you after school." The class had been hushed into submission. And remained that way until the end of class.

Howie noticed how disturbed I had been by the kids' stares, so he suggested we eat lunch by ourselves. I was relieved, until Flash approached us.

"Ruby," Flash said, towering over me.

"What do you want?" I said, face tightening, ready to run if need be.

"I don't want anything," he said, getting angry.

"Then leave."

"I wanted to apologize for all the things I said before the sign stuff. I shouldn't have said 'em. That's all I wanted to say." He turned, his arm still in a cast, and walked quickly back toward the metal shed. Howie laughed beside me once Flash was out of earshot.

"What are you laughing at? Did he just apologize? To me?"

"Don't you get it?"

"Get what?"

"That's all anyone's been talking about. Everyone's terrified of you."

"Terrified of me?"

"They think your father is a murderer."

"But he didn't do it. It's been on the news. No one in my family would—"

"That doesn't matter, R.T. His name was connected with all of it, so, you know, people kind of got hung up on it."

"But that's not fair. That's terrible."

"Oh, who cares? The people who know you aren't gonna believe it. I don't believe it. And if it makes someone like Flash afraid of you, it's not all bad, right?"

I longed for the days when Hollis was *just* a gambler.

"How would you like it?"

"I'm not saying it's easy, but who cares?" The bell rang and lunch had ended.

The last two periods of the day sailed by—I busied myself with thoughts of how school was going to change for me. Flash Gray, at least, was going to be a lot more accommodating. When the final bell rang, I sat in my chair and watched everyone file out. I was surrounded by rows of empty desks in the middle of the classroom. Soon Miss Sharpe and I were alone, and I was nervous.

"How was your vacation, Ruby?"

Hadn't she turned on the television? Or read the *Laguna Ledger*? I didn't resist the temptation to lay everything out for her.

"Other than the whole murder thing and a stressful trip to Vegas where we were followed and my grandmother died, I guess it was fine." It felt good to say it out loud. Miss

Sharpe faced the chalkboard. When she turned to me, she was smiling brightly.

"I'm glad you decided to come back to school today, Ruby. I was worried about you."

"My mother made me. I didn't want to."

"Your mother?"

"She thinks it's important."

"It is." Miss Sharpe looked at me expectantly.

"Can I ask you a question, Miss Sharpe?"

"Yes. You know you can talk to me about anything."

"Do you think my father is a murderer? That he brought crime with him from Vegas to Laguna?"

"Why, of course not."

"A lot of people seem to."

"That doesn't matter."

"It doesn't?"

"Of course it doesn't. Do you remember when I spoke to your father at Open House?"

"Yes. You two were fighting."

"We weren't fighting, Ruby. We were talking about you. Do you know what he said when I told him that he was making things hard on you at school with all his gambling business?" She paused. "He said that no one knew better than he did how hard it was for you or how much he had struggled to make things right. He said he was doing the best he could, and that he was sure it was going to be good enough. And then he told me to mind my own business and do my job." I had no idea what she was getting at. It showed on my face. "What I'm trying to say, Ruby, is that your father is protective of you. It really is none of my business. That kind of dedication—someone who'll do anything for you—that's really all you need in a family. The other stuff comes in so many variations. Who's to say what's okay?"

She stopped and, without hesitation, moved seamlessly into *A Separate Peace*.

"Have you gotten through much of it?" She looked at me and smirked. "I suppose you've had other things on your mind. Well, read it when you can. I feel as if I've done too much talking today. I'll see you tomorrow. Same time?"

"Same place."

As soon as I cleared the threshold of Miss Sharpe's classroom, I sprinted out of school. Darlene was waiting for me in someone's driveway, in her mint-green Thunderbird.

"Darlene, you're not allowed to park here," I said peering in the open window at my mother. "This is someone's house."

"Oh, it's fine. No one seems to mind." She looked glamorous with her delicate arm dangling out the open window. Her hair fell to her shoulders in large blonde curls.

She had dressed up since dropping me off. This time her sunglasses were boxy red with small rhinestones adorning every inch. Mine rested on the passenger seat—I secretly hoped she had set them there for me. I hopped in the car and put them on. Darlene pulled out of the driveway, turning her wheel with such force that we squealed down the street. I sunk low in my seat.

"How was school?" Darlene asked. It was as normal as a question could be; it was just that I couldn't remember my mother asking it before.

"It was fine."

"Fine? Your father makes the seven o'clock news three days in a row and it was just fine?"

"Well, yeah. No one really talked about it."

"No one?"

"I think people were avoiding me."

"Well, you know what, Ruby Tuesday?" I readied myself for one of Darlene's skewed rants.

"This may be a problem for you for one, maybe two weeks on the outside." Her take was different from Miss Sharpe's, but I was beginning to think no less valuable.

"Really?"

"Honey, tomorrow it'll be Mrs. Jennings's botched boob job or how the Sandersons had to move because Mr. Sanderson wasted the family fortune on hookers and cheap

Chablis. It's always something. Don't worry about what people think of you too much. Chances are, they aren't thinking about you at all." Darlene looked over at me, grinning proudly.

It was the right counsel at the right time. And as we pulled out of sight of Laguna Heights, I thought of how silent Flash Gray's corner would now be. Perhaps a little mystery surrounding the Sweet family wouldn't be such a terrible thing after all. Perhaps Nana Sue had known this all along. I smiled back at my mother without the slightest bit of hesitation.

Sixteen

It's hard to say, looking back, knowing all the things I now know, what I should have done with the package that Nana Sue sent my father shortly before she died. Some days I'm glad I opened it. Others, I'm positive I should have left it alone. Nana Sue always used to say that the past only haunts those who let it; I'm not sure she believed it herself. Few days pass when I don't think of her and that letter. That month of my life has never lost its vividness; it's easy to recall. That afternoon most of all.

"Why don't you hop out and get the mail," Darlene said as we pulled into the driveway on our way home from school. Darlene let me out and I walked to the bottom of the driveway toward the mailbox. The sun had burned through the marine layer; it was a bright spot shining through the clouds above me. The mailbox was stuffed to capacity.

No one had retrieved the mail in four days.

I shuffled through magazines, bills, junk mail, until I got to a large manila envelope. Its return address was the Fremont Hotel. There seemed to be something heavy in it. I remember the exact way Hollis Sweet was written in large loopy letters. I stopped in the middle of the driveway and I immediately recognized the importance of what I held in my hands. This was probably the last package Nana Sue ever mailed—maybe one of the final things she did before she died.

The envelope could have contained anything—from something I had left behind at the Fremont to a knickknack that made Nana Sue think of Hollis. It was addressed to my father, but I knew that if I opened it and taped it back shut, no one would be the wiser. After all, Nana Sue had told me several times that nothing should be kept from me. That I should have my eyes open. Before I realized that I had made the decision to open it, my fingers ripped the back seal of the envelope and fished out three loose pages covered with scribbled handwriting.

It began *Hollis*. My stomach jumped. Inside the envelope was a rectangular bubble-wrapped object. This was wrong, and I knew it. Yet something about being the first of the Sweets to receive information had an irresistible appeal—an appeal that overrode any worry of disappointing Hollis. If these were some of Nana Sue's last words, I had a right to know what they said, didn't I?

I put the thick manila envelope inside my jean jacket and walked into the house and into the kitchen. Darlene was there with her feet up on the table and her sunglasses still on, reclining as she read the paper. I tried to hide the envelope between my arm and body without appearing awkward.

"Anything interesting in the mail, Ruby?"

"Nope. Bills, junk, and a few magazines." I dropped everything but Nana Sue's envelope on the table by Darlene's feet. I wondered if she noticed my hand trembling.

"Hungry? You want a snack or something?"

"I think I'm going to have some ice cream outside. It's cold in here."

"Does Hollis normally let you have ice cream before dinner?"

"He lets me eat what I want. Where is he, by the way?"

"I think he's meeting with Nana Sue's lawyer about her will."

Perhaps that was what the package held. I could hardly focus on conversation. My stomach rumbled with nervous energy and paranoia that Darlene could sense what I was up to.

"Is he trying to find out what Nana Sue did with the money?"

"What money?"

I knew I had to keep the conversation going. If it stalled, I might lose steam and drop the package or come clean and miss my opportunity. I hardly realized what I was saying.

"I know about the money and I know Nana Sue probably had it. The two million dollars—the reason for all of this." Darlene stared at me, half quizzical, half coy, and answered without hesitation.

"Well, well. The check was made out to Sue Sweet, so I'm sure she left it to Hollis in her will, if you must know. But," she said, puzzling over my newfound boldness, "you shouldn't worry yourself with that now. When Hollis gets home, let's be extra helpful. This all has been too much for him, I'm afraid."

"Okay," I said, opening the fridge. I awkwardly scooped two large mint-chip balls into a plastic bowl, keeping one arm close to my side to steady the package. I couldn't take so much excitement on an empty stomach.

Darlene looked up, casually flipping through the entertainment section. "Make sure you bring that bowl in from the veranda when you're done, alright, Ruby?" She was always doing that—coming up with fancier names for normal things. The deck was a veranda, the hallway was a foyer, the view a vista. "I don't want a full-blown ant attack out there."

"Sure." I tried not to rush to the deck. I looked behind me, positive that Darlene couldn't see me, double-checking anyway. I felt guilty that I didn't hand the letter over to Darlene, but I figured I would take the first look at it and we could sit and discuss it, mother to daughter, later. As soon as I sat down, I took out the three pages of Fremont Hotel stationery and began devouring Nana Sue's words along with the occasional spoonful of ice cream.

Hollis,

I'm sure this letter has caught you by surprise. I've never been much of a writer, as you know, but I came across a few things you should have. The first is an audiotape. It's a recording of an old woman having lunch with Ty Pickford. On it she tells him key information about Larry Brenn, about where to find him in Laguna. She tells him that he's keeping the two-million-dollar ticket on his body, and that it would be easy to eliminate Larry and cash the ticket in for himself. Maybe the voice is familiar to you. Maybe she shouldn't have interfered. Maybe it was the right thing to do.

The second item is a videotape that shows Larry's murder at the hands of Ty Pickford. Don't watch it if you don't have to. The rumble among the wise guys in Vegas is that Pickford was going after Larry's claim on the future bet—the two million all for himself. I guess someone followed him, maybe someone who knew what he was going to do. At best, someone got to Larry before Larry got to Middleman. You may be wondering how I came by all this—but you live in Vegas long enough and you figure out how to get most anything from most anybody. I know you'll never stop setting odds—you're too good at it—but choose your company wisely.

Information is a handicapper's best friend, Hollis, and in this world it can get you a long way. But grant a tired soul one last wish and keep this to yourself—none of this business makes a weary woman especially proud. The way I figured it, I was close to playing my last hand and anted up one last time. I'm sorry you had to go through all this, but Larry's dead, you're alive, and I'm thankful.

As for the future bet, I have a feeling that the money, as money often does, will take care of itself.

Forever,

Sue

I read the letter twice to make sure I hadn't misunderstood. Then I put the envelope, with all of its original contents, back in my jacket. What remained of my ice cream was now a thick pool of brown-flecked light green goop. I took it inside and put it on the kitchen counter.

Removing the bubble-wrapped tapes from the envelope, I placed them in the far back of the bowl cupboard. I needed time to think, time to figure out what to do next. My first instinct was to show the letter to Darlene. A week ago, this would have been the furthest thing from my mind, but I had been forced to depend on her and it seemed like the natural thing to do.

Darlene sat silent, eyes down, still reading the paper. In the living room, the fire blazed bright. The way *I* figured it, Nana Sue had conned Ty Pickford into killing Uncle Larry to protect Hollis. But that meant she was partly responsible for the whole mess, including Hollis's stint in jail. I knew I would hear her voice if I played the tape. Here I was, alone in the living room, fairly sure that my grandmother had set a murder plot in motion to save my father. All this while my mother read the paper, clueless, in the kitchen.

I walked over to the fire. The gas logs produced a heat that was not as warm as I expected, allowing me to press myself flush against the wire screen. I could easily slip the envelope in between the screen and make it catch on fire; I would push it farther and farther toward the center, sending it from the orange flames to the blue ones until the entire letter was engulfed and only dark smoke remained. I could protect Hollis, just as Nana Sue had. His grief wouldn't have to be clouded with Nana Sue's dark secret. The knowledge of Nana Sue's role in Uncle Larry's murder would be mine alone. The line between wanting to have my own family secret and wanting to protect Hollis blurred in my mind.

"Ruby?" Hollis said it softly. He stood in the doorway between the kitchen and the living room. I gasped, fumbling with the letter, crinkling it as I shoved it back into my pocket. My heart felt like it might pound through my rib cage.

"When did you get back?"

"Just now. Ruby, come into the kitchen for a second, will you?" His voice was full of kindness. Hollis moved to one of the metal stools at the counter. I sat next to him. We both looked over at Darlene seated at the kitchen table. She put the paper down.

"I just met with the executor of Nana Sue's will," Hollis said.

"And?" Darlene's eyebrows jumped up and hovered above her studded red frames.

"And her will was short. But specific. She had revised it within the last couple days." Hollis turned toward me. "Ruby, I don't know how to tell you this, but Nana Sue's left you half of the winnings from the future bet in a trust. Jack's to have the other half. *The future should be Jack's. The future should be Ruby Tuesday's.* That's what she wrote in her will. It's absolutely clear." Hollis looked at me, shaking his head with a grin, equal parts shock and amusement. Darlene said it before I could.

"*What?*"

"It makes perfect sense, Darlene. Danny made out the check to Sue Sweet, just as I asked him to, so the money couldn't be easily traced if things heated up. And I guess she did what she saw fit."

"But she shouldn't have done that," I said, buckling under the weight of it all. "How could my future be the result of a Kirk Gibson home run and an old lady's last wish?"

"She wanted you to have the money, Ruby, plain and simple." *One million dollars.* I searched for jealous pangs in my father's face.

"My daughter the millionaire," Darlene said. She could have been resentful, but her white-toothed smile said otherwise. Which made me feel even guiltier about hiding the letter. It didn't seem real. In some way, I didn't want it to be. I hadn't asked for this.

"Actually, Darlene, after Uncle Sam's taken his cut, the sum'll be closer to half a million, I'm afraid."

Darlene raised her sunglasses and focused her jade-colored eyes on me.

"Don't spend it all in one place, Ruby darling."

"I'm afraid she's not going to be spending any of it

anytime soon. Nana Sue's put it in a trust she can't touch for a long time. Don't get any big ideas—you're still as poor as a pauper for now, Ruby Tuesday."

My mind raced to play along.

"Actually I'd prefer it if you referred to me by my new name: Heiress." The three of us were suddenly more than a little giddy and it seemed to shrink the distance between us. Darlene excused herself, chuckling down the hallway, and I was left alone with my father.

We faced each other, on our stools, knees almost brushing.

"Hollis, you aren't mad, are you?"

"Mad? Why would I be mad?"

"Because that future bet was yours. The money should be yours. Or Darlene's."

"Oh, Ruby. You're not going to have to worry about me anymore. And your mother has never needed that kind of thing—as long as that old Thunderbird keeps running, she'll be happy."

"And her royalty checks keep coming."

"How. . . how do you know about that?"

"You've been away for a while, Hollis. And I've been asking lots of questions."

"Is that right? Well, anyway, Nana Sue was a pretty good gambler—over twenty years that kind of loot adds up, you know?" Hollis winked and smirked. "Who's to say that what she left me wasn't more than your treasure, huh? Maybe you got a little shortchanged." I felt Nana Sue's letter crumple against my stomach.

"Hollis, after all this I still have some questions."

"Shoot."

"Why do they still call you Middleman in Vegas? And why'd you have to leave? Nana Sue wouldn't tell me."

"Why wouldn't she tell you?"

"She said that you'd want me to hear it from you."

"Well, I guess hiding things from you is pointless these days, right?" I let him continue. "I was living in Laguna here, with your mother, Jack, and you in some beat-up old apartment with a leaking roof. It was a few days before the 1979 Super Bowl and Pittsburgh was favored by two and a half over Dallas. I bet a lot of money at a lot of sports books on Pittsburgh laying the points. I don't know if you know this, but people respected my moves—I was quite famous in Vegas for a while."

"I know all about that."

"Oh, really? Is there anything you haven't found out?" Hollis said, amused. The letter turned hot against my stomach. I was bursting.

"Not really."

"Well, then I don't have to explain to you that when a

sharpie bets early, and word gets out, a lot of people follow his move." I wasn't quite understanding, but I nodded anyway.

"So the lines makers in Vegas moved the line to three, then four, and then to four and a half to get the bets evened out and bring more money in on Dallas. When the line hit four and a half, I went the other way and bet the same amount on Dallas plus the points at a lot of sports books. It's frowned upon. It's called trying to catch a middle. You bet both sides, Dallas and Pittsburgh, when the line moves. So say you have five hundred grand on each side, the most you risk is the vigorish, the casino's take (fifty grand in this case). If you catch the middle and Pittsburgh wins by three or four, you win a cool million. Middling bets in football only make sense with likely results—three, four, seven. In this case I had both three and four in the middle." Hollis talking so frankly, figuring I could understand him, was wonderful. I wanted to rush to my Fort Worth dictionary.

"It's not illegal or anything, but I saw an opportunity and I took it. I had studied it, Ruby, and well, with a little luck, Pittsburgh beat Dallas by four points." I quickly did the math in my head.

"So you won both sides?"

"Exactly. Pittsburgh won 35–31 covering the two and a half points I was laying and Dallas, with the four and a half points I was getting on my other bets, covered as well."

"How much did you make?"

"Well, Ruby. A lot. Enough to buy this house and for us to live pretty comfortably if I kept working small time."

"So why'd everyone in Vegas care, then? Why'd you get kicked out?"

"Word got out that I had started a move. Sharpies all across the nation followed my lead—and my initial action caused it all. Almost every sports book in Vegas lost millions and millions of dollars on that game. Not to mention all the illegal books around the country."

"And you got blamed?"

"They looked at it as if I'd orchestrated some kind of huge betting coup—as if I was responsible for the millions of dollars lost. Even the strip casinos upheld the ban, saying I was crooked. I 'middled' the Super Bowl. Hence the name 'Middleman.' And I'm not supposed to show my face in Vegas anymore."

"So you didn't murder anyone?"

Hollis was really laughing now.

"No, no. Of course not. But I haven't stopped playing with numbers and lines. I don't know if I ever will, Ruby."

The fact that Hollis was being forthcoming was eating away at me. I couldn't handle the guilt when I looked him in the eye. He had no idea. The money was enough pressure. The letter put me over the edge—I didn't want a family secret all my own anymore. I pulled the wrinkled pages from my jacket and placed them on the green marble countertop in front of Hollis.

"This is a letter from Nana Sue."

Hollis stared at me blankly. I continued.

"I saw it in the mail and I opened it. I know I shouldn't have. I left the tapes in the cupboard, behind the bowls. I'll be in my room. I'm sorry, Hollis. I'm sorry." It was like I was reading a script of the things I had wanted to say. I got them out in choppy bursts and then I went to my room, knowing full well that I would probably cry for a while. About Nana Sue. About the money. About the murder.

I stayed, bedroom door closed, waiting for Hollis to find me after he had read the letter. The afternoon softened to dusk. Through my door to the patio, I could see the sky beyond the veranda. The setting sun turned the clouds a psychedelic pink against the blue. The sky dissolved into darkness. I was afraid that Hollis would never come.

Five minutes past midnight, there was a knock at the door and Hollis entered. He clutched something in his hand and spoke to me through the darkness.

"You know what, Ruby? We've been letting this Monopoly game fester, and I'm feeling ready for a comeback." I could have kissed that Monopoly board.

"You're not angry at me, are you?"

"Well, I don't know. I came in here because I know we should talk about it—I've been trying to figure out what in the world I'm supposed to say to you."

"I'm so sorry, Hollis. I kept finding things out this week; I was curious. I never expected the letter to—"

"You shouldn't have opened my mail."

"I know."

"That letter wasn't meant for a thirteen-year-old girl."

"I know. I wish I had never opened it."

"Ruby, have you ever heard of a pitcher named Juan Marichal, played for the Giants in the sixties?"

"No."

"They called him the Dominican Dandy, and he is one of the best to play the game."

"Did he make the Hall of Fame?"

"You bet he did. Anyhow, the reason I bring him up is because he was responsible for one of the most violent brawls in major league history. Koufax and his Dodgers were facing Marichal and his Giants at Candlestick Park in late August of sixty-five, in the midst of a tight pennant race. The Dodgers and Giants rivalry had never been fiercer. Marichal had thrown some of his pitches at a couple Dodger batters in earlier innings. So when Marichal came to bat late in the game, Dodger catcher John Roseboro threw the ball back to Koufax, and it nearly hit Marichal on the head. Heated words were exchanged, and Roseboro ripped off his catcher's mask and got in Marichal's face. And then, Marichal took his bat and slammed Roseboro over the head with it."

"Did he hurt Roseboro?"

"Gave Roseboro a concussion. Marichal had to pay a big fine and was suspended for a week. Some of the press said it was malicious and unforgivable. Most agreed he cost the Giants the pennant because he missed two of his starts and the Giants had to finish the season shorthanded. They lost the pennant by two games to the Dodgers."

"Did Roseboro deserve it?"

"It's hard to truly say. Marichal felt like he was defending his team and Dodger pitchers had been throwing at the Giants all game. But it certainly tarnished his reputation."

"Did he apologize later?"

"Yes, he did, the Dodgers even picked him up in free agency and he ended his career in LA. My point is, he did a terrible thing that day in 1965, but that doesn't mean he wasn't one of the best pitchers to ever step on the mound. Do you understand?"

"I understand."

"I also . . ." Hollis was struggling. "I also want you to

realize that however wrong Nana Sue was, she thought she was protecting her family. And she was still a great lady." He reached across the Monopoly board resting on my bed and grabbed my hand.

We sat in the darkness of my room. Hollis fiddled with his piece, the thimble, resting on Kentucky Avenue, until he was ready to roll the dice and make his move. When Hollis pulled a "Get Out of Jail Free" card, we laughed until tears rolled down our faces. But we played most of our game in silence, fighting fatigue, until Hollis tucked me in, exactly as he had done thousands of nights before.

Seventeen

There is little worse in this world than a shabbily dressed person at a funeral. It takes someone greatly skilled in the art of bad taste to make black look vulgar.

I have no doubt, had Nana Sue been standing next to me at her own funeral, she would have muttered this as she scanned the crowd atop the highest mound at Paradise Memorial Gardens that blistering afternoon. The most unpredictable forces, I would learn, brought the strangest people together. This time, it was respect for the life and death of a venerable old gambler—a Vegas fixture. This was a group of people who had established a home in the glimmering oasis that made them feel they were vacationing and settled all at once. All these people had been close to Nana Sue, but I couldn't help but focus on the idea that she had died alone in a casino, among thousands of strangers. She must have wanted it that way.

A woman, almost the spitting image of Nana Sue, stood two paces behind everyone else. I did a double take, and the possibility of Nana Sue attending her own funeral went through my mind.

"Hollis," I whispered.

"Yes?"

"Who is that woman over there? She looks exactly like—"

"That's Nana Sue's younger sister, Bess."

"How come I never heard of her?"

"She and Nana Sue had a falling out." I could tell Hollis didn't want to talk about it.

"Why?"

"No one knows for sure. Some say it was a hand of poker." His tone told me that he would answer no more questions. I would have to learn about Nana Sue's sister later.

Darlene and two insufficiently clothed lounge waitresses surrounded my brother and his wife. Sandy stood to Jack's left, holding a black leash with a placid Twenty-one in a menacing spiked collar. Next to the iguana was Danny, chewing an unlit cigar, in yellow pants, suspenders, and his traditional bowler hat. Sammy and a few other dealers I vaguely recognized from the Fremont and Caesars were in the crowd, too. A rent-a-pastor in an Elvis Lives T-shirt, whose main occupation, we would find out later, was conducting weddings while jumping out of airplanes, stood at the foot of Nana Sue's closed wooden casket.

I was behind Sandy, who was clad in a bejeweled bustier that looked like something from the sale racks at Frederick's of Hollywood. Less than a week after I had sworn off Las Vegas, telling Nana Sue I would probably never return, here I was, with a view of the entire city behind me. She must have known all along.

I tried to look up and make eye contact with my father. I wondered if Nana Sue's letter had affected the way he felt about having lost her. He hadn't uttered more than a few cursory words since the night before, and our trip from Laguna to Las Vegas was filled with silence.

Now, though, my father was grimacing. When the pale, sweaty pastor intoned "as Sue Sweet looks down on us," I knew Hollis was secretly hoping his mother wasn't actually looking anywhere in the vicinity. But this was exactly as Nana Sue planned it—she had specified every detail of her own funeral down to the pastor, no doubt a friend she had made during her two-decade visit to Vegas.

Sandy dabbed her eyes as Sue's coffin was slowly lowered into the ovenlike grave below the shiny carpet of iridescent fake green grass. I couldn't tell if she was crying or sweating under the Vegas sun, as her overabundance of mascara formed mimelike tears under her lavender-tinted eyes. It was just like Nana Sue to die right smack in the middle of a one-hundred-plus-degree Sin City heat wave and then request that her remains be buried in the airless hills, high above the city.

Gum-chewing Ginger, sometimes a waitress on the floor of Caesars, wore less makeup than Sandy, but made up for it in the sheer quantity of gleaming cleavage waiting to explode from her one-shoulder asphalt-colored knit top. These women were Nana Sue's favorites—always making certain her tumbler remained filled with a generous complimentary splash of bourbon. Sandy and Ginger stood in their stilettos, three inches taller than anyone else in the group. They looked even more inappropriate than usual here, outside the neon glow of the Strip—like misplaced monuments to Vegas's particular brand of tacky living.

"I think it's right for her to be buried here in Vegas. Vegas is where she belongs," Sandy whispered to Ginger between sobs.

Jack and Mae, having driven in Jack's jeep, looked posh but windblown standing next to the Vegas stalwarts. Darlene wore a huge straw hat that looked as if a small flying saucer had perched itself on her perfectly coiffed faux-platinum blonde head. Somehow it worked—she looked fashionable, as always. Hollis, in a simple tie and slacks, carrying dozens of red roses in his arms, was a portrait of somber distinction. The plain black sleeveless dress Darlene had insisted I wear clung to me, soaking up all the moisture from my skin.

I looked around. One of these people must have helped Nana Sue follow Pickford and record Uncle Larry's murder on film. I glanced at Darlene and Hollis, my father's jaw quivering in that distinctly human way and my mother's eyes glistening beneath her enormous hat.

On top of the sinking casket were wreaths of plastic flowers, one carefully arranged in the shape of an ace of spades, which seemed to be melting in the dripping heat. Soon Darlene, now carrying a guitar, moved to the plot of Astroturf behind the sunken grave and unfolded a tiny sheet of paper. We waited for her to begin.

"We're all moved by the number of people here who braved the heat and the long drive in tribute to a woman who touched so many lives. I have a little something to sing. It's a song I wrote a long, long time ago, and it's about a courageous woman much like Nana Sue. After I'm done, if any of y'all would like to take a red rose from Nana Sue's son, Hollis, and place it in her grave, please do so. Here it is, 'Whiskey-Eyed Woman.'" It was the song Shade Roberts had ended his concert with. It was also his biggest

hit. I stood awestruck, staring at my mother. She picked up
her guitar and sang softly, in a low, sweet voice. I had never
heard my mother play guitar before.

Sittin' at the table
  she was splittin' aces
She settled there
  loneliest of all the faces
Wore out her youth trying to viva Las Vegas
  acting her whole life through

Hid behind her whiskey-eyes, alright
Never left well enough all alone,
Never turned away from a fight
No matter if it was wrong, she loved headlong,
She loved headlong.

Whiskey-eyed woman spent her life
  running from convention
Burned out so much rubber
  on that road called Good Intention
Knowing the difference between a win and a lose
  was only a Jack away.

Hid behind her whiskey-eyes, alright

Never left well enough all alone,
Never turned away from a fight
No matter if it was wrong, she loved headlong
She loved headlong.

Darlene had finished. The lack of acoustics on the hilltop lent the song a haunting beauty; it was as if Darlene wrote it for this occasion. I was moved. As I looked around me, I realized everyone else had been affected too. We all stood silent, all terribly miscast for such an occasion, bathing in the raw energy of the moment. Nana Sue would have approved.

My mother took a single rose from Hollis's arms, and with deliberate slow paces to the edge of the grave, let the rose fall toward the descending coffin. Sandy, gasping harder for air with each inch the coffin sank into the ground, let out a piercing wail and braced her hands, bright with orange acrylic fingernails, on the frail shoulder of an older woman next to her. Sobbing, she followed Darlene's example. As each person passed Hollis, they gave him a look of pity. No silent tears fell from his sad eyes. It was over in minutes. I approached Hollis, the last in line to pay my respects.

"Take one, Ruby," he said, holding out the remaining three roses. I plucked one from his arms, careful to avoid any thorns. He reached into his jacket pocket and pulled out the envelope containing Nana Sue's letter and accompanying tapes. Then he handed it to me.

"Are you sure?"

"Bury it with her." Hollis's mouth shut with unyielding resolve. He nudged me toward Nana Sue's grave. Taking the rose and the battered package in my hand, I extended my arm straight out, parallel with the casket. I opened my clenched fist and watched the rose fall, hitting the tomb softly. The package landed with a thud. The coffin had sunk completely into the ground. As I turned from the grave, my eyes met my father's.

It was to be the last time we would ever acknowledge the evidence Nana Sue had left behind.

My mother, electing to stay in Vegas, said good-bye to me at Paradise Hills.

"I just have to tie up some things here, Ruby," she said, grabbing my shoulders, with moist pools forming under her eyes. She said this every time she left me to go off on one of her adventures. "I'm going to miss you, Ruby Tuesday." She said this every time too.

Having just bid the only grandmother I had ever known good-bye, I couldn't help thinking that she and Darlene were two of a kind in a very mixed deck: These women loved headlong. Nana Sue had gotten Larry Brenn killed because of it, right or wrong. And my time with Darlene had revealed that she was Nana Sue's equal in every way—whether she was pulling me fiercely from the veranda, feeding me my first drink, or wheeling me through the hills of Laguna. Maybe it had never been about her *not* loving me; maybe it had always been about not knowing *how* to love me. She couldn't handle the thought that she might ruin me with it.

As I stood in front of my mother, I found myself longing for her to stay, for the cycle of coming and then leaving to end forever.

"I finally got to hear your song," I said. "You didn't tell me it was 'Whiskey-Eyed Woman.' That song is a huge hit."

"Yes, well, it was never *my* hit. Anyway, I thought it might be a nice gesture. . . . I know that Nana Sue had her problems with me but—"

"No, it was great. Nana Sue would have loved it."

Darlene's face lit up. "Why, that's nice of you to say. You know, maybe I'll write my next song about you and our Vegas adventures."

"You think a thirteen-year-old's trip to Vegas has the stuff rock and roll is made of?"

"Oh, Ruby Tuesday, of course it does. Haven't you

learned anything this week? Rock and roll is about singing the truth. It's art's great equalizer." She held tight to my shoulders. "And you've got just as much truth to offer as anybody."

"Well, I'll leave the songwriting to you, if that's alright."

"Fine. I'll bring out the talent in you yet. In fact, I'm looking forward to it." She paused. "Now take care of Hollis while I'm gone. It's been an adventure I won't forget, and I'm glad we lived it together. I'll be back soon." She gave me a fierce hug. I could see why Hollis loved her in spite of everything—my mother was an easy addiction. The recognition that she might not ever change completely, that she was leaving me once again, saddened me, but this time things were different. This time I knew she'd be back.

Glossary

bad beat: a rough betting loss that a person blames on bad luck

bookie: a person who takes bets (also called a bookmaker)

chalk: the team favored to win

dime: a thousand dollars

dog: the team nobody thinks will win; the team predicted to lose (also called the underdog)

double sawbuck: a twenty dollar bill

exacta: a bet where you predict the horses that will finish first and second

future: a bet placed before a sports season that predicts the outcome of that season

gee gee: a horse

greenie: a sucker or novice

handicapper: a person who analyzes and predicts who will win sporting events and by how much

hedging: betting the opposite team or side of a bet so that you can minimize losses

hipster: someone who has a lot of gambling know-how

in the hole: to be in debt to a bookie or a sports book

maiden: a horse that hasn't won a single race

middle a bet: to bet both sides in a game and win both sides because the number of points a team is favored by changes after you placed your original bet

nickel: five hundred dollars

over/under: a bet placed on the total number of points scored in a game

parlay: a bet on two or more teams at once where every team involved must win for a payment to occur

pheasant: *see "greenie"*

push: a bet where no money is won because of a tie

railbird: a person who goes to a lot of horse races

runner: a person who places bets or collects winnings for someone else

shopping odds: checking with different sports books or bookies to see who has the most favorable lines and odds

slicker: a dishonest gambler

spread: how many points one team is favored to win by over another

stooper: a person who looks for thrown-away tickets that are winners at the racetrack

teaser: a bet where a person can add or subtract points to/from the spread in return for less favorable odds

tout: a person who tries to sell inside information on a bet

vig (vigorish): the percentage that a bookie or sports book takes on a bet; also known as "juice"

welch on a bet: not paying a debt owed

6268